Return to Us

Cover Design: Sommer Stein, Perfect Pear Creative

Editing: Ashley Williams, AW Editing

Proofreading: Michele Ficht & Julia Griffis

Cover photo © Henry Jimenez

Model: Michael Yerger

Formatter: Alyssa Garica, Uplifting Author Services

Willow Creek Valley Series

Return to Us
Could Have Been Us
A Moment for Us
A Chance for Us
Truth Between Us

Return to Us

NEW YORK TIMES BESTSELLING AUTHOR
CORINNE MICHAELS

To Carrie Ann Ryan and Chelle Bliss. Without you two, this book would've never been written. There are no words to describe the gratitude I have for our friendship and our mornings spent writing together. Thank you.

One

JESSICA

I hear the *bing* from the cockpit, the one that we train for. The one that makes my heart fall to the pit of my stomach because I know everything in my life is about to change. Training is great, but reality is a bitch.

There is a problem with the plane.

I lift the receiver and hear the pilot's voice. "Engine failure. Emergency landing. It's going to be rough, Jessica. Brace."

I don't reply to Elliot. I just slip into survival mode. There's only one passenger on the plane, and I need to ensure that we're both safe. Of course, he happens to be a famous celebrity, so I guess if I'm going to die, at least it'll be with Jacob Arrowood.

"What the hell is going on?" Jacob asks as I approach.

Somehow, I keep my voice calm. "There is an engine failure. We are going to make an emergency landing. I need you to get into a bracing position and try to stay calm."

I want to laugh because, on the inside, I'm anything but calm. However, if I don't do what I've been trained to do, we will die. There's a chance that Elliot and Jose can land the plane safely. There's also a chance they will not, and for that, I have to give him instructions.

"Where are you going?" he asks.

Keeping my eyes on him, I speak clearly and with as much confidence as I can muster. "I need to go to my jump seat, but I'm going to be right here with you. I need you to know how to get out of the plane if something happens to me. This is the door. You need to pull the lever up and then you're going to push. If I'm incapacitated, I need you to unbuckle me and take me out of this aircraft with you if you're able to."

"We're going to crash?"

"We're going to make an emergency landing."

I buckle the first of two seatbelts, and thank God that if I die, I won't be leaving behind a spouse or kids.

But my heart sinks because if I don't make it, then my sister will be left to deal with my mother by herself. I hope she finds someone strong who can help shoulder her burdens. I've tried to help financially, but I haven't been back to Willow Creek Valley in years, and now, I probably never will be again.

And then there's Grayson. Grayson Parkerson is my one regret in life. I loved him so much, and yet, I let him go. Now I'm going to die, and he'll never know that leaving him is my biggest regret.

All these thoughts jumble in my head as I try to buckle the second connector. My fingers are trembling as I fumble with the latch.

I close my eyes, trying to focus. I have to get strapped in

or death is a certainty.

I check over the panels, making sure everything is locked. The door handle slides up and I look at it, visualizing what I'll do if I need to. My job is to get off this plane, not worry about all the things I haven't done or the love I lost.

"Jacob?" I say, needing him to focus on what matters. "Do you remember what I said about the door?"

He nods, and I see the fear in his eyes. I pray he doesn't see mine. "Stay calm and just follow my directions," I instruct.

Jacob's gaze stays on me. "What's your name?"

"Jessica."

My heart is pounding, and the only thing holding me together is my training. If we panic, we don't make it out of here. All of us will have to be a team, and that means one of us has to be the voice of reason. I'm shaking, feeling a sense of dread like I've never known, but there's nothing I can do but pray.

Jacob's voice is much stronger as he speaks again. "Okay, Jessica, it's great meeting you, and we're about to go down in a plane crash together, so that means we'll be lifelong friends if we survive."

I try to smile, but it feels mangled. "Get in your position, Jacob."

He nods. "If I don't make it, I need you to tell Brenna I loved her and I was thinking of her."

"Don't think that way."

"My family. I need them all to know that I love them."

"Focus, Jacob. Remember, getting off the aircraft is imperative."

"Will you tell them?"

I'm not making that promise. We aren't going to even discuss it. There is one final ping, alerting me that it's time and we're nearing the ground.

"Jacob." My voice is strong and forceful.

"I'm ready."

I look to Jacob, keeping my gaze on his. He mimics my position, and I start to chant, all the while praying this isn't our last moment. "Brace. Brace. Brace."

I sit up, gasping for air, clutching my throat as I struggle to breathe. Sweat soaks my shirt, and my heart is beating so hard I wonder if it'll bruise my chest.

It was just a dream.

It's okay. I'm okay. I survived.

I'm in my room, in my bed, and I'm safe.

I repeat that over and over until I can feel my heart rate starting to decrease. Every night, it's the same dream. The same panic that makes it so I have to fight for air. Then it's the same inability to sleep for the rest of the night.

The last three weeks have been absolute hell. I'm so tired of being tired. The crash haunts me. The memories, fear, and darkness make it impossible for me to move on when all I really want is to move forward.

I throw the covers off my legs and head downstairs.

Over the last few weeks, my mother has grown accustomed to the nightmares, no longer waking when she hears me—or maybe I'm not screaming anymore. If that's the case, I'd really love it if the dreams would just stop. Since tonight is not that night, I start my ritual of coping with a few hours of rest.

I make myself a cup of tea, grab the blanket off the back of the couch, and head out to the front porch. The swing that my father hung the weekend before he walked out on us is still there, welcoming me to rock and ignore the world.

I curl up, holding the warm mug in my hands, and slowly

sip while surrounded by silence.

Willow Creek Valley used to be my favorite place in the world. It's quiet, beautiful, and allows total seclusion. We're surrounded by woods, and even the poorest members of the town—my family—get to feel as if we at least have privacy.

I would sit on this very swing, dreaming of a life just like my mama and daddy had. I wanted the husband, kids, and the perfect Southern life.

It was all there. In a perfect world, I would've opened an inn with Grayson and lived the life we talked about. It was all within reach. And then I realized that dreams are lies we feed ourselves.

Husbands leave.

Daddies never call.

Kids are destroyed by it.

And I want no part of it.

Instead, I wanted to see the world, which I did until it ended with the plane coming down.

My head is beginning to ache, and I start to rub my temples.

Please don't let this be a crippling one this time.

My phone pings with a text from the only friend I kept in touch with from Willow Creek.

Delia: Want to get breakfast?

Me: Why are you awake?

Delia: I never went to sleep. So . . . food?

She works in the factory a few towns over, which is one of the few job options around here. The thing is, the idea of leaving the house makes tears form in my eyes. For weeks now, since I've been back in Willow Creek Valley, I haven't left unless it was to see the doctor. I've been here, and no one really knows I am in town other than my mother, my sister Winnie, and Delia. Going out and seeing others will solidify that I failed and had to come back.

Going to get food early, though, might be the safest way to ease myself out.

My therapist has been trying to encourage me to take one small step, and in the back of my mind, I hear Dr. Warvel saying, *"Take the hand outstretched when you're weak and let it lend you strength."*

I gnaw on my thumbnail, take two deep breaths, and reply.

Me: Sure, but you'll have to pick me up. You know, TBI and all means no driving.

Until the fainting, debilitating migraines, and periods of confusion go away, I'm not allowed to drive, ride a bike, or do anything that could throw my equilibrium off. Yet another awesome side effect of my plane crash.

Delia: Be there in fifteen.

More like ten if I know her driving. I head back inside and throw on a sweatshirt, brush my hair and teeth, and sigh as I see my reflection in the mirror. The dreams may make me feel as if it were just yesterday, but all my visible injuries have healed.

There are no more bruises on my face, and the scar from where they had to drain the fluid from my brain is still healing but hidden beneath my hair. My ribs are still healing, but again, that isn't something you would look at me and know. To anyone on the street, I look like the same Jessica Walker who was ready to take the world by storm.

Inside, however, I'm something else.

I'm broken.

I can't always speak correctly, I can't drive, and I will probably never be able to fly again due to the air pressure changes.

Being here is a different sort of pressure. The kind that gives me a whole other thing to be anxious about, the boy I left. The man he's become and the people who made me feel small, all of them are still here and probably salivating over the chance to be cruel.

"She's not good enough. She'll never fit in to do more than scrub the floors. You'll see, she'll never amount to anything and will end up just like her mother."

I hear the words, the voice of a woman so disgusted with the idea of being in my presence, playing in my head like a lyric that won't be forgotten.

There's a knock on the bathroom door. I open it to see my mother. "Oh," she says looking startled. "I didn't know you were awake."

"Had another nightmare."

She gives me a sad smile. "I thought they ended."

"No, I wish."

"Where are you going this early?" she asks as she looks over my outfit.

"Delia is calling in. Eating." I stop myself, knowing the words aren't right, and take a few seconds. This is what I can't handle. My brain says: Delia is coming over so we can go get breakfast, but my mouth says something else. My mother doesn't say a word, she allows me the time I need to collect myself and try again. "Delia is taking me to breakfast."

"Is that a good idea? To go out and see the people in town?"

And here is where I want to rail against the world. For the last fourteen years, I've been on my own. The day I left for college, I learned how to survive on my own and be worth—something. I've spent my time taking care of myself, proving that I don't need anyone to make it.

More than that, I'm getting better each day. I'm trying to do more so that I can stop living in this prison and get back to the life I want. "Mom . . ."

She raises her hands. "I know, I know, you're grown now and don't need me to worry over you. I just don't want to see you struggle, honey. That's all. I know how the people here are, and there's a lot of gossip around you returning."

I exit the bathroom and lean against the wall. "I have to try."

"Yes. You do." There's defeat in each word, but there's also a bit of pride. "Did you take your medicine?"

I swear she just said I didn't need her to worry.

"Yes."

If I don't, I'll be curled in a ball, begging for someone to put me out of my misery.

"Then I guess have a good time."

I walk over, squeeze her hand, and smile. "Thank you, Mom."

She sighs. "I'm trying, sweet girl."

"I know. We both are."

"Go on now." Mom kisses my cheek. "I love you."

"I love you too."

For all the things that my mother has struggled through, giving love has never been one. My father leaving her was a blow she never recovered from. Winnie and I knew that my mother was doing her best. She loved us and did everything she had to in order to make sure we survived. Her heart was broken, but all we saw was strength.

My father, on the other hand, is a piece of shit. He walked away from his daughters without a second glance.

I get downstairs in time to see the headlights shining through the window. Delia made it in fewer than ten minutes, which is somewhat impressive.

Since I've been back, she's the only person outside of my family who I've allowed to see me. The first few days were terrible because I was in so much pain and the bruising was awful. As all of it started to heal, it became more of a protective shell. Staying here meant I didn't have to explain what happened.

I could pretend this was just an extended vacation.

As soon as I'm in the car, my hands tremble as fear starts to grip me.

Delia reaches over, taking both of them in her hands. "You're okay. We're just getting breakfast on a random Tuesday morning."

I release a deep breath and force a smile. "It'll be fine."

"Yes. It will."

I do the breathing exercise, and Delia backs the car up. Thankfully, she doesn't give me time to work myself up too much as she drives toward town. I close my eyes, allowing my thoughts to center on the techniques I've been learning the last few weeks.

The drive doesn't take very long to get to the diner since we are not considered to be on the wealthy side of Willow Creek Valley. Those houses are far away from the center of town. Which is not where Delia and I grew up. We're from *that* side of town. The one the rich kids avoid at all costs because they don't want to be seen with us.

However, there was always one boy who never treated me that way. Regardless of his parents absolutely hating that we were together, Grayson Parkerson didn't care. He loved me even though my mother worked at the grocery store, cleaned rooms at the inn, and then at the bar just to cover our bills. He didn't see rich or poor, he just saw me.

Well, if he could see me now.

Last I heard, he was married and had a beautiful little girl, running one of his family's inns somewhere in the country.

I sure showed him.

I could always ask Delia, but we made a promise not to ask a question we really didn't want the answer to, and I definitely don't want to know this one.

Leaving him was the hardest thing I've ever done, but I saw what our future would be after his mother told me I'd never be a part of their family. He would leave me, so I left him first, and it broke me in half.

Delia parks the car and turns to me. "All right, let's go get some food, I'm starving."

Inhale. Five, four, three, two, one. Exhale.

I repeat that three times and then nod. "Okay, let's go."

We enter, and sure enough, Ms. Jennie is still working as the waitress. "Well, if it isn't Jessica Walker! As I live and breathe, my God. You are just as beautiful as the last time I saw you."

I smile as her warmth fills the space around us. She's always sweet and loving. I doubted the woman had a mean word to say about a soul. "You are the best part of this town," I say with a smile.

"Vernon!" she yells over her shoulder toward the kitchen. "You come out here and see who came for your famous breakfast."

Her husband peeks his head out of the door. "Hello there, Miss Jessica."

A sense of calm settles over me as I realize that I had been worried about a town that loved me and wished me well as I ran away to avoid having my heart broken. "It's good to see you, Mr. Vernon."

He gives me a wink and then heads back in.

"I'll give you my best table. Come on, girls." Jennie grabs two menus and walks us over to the only open table.

"This place hasn't changed," I muse as I look around.

There are still the same deep-red booths with black-lacquer tables, checkered black-and-white floors, and football jerseys hung on the wall.

Jennie smiles. "No need to fix things that aren't broken. This town hasn't changed because we don't need it to."

I smile at her, taking the menu from her hand. "It's good to see you."

"It's good to see you too, honey."

"Table three!" Vernon yells from the kitchen.

"I'll be back with your food in a few. I'll just get you your usual." Jennie rushes off before I could give her another option.

It shouldn't surprise me that she would think I still ate pancakes, but when we pulled up, it was all I wanted.

After Grayson's games, we would all pile into his truck and head here, craving carbs and sweets. He and I would sit in the corner booth, his arm around me while I wore his letterman jacket. If I had been a cheerleader, we would've been that all-American couple everyone talked about. I couldn't afford to play sports, and there wasn't any way around it. I didn't get to sit in the stands each Friday because I was usually working, but Grayson was always there at the end of my shift.

I didn't have to be embarrassed, he just loved me. The poor, sad, and angry parts were held together by him.

It just wasn't enough in the end.

Delia looks at me, a smile on her lips. "Thinking of something?"

My hands are folded in front of me, resting on the menu. "The past."

"It's in every crevice of this place."

"That it is."

Her past is still the present, unfortunately. She's been in love with Joshua Parkerson since we were kids. The oldest and most elusive of the Parkerson brothers. She has watched, wondered, dreamed of a time when he would see her as more. Joshua has always pushed her away, except for one night when he kissed her in the hallway by the payphone in the diner. A moment she's clung to for years.

I watch as her gaze moves there, almost as though the memory calls to both of us.

"How is Josh?" I ask.

"I wouldn't know."

"He's gone too?"

Her eyes narrow, and she shifts. "Too?"

I nod. "Well, yeah. Aren't the Parkersons all scattered now? You don't need an entire family to work at the same location. Their parents always had the grand plan of having their own chain. Last time my mother said they opened another location in Wyoming and Oliver went to run it."

Delia shakes her head subtly. "Yeah, but . . . I mean, they're not all gone."

"I'm sure Stella stayed here." She was the baby, even if only by six minutes of her twin, Oliver, and spoiled beyond belief. I can't imagine their father allowed her to leave his side. "She and Winnie still hang out."

She bites her lower lip. "Well, Stella is here, yes, but . . ."

"Did Alex stay?" I ask.

"No, Alex went to their Savannah location," she says.

I can picture him loving that. Alex is our age and he used to love to party. Savannah would be the perfect mix of fun and seriousness for him. "How is he?"

Delia leans back in the seat, watching me. "Last time we talked, he was doing really well."

"I always loved him."

Delia grins. "Alex is the best."

I would argue that. In my heart, Grayson was the best, but she was very close with Alex and always hung out at his house. Partially because it meant she could be around Josh, but that was beside the point. We were Alex's friends . . . annoying, young, and stupid.

"Yeah, he's probably coming back to visit soon, they all do around their parents' anniversary."

"It was always a big deal for them."

Delia pushes the salt shaker back and forth. "Can I ask you something?"

"Of course."

"Why did you break up with Grayson?"

I feel the blood drain from my face. "You know why."

"I know what I heard, which was that you ended things when you went to college because it wasn't going to work long distance with him being in a different state."

He was two years older, and I was so sure we'd always be together. Not because of any other reason than we loved each other that much. Surely, two people couldn't love each other the way we did and not work. It was unfathomable.

But loving someone when their family despises you is something else. Grayson shielded me, or he tried to, but I heard their barbs. I felt their disdain, and when push came to shove, I knew he'd choose them because they held the keys to his future. Like my father had, Grayson would've chosen his happiness over the people in his life. I was young and dumb and thought if I left him first, it wouldn't hurt.

That proved wrong. It hurt and I was too immature to go back to him.

"Does it really matter? Do any high school sweethearts ever last?" I ask. "He's gone and living what I'm sure is a perfect life."

She looks down, blowing a long breath through her nose. "How does your sister literally spend every other day with Stella and you know nothing?"

Before I can answer or clarify, Jennie brings our plates and my stomach growls. It's been so long since I've had breakfast like this.

I stare at the plate, touching the rim, not sure how to start or if this is real. Before the crash, life was about efficiency. I was often flying early in the morning, which meant I needed to work out and then prepare for whatever trip the celebrity we were flying requested. I can't remember the last time I sat down to eat where it wasn't about running to the next thing. Let alone that I got to have carbs like this.

"Are you planning to eat it or make love to it?" Delia asks

with a snort.

"Both."

We giggle and then the chime rings on the door.

I look up, not knowing what possessed me to care, but when I do, it's as though not only the plane is crashing around me but also the world. A pair of blue eyes, dark brown hair, and a smile that I couldn't forget if I tried is there, and I can't breathe.

Grayson Parkerson is in town and staring back at me.

Two

GRAYSON

I stand here, looking at the woman I loved, not sure if I'm imagining it. Stella told me she was back, but I've spent the last three weeks waiting to see her and . . . nothing. I figured she was gone just as quick as she returned.

A hand clasps my shoulder, and I look away. I shouldn't care if Jessica is here. It has been fourteen years and we've both moved on, but then, if that were the case, it wouldn't feel as if I were just punched in my gut.

"You ready to eat?" Jack asks.

"Yeah."

"Good, the call we just had left me fucking starving."

I chuckle. "You're always starving."

It doesn't matter if we respond to a false alarm or four-alarm fire, Jack believes that getting out of bed earns him some food as a reward. Tonight, we responded to a brush fire that, thankfully, had been called in before it got out of control. Probably the football guys having a bonfire where they shouldn't have. Of course, it wasn't as if Jack and I ever did stupid shit like that when we were kids . . .

"Fact."

I use every ounce of willpower I have not to glance over at her. Not that I can't, at any time, recall how she looks in perfect detail. Her dark brown hair lays straight, rich honey-colored eyes, and freckles across her cheekbones that she tries to hide. How is it that she's even more beautiful than I remembered?

We get to our seats, and I purposely make sure my back is to her. If I don't, I'll end up staring at her and failing in my plan to pretend she doesn't exist.

She left me.

She decided we weren't worth the effort. Four years I loved her, and it took her four minutes to wreck it all.

Jack slaps his menu against mine. "You all right?"

"I'm fine."

"Yeah? Because you're acting weird. Couldn't be because Jessica is three tables back, could it?"

I shake my head with my lips in a firm line. "Nope."

"No, I mean, it's not like she was the one who got away."

"She left."

"She did, and now she's back."

"It appears she is. I don't give a shit," I say, looking at the menu.

He laughs once. "Yeah, you look like you don't care. I mean, you're the epitome of not caring right now."

"Drop it, Jack."

I'm really not in the mood for this. Jessica Walker is not

my concern anymore. She made her choice when she ran out of here like her feet were on fire. It didn't matter that I would've given her everything, including time while we were both in school.

He chuckles and starts looking over the menu. "I hear she's back for good."

I release a heavy sigh, knowing he's like a dog with a bone. "Stella said as much."

He doesn't lift his gaze as he nods. "Yeah, did she tell you why or did you cut her off before she could get the story out?"

"It doesn't matter if she's back for a day, an hour, or the rest of her life. It makes zero difference to me."

He laughs under his breath. "Fucking idiot."

Just as I'm about to tell him off, I can feel her standing there. I turn my head, steeling myself against finally getting a closer look at her.

She has a smile on her face, but I can see the hesitation in her eyes. "Hi, Gray."

"Jess."

"I . . . well, I wanted to say hello. How loud to go—" She closes her eyes, breathes a few times, and then speaks again, "How have you been?"

"Just fine." I give her a quick look before focusing on something else. This doesn't have to happen. We can live here and go about our lives not talking. We spent fourteen years not saying a word to each other, this should be simple enough.

"Oh. Good." She looks at Jack and then back to me.

Jack gets up and gives her a hug. "Jess, it's so good to see you."

She winces and then takes a step back.

"Sorry. Shit. I forgot you're hurt." Jack looks stricken.

"It's fine. It's good to see you, too."

He sits back down, shoots me a glare, and then jerks his head toward her.

"So, how are you?" I ask, not really wanting to have this conversation. I feel like an asshole, but I can't seem to stop myself. I'm pissed. She shows up here after all this time, and I feel like I've been thrown back in time. It took me years to get over her, and now, one fucking appearance and my heart is racing.

"I'm . . . okay."

"Glad to hear it."

Delia walks over and rests her hand on Jessica's arm. "Hey, guys. Jess, I got a call from my mother and need to head home to help her. Jennie is packing up the food."

She nods and then turns back to me. "It was good to see you, Gray."

"Yeah. Sure. Good to see you too."

I let out a low breath while my best friend stares at me. A few seconds pass, and he doesn't say a word or look away. "What?" I ask.

"You were a dick."

"Does she deserve my kindness? She fucking left me."

He laughs once. "What are you, a fifteen-year-old girl? Get over it and put your big girl panties on, pumpkin. That girl has been through hell, and you were a prick, which . . . you're not. Since when do you act like *that*?"

As Jessica and Delia walk out, Jess gives me a small wave, and I lift my head. I'm not sure what anyone expected regarding our reunion. I loved that girl. I would've fucking given up anything for her, but she walked away without a second glance.

So, now that her life didn't work out and she's back, I'm supposed to forget what she did? Too bad. Life didn't exactly go *my* way either.

But something Jack said bugs me. "What hell did she go through?"

Jack crosses his arms over his chest, a smirk on his face. Clearly, I'm missing something that everyone is aware of. "Do you remember that plane crash the guy playing the Navigator was in a few weeks ago?"

"Jacob Arrowood?" He's one of the new top celebrities that everyone is going nuts over. His last action movie was top in the box office for weeks and the plane crash only added to his fame. It was all over the news for days as they searched for him and the crew.

He nods. "Do you know who else was in that crash?"

It takes me a second to put two and two together. Jessica was a flight attendant. I'd heard that much when Winnie was babbling to Stella about her sister. I normally could avoid anything relating to her, but they were discussing how cool it was that she flew with celebrities. Of course, she'd just done a flight with Stella's favorite musician and Jessica had sent Winnie a photo.

"What?" I ask, nearly spilling my coffee. "She was in a plane crash? Why didn't anyone say anything to me?"

Jack's smug grin makes me want to punch him.

"Hey now, you didn't *want* to know anything. Jessica Walker is on your do-not-mention list along with—"

"Yes, her too."

"Ever think it's you, buddy? I mean, two girls, two horrible endings to your love story. I'm noticing a pattern."

I tilt my head back because I wonder the same thing every day. I loved two women and they both left. Jessica and I were young and as much as I wanted to marry her, give her everything, we weren't ready. When I met Yvonne, though, it was different. I was in grad school and she was pursuing her singing career, both from the same lifestyle and she was everything my mother wanted but I fought against—only I knew I wasn't ready to date her, but I did anyway.

"At least Yvonne left me with something I love and was worth the hell."

Jack grins. "Amelia is definitely worth it."

While I never pictured life being this way, I wouldn't trade my daughter for every star in the sky.

"Jessica left me with nothing."

He shrugs. "If it weren't for her doing that, you wouldn't have Melia."

"True."

"Is she with Stella?" he asks.

"Yeah, she's having another sleepover. It's why I was able to answer the fire tones tonight."

The food arrives and Jennie gives us a warm smile. "You boys eat up. You have to keep your strength if you want to keep saving the town."

Jack grins. "See, Jennie gets it."

"Jennie thinks food fixes any problem."

She stares at me, one brow raised as she smiles. "It does. My Vernon and I have been married for fifty-three years. There's nothing in this world that can't be fixed with love, understanding, and some food from the heart."

My head turns to where Jessica was sitting before. "You think?"

Jennie winks. "Oh, I know so, son. Sometimes what's

missing when it comes to forgiveness is love." Before I can reply, she laughs. "Or it could be that you can't cook worth a shit and need someone else to make the food."

Jack and I both chuckle. "Well, we're glad we can always come here," Jack says as he digs into his eggs.

"Always, and who knows, sometimes you find what you need even when you aren't looking." She leaves, and I'm sitting here, a little off balance for the first time in four years. Not since the day Amelia was placed in my arms as Yvonne ran out the door to catch a flight to France.

"Breakfast and life advice," Jack muses. "I need to tip her more."

"It's not that easy . . . what she said."

"You cooking? Oh, I know, I've eaten the crap you try to pass off as food."

I roll my eyes. "The forgiveness."

Jack leans back, his fork resting on the plate. "And what is holding on to all that shit doing to you, Gray? Nothing. It's making you live in this constant state of pissed off."

"You know why I'm pissed—and it's not constant."

For the most part, I just deal with it. Sure, the two women I loved left me. Sure, I basically refuse to date and have been close to monk status for a few years. Sure, I'm raising my daughter on my own and have nothing other than her and work. It's fine.

It's all fine.

"Yeah, and I get it. But you have Amelia and"—he lifts the fork, pointing it at me—"if you ask me, you were given a gift, my friend. Yvonne wanted your money, connections, and whatever she could take. Her leaving was rough, but she did you a favor by being a selfish bitch and not sticking around."

This isn't the first time I've heard this. My friends, siblings—hell, even her own family said it. We would've made each other miserable, but I didn't see that at the time . . . or care. I wanted what I lost with Jess, and I fell for her lies.

"Maybe she did, but you tell Amelia that when she asks why she doesn't have a mom."

Jack loves my daughter, everyone does. She's smart, funny, tenacious, and has an ability to make everyone smile. Equally, she can break your heart when she cries.

"Yeah right, I'll never be the one to hurt her. One day, though, she'll see it for herself. Your ex wasn't worth your time, and she never was the right girl for you."

I release a deep, slow breath. "They said the same about another person too."

Jessica. My mother couldn't have been happier when we ended things.

"What's that saying about if something is right for you, you should let it go?"

"And if it's meant to be, it might just come back," I finish and then look at the door where Jessica exited.

It seems she did, but I'm not sure either of us are right for each other.

Three

JESSICA

"And how did you feel seeing him again?" Dr. Warvel asks as I play with the fringe on the blanket.

"It was fine."

"Fine, how?"

"I'm not sure. A part of me is glad it is over. The other part of me is happy that it went as shitty as it did. Your moving work less."

As soon as the words are out of my mouth, I can feel the rage burning. It is frustrating and makes me feel inept that I can't get my mouth to work right. All day, I struggle to keep it together and not allow it to bother me, but in this room, I can be angry.

She leans forward. "Try again, remember to go slow and stay calm."

"I hate this."

"I know. Part of what we're working on is getting your brain to push against itself while also handling all the changes in your life. It's a lot to deal with, Jessica. You've done great so far, but the more you can control your anger, the more likely it will be that your words come out correctly."

She's right. When I'm able to breathe, think it through, and focus, the words come out better.

Allowing my anger to leave my body in a long breath, I try again. "It was hard seeing him."

"Because you have avoided it?"

"Yes. There was always a part of me that regretted ending things."

Dr. Warvel sits back in her chair. "Your first love is always one that hurts the most. At least, for most people. Losing him was your choice, though, correct?"

"It was the right one."

Grayson and I would've ended, it was inevitable. We were two kids from very different places, even though we were in the same town. He was two years into the college he was attending in Charlotte, and I was headed to school in Massachusetts. While we could do the distance from Charlotte to Willow Creek, going states away was going to be our demise. Even though I loved him, I needed to end things. I needed to be free from his family and the fear of him leaving me when he saw I wasn't the girl for him.

"How did things end?" she asks.

I focus, keeping my body loose as I start to talk, preparing for my words to jumble but hoping they won't. "When I went to Massachusetts, I told him that I wouldn't be returning to Willow Creek—ever. He was always set to take over one of his family's properties, and that wasn't what I wanted."

Grayson's family's properties came with strings, Mr. Parkerson made sure of it. His children were to be with likeminded and financially stable families. Their kids were to elevate them in society, not bring them down with gutter trash like me.

Never mind that I loved his son. Never mind that I treated him with respect and it wasn't about the money.

It didn't matter. My father was a piece of trash who left. My mother was a member of the Park Inn's housekeeping staff, which meant I was completely unsuitable.

"Why wouldn't you want that?"

"Because they told me that I was no better than my mother who cleaned their toilets. I was poor, and they would never accept me. And . . . I don't know . . . he'd leave when he realized I wasn't good enough. I wanted us to build our own life, travel, get out of this town. I wanted to start new, and he didn't."

"Did you and Grayson ever talk about that?"

I shake my head. "He was born and bred to take over. That was part of their legacy and each of the kids in his family have something to run. He would always choose them."

She writes something in her notepad and then places it on the side table. "You know, I've known the Parkersons for a while. I don't know them well, but I know a bit and then what I've observed. Family is important to them, but it's not everything."

"It was back then."

"So, you prevented him from hurting you?"

I nod. "Exactly. I was being strong, making it so he didn't have to leave me. I left him. And we were young, so it wasn't going to work anyway."

"It doesn't sound like Grayson chose them. It sounds like

you chose for him and then left before he could prove you wrong."

"Yeah, I guess I did."

Dr. Warvel's smile is triumphant. "That was easy."

"I know what I did. I was young and scared. Also, my father leaving was horrible on my sister and me. It really screwed us up on the rules of dating."

"That's the thing about dating, the rules change, and sometimes, we don't even know it." She looks at her watch. "Our time is just about up, but let's talk about your nightmares. Are they still causing you problems?"

"Yes."

The crash is constant, and I'm exhausted. I'm ready for this nightmare to be over, but no matter what techniques I use, it continues.

"I see. And the methods we talked about aren't helping? Are they at least less intense?"

"No, they're worse. I hover on the edge of consciousness most of the time. Like, I can feel them as though it's real."

"Okay. I want you to try something. When you wake up, I want you to write it all down. Every detail from the dream, not what you remember from the actual crash, but only what you recall from the dream."

"Well, the dream is the memory of the crash."

She lifts one shoulder. "Humor me."

"Okay." I get to my feet and take a step before she stops me.

"I'd like to tell you we had a very intense conversation and you were able to control your speech very well."

There is a huge sense of victory running through my veins. I was able to get through this session much better than the last.

"Thank you."

"You're welcome. Part of what we do here is deal with the things that we've buried or don't like to discuss. I'm giving you some time so you're not blindsided, but we need to discuss your father next session."

My entire body tightens. I've done everything I can in the last sixteen years to rid that man from my life. "There's nothing to talk about."

"Then we'll talk about that next week."

I'm lying on the couch, trying to watch the movie Jacob sent me when I admitted I'd never really watched his movies.

I grab my phone and send him a text.

Me: They paid you far too much to make this film.

Jacob: Ha! Don't I know it.

Me: You're very lucky you're so pretty.

Jacob: Don't forget I smell like oak and whiskey. It was probably that.

And now I want to die. Of all the things he remembers, it has to be that I said that. I blame my brain bleed for it.

Me: What is said during a near-death experience should not be held against those who almost died.

Jacob: But you didn't die, therefore that rule is null and void.

Me: Tell Brenna I said you're a pain in the ass.

Jacob: I don't have to tell her, she knows.

Since the crash, Jacob and I have kept in touch. The entire flight crew has. He offered to have me stay on his family farm in Pennsylvania while I recovered, but that was far too much of an inconvenience for him. Instead, I'm here, living it up on my mother's couch in North Carolina. Lucky me.

Me: Well, I just wanted to let you know your movie is subpar.

Jacob: Noted. How was therapy today?

It's really sad that a Hollywood star knows my entire life's schedule.

Me: It was fine.

Jacob: Brenna said you're always welcome to talk to her.

Because that wouldn't be awkward at all. There is nothing even remotely inappropriate about my and Jacob's friendship, but there's no way I want to spill my guts about the crash to her. She's dealing with his trauma, whether he wants to think he has any or not.

Me: I appreciate it.

There's a slight ringing in my ear, which is the early signs of a possible migraine. I am so fucking over this. I'm tired of my head and all the nonsense that comes along with this injury. There's no timeline to recovery either. I could wake up tomorrow and be healed or I could still be dealing with it years from now.

My neurologist keeps saying how the brain doesn't work like a broken bone. There's no telling how long it'll take to heal. Or if it ever will.

I get up, turn the television off, and go to the kitchen. I drain two big glasses of water, knowing that, if I'm dehydrated, it makes it worse. Then I take my medication and head out to the porch swing.

I grab the pillow and blanket, close my eyes, and let the quiet surround me.

"And I thought you never napped?" A deep voice causes my eyes to fly open.

I sit up much too fast, hand resting on my throat. "Jesus!"

"Sorry," Grayson says with a smile. "I knocked and was getting ready to leave when I heard you snore."

"I don't snore," I say as I try to focus on a fixed point to stop the spinning.

"Next time, I'll record you to prove otherwise."

I should've picked something other than Grayson to be my fixed point. Now, I look like I'm staring, which I am just not for the reason he probably thinks I am.

The aqua-blue in his eyes mixes with the green, making them look like the ocean as you fly over. My lips part, and I'm taken back to when those eyes did strange things to my belly. One look from him would make any girl feel cherished.

And he did cherish me. He was a great boyfriend, I was just too young to know how to handle the obstacles thrown our way.

"What are you doing here?" I ask, my voice a little breathy.

"I wanted to come and actually talk. Last week . . . wasn't

my finest moment." He leans against the rail, head tilted so it rests on the pillar as though he's got nothing but time. The casual stance is at war with the apprehension in his eyes.

"I appreciate that, but it's fine. You didn't say anything wrong."

"No, Jess, we were friends and I cared about you. I was a complete and total asshole."

"Yeah, you kind of were."

He looks at his feet. "I'm sorry."

"I appreciate it."

"I didn't know," he says, looking away. "I didn't know about the crash."

"Oh."

I'm not sure what to say to that. It doesn't really matter either way. Him knowing or not knowing doesn't change anything.

He pushes off the rail, coming a little closer and then stopping. "Are you okay?"

No. Not even a little. "I'm getting there."

And I guess I am. Little by little, I'm going to find my way through it. I have a great support system and doctors who are all doing what they can. As I heal, I'll find ways to be better and stronger. At least, that's the bullshit I'm feeding myself.

"Good. So, like I said, I don't want things to be awkward."

"You really don't have to worry. It was a shock to both of us—seeing each other after all these years."

Grayson runs his hands through his thick, dark hair. It's longer than he wore it when we were kids. It's not long, but it curls right at the ends, giving him a sexy-but-serious look.

After seeing him, I made Delia unload about everything she knows. It was years of gossip around the Parkerson family that left me shocked. I can only imagine how they handled the drama of his girlfriend getting pregnant and then leaving. His father was all about propriety.

"It was, but this town is small, so we're bound to see each other a lot."

"That's a shame," I say with a shrug.

"Yeah? Why is that?" He stands up straight, no longer looking like he had nothing but time.

I grin, hoping that maybe if we can joke with each other, we'll find a way onto neutral ground. "You were much cuter back then."

Grayson's laughter is deep and rich. "You were sweeter then."

"You were smarter than to say something like that."

"I was also trying to get into your pants."

"Which you did," I remind him.

"Many times."

I roll my eyes with a smile. "Yeah, and if I recall you were not—"

"Don't say it!" He chuckles as he moves closer. "I was terrible, but in my defense, I was sixteen and we were both a little bad at it."

God, we were just two fumbling teenagers, watching really bad movies on what to do and not mimicking the act all that well.

"We were, but we loved each other."

Grayson's laugh is more like a huff. "We did. And then you left."

No point in either of us trying to beat around the bush. I hurt him, and regardless of how much time has passed, there was never closure. "I'm sorry."

Grayson looks over. "I'm sorry that I didn't stop by when you got back. I didn't know, Jess—about the crash. I would've come to see if you were okay."

I glance over at his profile. "Why? I left you. You owe me nothing, and I didn't take offense to it."

"You leaving me was a million years ago, right?"

"It sure—" The words get caught in my throat. I know this will pass, but it has been so nice feeling a little like myself. "Sorry. Sometimes my brain needs to pause so I can speak again," I explain.

"Take all the time you need."

"Since I never plan to venture off this porch again, I may take longer than you want."

"You're planning to stay here?" Grayson asks with a smirk.

I shrug. "It's better than going out there right now when I can't speak or drive or anything. All I want is to work or have something meaningful, but I'm broken, so I'll stay put."

Grayson sits beside me, nudging me gently. "That's not the girl I knew. She was fearless, ready to conquer the world."

Sadness creeps over me, blanketing the joyful banter we were just having. "She isn't the same anymore."

"Are any of us?"

I look at him, wondering what has made Grayson who he is now. "No, I guess not."

He gives me a sad smile and then gets back up. "I should go. I have to pick up Amelia."

"Is that your daughter?"

Delia filled me in, but she never mentioned her name.

A bright smile warms his face. God, he's still insanely attractive when he smiles. The dimple on his left cheek makes my heart ache.

"She is. She's four." He takes out his phone, swiping to show the little girl on his home screen.

"She's beautiful."

"And a handful."

I laugh, imagining how much she probably has him wrapped around her finger. I know that, at her age, I was all Daddy's girl. There was nothing he would deny me as long as I batted my eyelashes and grinned.

"Most girls know how to work their fathers."

"Oh, she's got my number."

"She's lucky she has you, Gray."

"I hope so because I'm all she has."

I want to ask all the questions, but I'm exhausted, and I'm not sure how much longer I can keep my brain cooperating. I lean back against the pillow and exhale.

"Take a nap. It was good to see you. I mean that." Grayson heads down the porch steps and gets to his car. "Now that you're back in town and we've talked, I'll stop by again."

I sit up and raise my voice so he can hear. "I'd like that, bring Amelia, I'd love to meet her and tell her all the stories you would rather she never know."

His deep laughter fills the air and then he gets in his car, driving away.

What a strange but hopeful day.

GRAYSON

"Thanks for watching her, Stella."

My sister leans down, tapping Amelia's nose. "It's nothing. I love spending time with my Melia. Not to mention, she loves her auntie."

She does because my sister spoils her rotten, which I guess is one of the perks of being an aunt.

"Still, you dropped everything, and I appreciate it."

"I was going shopping with Winnie, not solving world peace. Plus, doing these things allows me opportunities to collect debts in the future from you four boneheads."

Regardless of what she says, Stella is the princess of the family and has loved having four brothers who are willing to slay any dragon for her. Joshua would've killed me, Alexander, or Oliver if anything happened to her.

This girl is able to get whatever she wants and loves every

second of it.

"You have a very skewed memory of your childhood."

She laughs once. "Please, you all made it so I could never have any fun!"

"I recall you having a little too much fun at a few parties."

As much as my sister would like to think otherwise, she was a damn mess. If it weren't for us covering for her, she would've been in a lot of trouble.

"Because you all were a bunch of saints?"

"Not even close. That was why we *knew* what was going on when you tried to tell us one of your horrible excuses."

Stella shakes her head. "I feel bad for you, Gray. Melia is going to grow up and be just like me one day."

A shudder runs through me. "She'll date when I'm dead."

"Pretty sure Dad thought the same thing."

"Dad failed, I won't."

"Anyway," she draws the word out, "I heard you ran into Jessica."

This town is insane. I'm sure Winnie told her, since she's Jessica's sister.

"I actually stopped by and saw her on my way home."

"Oh. Oh! Wow. Okay. And? How did it go?"

I love that I caught her off guard. One thing she loves more than anything is being in the know, and her not being the first to know I'd run into Jessica probably grated on her.

"Fine." I pick Amelia up, kiss her cheek, and head into the kitchen.

My sister groans, and I fight back the urge to laugh.

"Daddy, I am so hungry."

"I'm sure you are. Aunt Stella's idea of a meal is M&M's and Twizzlers."

"The peanut ones!" she says as she follows me. "They have protein."

"How is it that you're as skinny as you are when you eat like a thirteen-year-old boy? Seriously, have you consumed a vegetable in the last ten years?"

Stella makes a face. "No thanks. And the reason I'm so slim is because I work out and have great genes."

Amelia takes my face in her hands. "I don't like vegetables neither."

"Auntie Stella loves them, she was kidding. She is going to eat some with you now."

"Auntie Stella has to go to work since your daddy stuck me on the night shift while our manager called out."

"How convenient that you have to leave so soon," I say with a grin.

"Isn't it? I love how that works out. But, anyway, was everything good at the Park Inn?"

The Park Inn is our flagship bed and breakfast as well as one of the top destinations. The way my father designed the building was smart. Instead of making the land curve to the structure, it seems as though the inn was formed from the mountain. It sits perfectly, giving the guests unobstructed views of the trees, sky, and nature.

"It was fine. The couple in room five was moved to eight because they didn't want the view of the right side of the mountain. Other than that, it was a quiet day."

Stella nods and then reaches for her purse. "Have you talked to Mom?"

"No, you do that so I don't have to."

"Yeah right. I'm sure you'll have no choice when she picks up Melia this week. She said that Dad is visiting Oliver this week and then will check on Joshua in New Orleans after that."

"And I care because?"

"Because that means we have two weeks where she's going to be up our asses and we'll have to entertain her. I dealt with it the last time he traveled, so you're it this time."

My mother is a brilliant, strong, and fierce women—as long as my father is by her side. When he's gone, she wilts.

She also pretends that his trips aren't to visit his mistresses that he has all around the properties he owns. It's too bad his kids don't have the same ability. Even if we don't discuss it around her, my father is well aware that we know and how we feel about it.

"When does Josh come back home for a visit?"

Stella shrugs. "Hell if I know."

"Hell is a bad word," Amelia cuts in.

"Yes, it is. We're going to have to wash Aunt Stella's mouth out with soap."

Amelia nods. "Uh-huh."

"I'm sorry, Melia, I won't say it again."

"Okay." Amelia forgives her without pause.

"Now, I have to go to work, you need to feed your child something that has nutritional value, and I'll see you tomorrow . . . at Mom's."

I walk her out, not commenting on that last part because if I have to see my mother this weekend, I'm not going tomorrow—no matter what threats my sister hangs over my head.

"Thanks again, Stell."

"Anything for my favorite brother." She kisses my cheek and then playfully slaps it. "Well, Alex really was, but you were a close second. Also, don't think I didn't notice you evading my questions about how it went with Jessica."

"I'm sure Winnie will tell you everything."

Stella's face brightens. "She most definitely will, but I was hoping you'd share."

"There's not much to say. It was awkward at the diner, so I went there to let her know there were no hard feelings."

Stella laughs. "Oh, I'm sorry. You're serious?"

"It was a long time ago."

"Yeah, but Jessica was that girl for you. The one who haunts your dreams, and even when you were with Yvonne, we all knew it was Jessica who had your heart."

Arguing with her about this will get me nowhere. "And on that note, you have to go."

"You have lost a rung on my favorite brother ladder."

I clutch my chest. "I'm crushed. As much as I'd like to continue our conversation, I have Daddy duty to ensure my kid doesn't survive on your version of food groups."

"All right. Love you, Gray."

"Love you too."

Once she's off, I head inside to find Amelia sitting on the floor with her dolls and an open container of cookies.

"Hey," I say and she looks up, "who gave you those?"

She ducks her head. "I found them."

"Are you allowed to have cookies before dinner?"

"No, but I was hungry, Daddy."

Her big blue eyes widen, proving that Stella was right—I'm totally screwed. I scoop her up, and we begin our normal routine. I get Amelia something healthy to eat, then it's bath time, and now it's time for bed. She's all tucked in her bed, the spinning cloud light that Stella bought her is on, and it's story time. We read the same book she loves every night, and I can recite it without even looking.

"Can you read with the silly voices, Daddy?"

"Do you promise to stay in bed if I do?"

"I promise!"

She lies, but I have a hard time denying her anything. "Okay."

I drop my voice deep as I get into the role of the elephant. "Do you have big dreams, little mouse?" I ask.

"I do, I do," I say, going much higher than is actually comfortable.

"And tell me what do you dream of?"

Amelia's eyes light up as she answers in her best mouse voice. "To be a singer."

I grin. "And what do you want to sing?"

"Opera, like my mom does in Paris."

My heart plummets. That's not the words to the book. Every now and then Amelia will ask about Yvonne, and I made a promise to tell her the truth. While it's hard for me, I can't imagine it's easy for her either. Still, if she always knows the truth, then there will never be a time I have to tell her that I wasn't honest.

"Melia, that's not the line."

She snuggles deeper under her covers. "I know."

I brush her cheek. "I love you more than the stars in the sky."

"I love you more than the clouds."

"I love you more than the books in the library."

She smiles. "I love you more than anyone in the world."

"You're the person I love the most, Amelia. Never doubt that."

Her long lashes rise and fall, and she launches herself into my arms. "I love you, Daddy."

"I love you more. I love you most."

I hug her, holding her tight because, while I can't fix the fact that her mother chose to leave her, I can love her harder and hope it's enough.

Today is one of those days I should've just stayed in bed. It's been a rough few days, but today, everything went to shit. I got to work to find out we had a pipe burst that flooded a guest room, my plumber can't get here until tomorrow, which means the repair people can't get the room fixed.

And then my front desk manager quit because her husband got a job in Charlotte and they're moving next week, which is why she called out.

Willow Creek Valley is great to visit, but not many people move here, which means finding a suitable replacement is going to be absolute torture.

Stella waltzes in late with bags in her hands. "Sorry, it was a crazy day. I got your voice mail. Seems we have a mess?"

"Yes. It is a mess. I could've used some help."

"I'm allowed a day off, Gray."

"When is the last time I had one?"

She scoffs. "That's your choice, brother. You're the one who works here constantly, and when you're not here, you're at the firehouse—of your own free will."

"Some of us have to be responsible."

I'm being a dick, I know it, and yet, I need to get this out.

Stella sets the bags down, her eyes narrow, and her lips purse. "Well, I can see you're going to be the asshole today. Fine. Go ahead. Tell me how spoiled, ridiculous, and childish

I am. Because I work just as hard as you do, but neither you or *them* ever acknowledge it. Who handled almost the entire renovation? Me. Who did it without any issues? Me. Who has grown our occupancy to full month in and month out? Oh, that's right . . . me!"

"No one calls you childish," I throw back.

She huffs. "Out of all that, you want to lead on that point?"

I run my hands through my hair and sigh. "I'm sorry."

"You should be."

"I am."

Stella sits in the chair across from me. "All right. Let's take it all one step at a time, and we'll divide and conquer. I know you hate the hiring process, so I'll handle it. Can you manage getting that room fixed as soon as possible?"

"That's a solid plan. What if we use the cottage as our spill over? I can get Mateo in there to work on fixing anything so we can move guests there."

"That's a great idea. I'll go look at it now too. Last I remember, it wasn't terrible and shouldn't need much work. It'll be great as a complimentary upgrade to the guests who booked for the other room."

The cottage has been on our shortlist forever. It's a bit away and most guests want privacy, but it also has that feeling of being in a home.

"Yeah, and we have a vacant room for the next two days, so right now we're okay. I'll get Mateo going right away. What are you going to do about hiring someone?" I ask.

She shrugs. "I'll figure it out."

"Okay."

"Don't worry, Gray. We endure."

I laugh as I get to my feet. "That should've been our family motto."

"Yeah, and don't ever fall in love, you'll end up shattered. And don't fuck the help should be another one."

"I've never fucked the help," I counter.

"Me either."

"No, Dad is far too busy doing that." I wink as I head out to find Mateo. On my way, I talk to a few guests, who tell me how much they love staying here, and then answer a few staff questions.

Then I see her.

Jessica is standing with her sister out by the overlook. Her dark brown hair moves in the wind, and her smile is wide as she laughs. I forgot how much I used to love making her laugh. She didn't do it with reserve. It was as if nothing could stop her from being happy, and I lived for it. I want to experience it again.

Our eyes meet, she lifts her hand in a wave, and I do the same. Winnie touches her arm and she turns away and I feel this ache in my chest.

Jesus. I'm not sixteen anymore. Stop it.

I came out here to handle the inn, not think about how to make her laugh so I can hear it again. Jessica wasn't made to stay in this town. She had bigger dreams that couldn't be contained.

She'll heal, and when she does, she'll leave.

Besides, I don't care about her like that anyway.

I find Mateo, who is all clear on his instructions. The cottage isn't great, but it's fixable. With Stella at the helm of decorating, she'll find a way to make the cracks part of the charm.

I head back to the office and look over to where Jessica was, but she's gone, and I force myself to be relieved by that.

We don't need to see each other again. We got all that out of the way a few days ago.

"Grayson?" I hear her call out as I'm rounding the corner.

"Hey, Jess."

She smiles. "You're the only person who still calls me that."

"Really?"

"Yeah, I don't know where along the way I stopped being Jess and became Jessica. Maybe it was when I got to Massachusetts or maybe when I . . ."

"When you?"

She shakes her head. "Nothing."

I'm not sure if this is another memory issue or she just doesn't want to say. Either way, I decide not to push.

"What are you doing here?"

"Well, I was here because I was abducted by Stella and Winnie to go shopping today. Then Stella said she had to get here right away."

I bob my head. "Ahh, I see."

"But, I . . . well, I wanted to thank you."

"For what?"

Her lower lip goes between her teeth and then slowly is released. "For hiring me. I know I'm still not at one hundred percent, but I think this is going to really help push me. I promise, I'll work hard before I start. My doctor said I needed to return to living and . . ."

Awareness hits like a freight train.

My sister.

She hired Jessica. Without talking to me.

The air becomes hard to draw into my lungs, but I manage to keep a smile on my face. If I tell her that Stella can't hire her because I'm going to kill my sister, then I look like there's a problem with Jessica working here, which there's not.

It's fine because I don't feel anything or care.

It's fine because, like I told my sister, Jessica and I are nothing and have left the past in the past.

It's fine because—well, I'm running out of reasons.

Mostly, though, the way she looks right now makes me want to give her the entire inn. She's nervous, excited, and there's a look of triumph that I don't want to diminish.

But fuck me, this is going to be torture.

Jessica stares at me, and I know I need to say something. "Yeah, of course. I'm glad this is going to work out for all of us."

The apprehension on her face disappears and she steps closer, her hand coming to my arm and squeezing slightly. "Thanks, Gray."

"I guess I'll see you on Monday?"

"First thing."

She walks away, leaving me standing here, staring at the horizon and wondering how I'm going to make my sister pay for this. And if this still means I've never fucked the help.

Five

JESSICA

The dream book is sitting on my lap, my hands resting over it as my leg bounces. Dr. Warvel is sitting in her chair, legs crossed as she waits.

I'm not sure if I have the strength to do this. I run my sweaty palms on my legs. "It's like opening Pandora's box," I finally say.

"The dreams aren't locked up, Jessica. You're living them every day."

"Maybe that's why I don't want to read it."

I *thought* that I would hand the book over and *she* would read it. Not that I was going to have to pour over every word. After I wrote in the book each morning, I didn't go back. I didn't want to see it in black and white. It's a damn movie in my brain.

She sits forward. "Part of healing is to face the trauma

you've endured."

"How am I not? I'm here and trying."

"Yes, you are. The point of reading it is to acknowledge it, but it's also to see if the dream is truly the same as the event or if you're experiencing things that you don't even realize are different. The point of journaling it is to give you a record of the dream to be able to compare it to the actual events."

My leg bounces faster. "I'm not ready."

"Okay then." She sits back in her chair and writes a note. "Tell me if anything new has happened this week."

I can do that. "I got a job."

Her eyes widen and a smile crosses her face. "Well, that's big news. Where, and doing what?"

"I'm going to run the front desk at the Park Inn."

"The Park Inn? The one that the Parkerson family owns?"

"The one and only."

I never imagined working for the Park Inn. The truth is, I sort of vowed I never would, but I was there and Stella offered it. It's been a month since the crash, and I need *something*. This is my first real taste of being my former self.

Dr. Warvel bobs her head slowly. "That's great, Jessica. You have spent the last month unsure of what the future held, and this will bring you one step closer to your goal of returning to normal."

I'm slightly impressed she didn't bring up Grayson or ask how I feel about working with him. I sure as hell am not going to be the one to mention it.

He didn't seem uneasy about being around me, we had that nice talk on my porch, and well, I don't plan to stick around here once I'm healed anyway.

"That's my hope."

"All of this is exciting. Do you have any concerns that you want to discuss?"

There's really just one. "I'm worried that my head and might . . . go . . . *this!*" I yell, frustrated because I couldn't speak again.

"And that's valid, but you can't control how your brain is healing. All you can do is be patient and work through the situations as they arise. Like you're doing right now."

I can't control my own mouth. "Why won't this stop?"

"Because, while you feel a month is a long time, it's not. Thirty days is a short blip, and you are not only working through new physical limitations but also an emotional trauma." Her eyes drop to the notebook on my lap.

I rub my fingers against the paper, feeling the anxiety coursing through me. A part of me wants to read it, to remember it in a different way. But this was all feeling. This isn't me just telling my story about the crash in a detached way—this is me at my rawest and most vulnerable.

"I'm scared."

"You're not alone. You're not in that plane. You're on the ground, safe, and alive," she tells me. "One step at a time."

"One page at a time."

She doesn't move, and I lift the cover, wanting to be brave. Wishing that for just a few minutes I can be the Jessica I was before the crash. The one who was strong, fearless, and ready to handle any situation. This version—the scared girl who wants to hide—isn't who I want to be.

I can feel the tremors moving through my body, but I use all my effort to focus on the words. I read, doing everything to just say the words without actually hearing them or taking them in. They're my memories, the dreams that haunt me each night, but I won't allow them to hurt me.

The words fall from me as I flip pages with shaky hands. I continue speaking, knowing that if I stop, I won't be able to go again. At some point, there is nothing left on the paper to read.

After a minute, Dr. Warvel reaches out, her hand grasping mine. "Jessica, I need you to look at me."

I feel cold and numb as tears fall down my face. When my eyes lift to hers, I can barely make out her features, and I turn away. Shame, anger, and frustration at the weakness I feel is too much. I should be over this, Jacob is. He's happy and enjoying his time with Brenna. Elliot just moved in with his girlfriend, and Jose reconciled with his wife. I'm the only one who is falling apart. Why can they all find a way through this but I'm . . . stuck?

"I can't," I confess. I can't . . . to it all.

"You can. You did great just now. Look at me." I force my-self to meet her gaze again. "You didn't live it just now, Jess. You told the story that was written on the paper. Each time you can read these words, you'll find it a little easier, and we'll see where the holes are, plug them, and keep working. I know you're frustrated, but you are making progress."

I wipe away the tears that continue to fall. "I d-don't feel l-like it."

She smiles softly and hands me a tissue. "Look at what has happened already. You've spoken to Grayson, who was a big part of your original story, and told him you were sorry for what happened all those years ago. You and your mother are spending time together again, and you're working. Those are not small feats. And the biggest one you still don't even realize."

"What's that?"

"You spoke that entire story with only two errors in your speech."

"Do you really think this is a good idea?" Winnie asks as she stands in the dressing room, disapproving over every outfit I try on.

"I do."

She sighs deeply, shaking her head as I turn, trying to show her how it's not that bad. Sure, it's a bit plain, but I'm running the front desk, not going to a board meeting.

"I'm not so sure, Jess. You just got back, give yourself some time. Why do you need to work anyway? Isn't the airline going to have to pay out a ton in settlements?"

That is going to be years down the line. I have savings, but with what I've been helping my mother with, that's going to run out in six months. She barely makes ends meet, so there is no way I would ask her to take care of me financially. The thing is, as much as I need the money, it's really about working, contributing, and living again.

I don't want to be dependent on anyone.

"It's not that simple, and I need to get out."

"But working for the Parkersons?"

"You love them."

"I love Stella. And even then, while she may be one of my best friends, I can only take her in small doses. We all know the way her family feels about us."

Winnie and Stella have been friends since they were kids. They ran in different circles, but were close in their own way. I guess it's fine for the Parkerson's daughter to be friends with us but it isn't okay for one of their sons to marry one of us.

"And here I am—the help."

"That's not funny," Winnie says, grabbing a coat that she likes.

I take it, knowing my sister won't relent unless I try it on. "It's the—" I struggle. The words again not forming.

"It's what?"

I follow the technique, but I can't get my mouth to cooperate. The words die on my lips. *It's the truth. It's what I am, and I'm okay with it because it's them helping me.*

I try and try. Angry tears fall down my cheeks, and then I feel the pressure of a headache come on stronger and faster than usual. God, this is going to be horrible.

"Jess?" Winnie steps forward as my hands grip the sides of my head. "Jess? What's wrong?"

I close my eyes and sink to the floor. "Head," I rasp the only thing I can say.

My sister closes the door of the dressing room as the pain comes on so fast I don't have time to prepare for it. The lights are so bright, and each sound feels as though it's being pushed through an amplifier. The metal hangers scraping, the cart rolling . . . it hurts so much.

"Jess, shhh," Winnie says, pulling me to her chest. "What do I do?"

"Lights. So much."

She cloaks me in darkness, wrapping something around me, but I won't open my eyes to see what it is. I need to calm myself.

"I'm going to tell the manager so I can get you out. Stay here."

I couldn't go anywhere if I tried. I need my medicine, darkness, and a few hours of complete silence. Winnie is gone, and I lie on the floor, clutching my skull, hating that the last few days have been amazing and now I'm crippled by the pain.

My doctor says a way to work through them is counting backward. To let the numbers help pass the time until I fall asleep.

I do that. I start at nine hundred ninety-nine and go back. Once I get to four hundred thirty-three, I hear the door open, and instead of Jessica's voice, it's deep, male, and familiar.

Before I can say or do anything, I'm lifted off the ground and tucked against Grayson's chest. God, he smells the same. It's a combination of fresh air, spice, and sandalwood that I would be able to pick out anywhere.

I stir, but he holds me tighter, his voice quiet. "I have you, Jess. Just relax, I'll get you home."

"I have her purse," Winnie says.

"Daddy?" a small, sweet voice says from beside me. "Is your friend okay?"

"She is," he whispers. "We have to be very quiet, though, can you do that?"

"Yes," the little girl whispers back.

I bury my head in his chest, allowing myself to take a small ounce of comfort from him. My head is still pounding, but it isn't as debilitating as it was seconds ago. I keep counting, not letting go of the monotony of the numbers.

"I'll take her," Grayson says.

"What?"

"My car has tinted windows, if it's light sensitivity that hurts her, your car is the worst."

Winnie drives a tiny convertible. There is no room to lie down and no hiding from the blinding sun.

"No," I croak, but Grayson tightens his grip on me.

"Don't argue, Jess," he whispers before directing his words to Winnie. "Take Melia's seat out." A few seconds pass, and then his voice changes. "Please, Winnie."

She makes a noise under her breath, but she must agree because a moment later, he settles me in a car. Not sure which one. The door closes, and I curl up on the backseat, no longer caring whose car I'm in, just that I'm lying down.

I can hear my sister outside. "Seriously, she's going to hate this when she's better."

"I have no doubt of that. Can you drive Melia to Stella's?"

"Stella's?"

"Yeah, I'll take Jess back home and stay with her for a bit."

"Gray that's not . . ."

"Daddy, can I come with you?" the little girl asks.

"Daddy is going to make sure his friend is okay and doesn't need to go to the hospital," he explains.

Jesus. This is not okay. I will be fine, I just need to sleep.

"Is she going to need surgery?"

"No, sweet girl, I just want to make sure she isn't in pain."

"So, you'll be there to watch her and make sure?"

"Grayson," Winnie cuts in again, "this is really not necessary."

The little girl's voice is musical as she says, "It's okay, Winnie. My daddy is a fireman and he saves people. He can help."

Winnie laughs. "Yes, I guess he does."

"Do you know his friend?"

"I sure do," Winnie says. "She's my sister."

"I wish I had a sister!"

Someone clears their throat. "You be good for Winnie and

Auntie Stella."

"I will, Daddy. Will I get to play with Auntie?"

"You sure will."

"Jess is going to be so pissed at us," Winnie says.

"I'm sure she'll let me know."

I count, trying not to focus on their conversation because the pain is throbbing again. I keep the jacket that smells like Grayson over my head, keeping myself in total darkness.

When he gets in, I struggle to say it loud enough so he can hear but not loud enough that it will make the headache worse. "Medicine."

Grayson is out of the car a moment later. Thankfully he doesn't close the door, but I hear him yell for Winnie.

After another eighty-three seconds, he returns. "I don't want to hurt you, but I have water and the pill Winnie got from your purse. Can you sit up to take it?"

I have to. I keep the jacket around my head, opening it just a little. I extend my hand, and he gives me the pill and water bottle. I toss it in my throat and chug the water. He lays me back down carefully before awkwardly buckling me into the seat.

I start counting backward from my starting point again, and I drift off, letting Grayson's scent surround me and knowing that, when this is over, I'm going to have to bury myself to avoid the embarrassment.

Six

JESSICA

The ache is back, but it's nothing like it was before. I shift to the side, nestling into my pillow, which causes me to open my eyes, not knowing where I am.

When I do, it all comes back, the pain, the headache, Grayson carrying me. The light causes my eyes to slam back shut. Too fast and too much to process. If there is a God, he will make sure that Grayson Parkerson is not here. That he dropped me off, my sister came, and she's the figure I swear I saw in the corner.

This time, I open my eyes slowly so as not to cause the headache to return with a vengeance. Once I'm acclimated a bit, I look around, avoiding the area where I know someone is, still praying it's Winnie, but there is no God because Grayson is there.

Great.

"Hey," I say, throat dry and hoarse.

He sits up. "Jess, hey, are you all right?"

The raging storm is now calm, just a few remnants, but nothing I can't handle. I nod, swallowing as I try to sit up. "I'm better. I . . . I don't remember the car or getting to the house."

"We got here and about two hours ago, I carried you in, and you've been sleeping since."

"You've been here for two hours?"

This is even worse than I thought.

He gets up and walks to my bed and sits at the edge. "I've never seen anything like that. You were in agony, Jess, and I couldn't leave you."

"It happens sometimes. It used to be daily, but it's not anymore."

"From the plane crash?"

I nod. "It's part of the concussion injury."

He releases a heavy sigh. "Daily?"

Those first few weeks were absolute hell. I couldn't move without pain so intense it would drop me to the floor. "The doctors say they'll become less frequent as I heal, but the brain works on its own time, and I can't do anything to move the process along. S-some days—" I stutter and then catch myself. "Some days were so bad I didn't get out of bed at all."

"Does your family know?"

"Of course," I say tentatively.

"Winnie must've told Stella, but . . ."

"But?"

He chuckles quietly. "I have a rule about not discussing women I love who left me."

"Ah, well, I guess both our sisters can keep their traps shut occasionally. I have the same rule about this town and people

I loved."

"So, you didn't want to know about me?"

I shake my head softly. "It was . . . I couldn't . . ." I had to pretend.

Pretend I didn't love you.

Pretend I didn't regret leaving and think of you.

Pretend that I didn't make a huge mistake.

He looks down at his hands. "I'm glad we were at the store today."

A niggling memory starts to surface. "You were with your daughter?"

Grayson smiles. "Yeah, that was her."

"I didn't get to see her."

"No," a soft chuckle escapes. "I guess you didn't."

"Where is she?"

"She's with your sister and Stella, doing makeovers and nails."

"While you sit here with me . . ."

Our eyes meet for a brief second, and it feels as if a million things are said without a single word. "I guess it's one of those things."

"One of what things?"

Why am I asking him this? Why do I care? He and I are nothing, and it doesn't matter that, when I thought the world was ending, he was one of the faces I saw. It's not the *only* reason I came back to Willow Creek Valley. It's home, and for all I knew, he didn't live here.

What we had ended years ago. I'm being stupid.

"Where you loved someone once and you can't quite walk away when you see them hurting."

And my heart races. I stare at him, wondering if this is

some medication-induced hallucination. It wouldn't be the first. Or maybe, maybe this is a dream. One that isn't filled with metal crunching and pain as the plane makes impact with the ground.

I blink a few times, seeing if I wake up.

"Winnie would've made sure I was okay," I say softly.

"I'm sure, but she couldn't have carried you out of the car. So, you'd be in the backseat right now instead of in bed."

I smile and close my eyes. "True."

Grayson leans closer. "Are you okay? Seriously?"

Slowly, I sigh and then look at him again. "I am. It's hard, and it usually takes a full day to recover."

"What brings them on?"

"It can be anything."

Grayson grips the back of his neck. "When is the last time you got one?"

I don't want to lie to Grayson, but at the same time, I don't want to lose the job before I even start. I am genuinely excited and ready to resume some sense of normal again. Working gives purpose and joy. I loved to fly, meet celebrities, and get to see new places. Now all of that is gone, and I'm not sure who I am anymore.

"It's been about a week, but when I'm triggered, there's no stopping it."

"Stress probably doesn't help," he notes. "Are you sure about going back to work?"

I knew it. Disappointment fills me as I prepare to have the job taken from me. "I can handle it, Gray."

"I didn't say you couldn't. I just worry that it's going to be a lot of stress, long days on your feet, running around and dealing with my family. I don't want it to end up hurting you."

I shake my head. "No, it's not like that. I need this. I have felt so useless and broken, please, don't take it away."

He moves quickly, hands taking mine. "I wasn't saying that. No, I wouldn't not *let* you work at the inn. It's that I'm worried it'll make things worse."

I sit up slowly, measuring the pain and light sensitivity. "The only thing that's making it worse is not living. Since the crash, I've been here—alone. I can't drive. My words . . . they get stuck. It's better though," I say quickly. "I'm doing better, and when Stella offered me the job, it was the first time I felt okay."

Saying it aloud makes me feel stupid, but I need him to see that this job is saving me.

"And if you get a headache?"

I release a breath through my nose and shrug. "I don't know."

He releases my hands, sighing deeply. "What if I find you another job? One where you don't have to worry about people or really much of anything, but you can still work."

"No. I'm not a charity case, and I swear, I can do this."

"I never said you were or that you couldn't."

"If I were just some girl and you didn't know me or about what happened to me, would you be worried like this?"

Grayson smirks. "You're not some girl. You were the first girl I ever loved, and trying to pretend otherwise is a mistake."

"Maybe so, but I got this job from your sister because you need a front desk manager."

He stands, pacing around my room. "I need a lot of things," he says so quietly I'm not sure I heard it right. After a few more turns around, he stops and looks at me. "Okay. One condition though."

"Name it."

"If you feel a headache coming on or that you need a break because you're tired . . . I mean anything weird, you tell me immediately. Don't wait until it's bad or because you're in the middle of something. Deal?"

I nod. "Deal."

"Good. Then I'll see you on Monday."

"Monday." I have one week to get prepared to be around this man all the time.

He sits back on the edge of my bed. "Okay then. Since you're doing better, I'm going to get my daughter, take her home, and do some damage control. I'm sure our sisters have corrupted her enough."

It's weird to think of Grayson as a father. He was always a great guy, caring, loyal, and giving, and it's good to know that hasn't changed about him. "Your daughter . . . is she like you?"

He grins. "I sure hope not."

"Why would you say that?" I ask with a yawn. The medicine usually causes me to sleep off and on for hours.

"Because I was stupid, trusting, and while I got Melia, who is the best thing to ever happen to me, the fight was hard, and I don't want her to struggle."

"Isn't everything worth fighting for hard?"

A flash of regret flashes across his face before the easygoing smile I remember from childhood is there. "And some things we have to let go because they aren't meant to be won, right?"

The words I said to him when I walked away.

"Jess, stop!" Grayson grabbed my arm as I walked back to my car.

This shouldn't hurt so bad. It was my decision to leave

him, and yet everything inside me was screaming out in pain.

But I heard his mother. I heard the anger as he said he wanted to marry me and her threaten to take everything from him. His father was there, too, agreeing because I was not good enough.

I was going to do this before we were ever faced with him having to choose between his family and me.

"Please just let me go."

"We have plans. We have plans, and you're just giving them up."

I turned, tears falling down my face. "We are kids! We have plans that will never work out. We both know it. I'm nineteen and I want to live, Grayson. I want out of this stupid town with its stupid judgment. I want to travel, eat strange foods, and make bad choices. I can't do that with you."

He took a step back. "Why? Why am I what's holding you back?"

"Because I love you! I love you, and I will never leave you or this place if I don't do it now."

"We can do it together."

My head shook so fast, wishing I could dispel the words out of my head. "All that will happen is we'll hate each other."

"Oh! And fucking leaving me like this will make us like each other?"

"I will always love you, Gray. Always."

And I would. He was the first boy I ever loved, gave myself to, and trusted to keep me safe, which he did. This moment was the only thing about us that I would regret. However, I knew it was the right choice. Grayson was destined for greatness, and he wouldn't achieve it if I was around.

Not only that, I needed to leave here. I couldn't stay and be like my mother. I couldn't love a man, give up my dreams, and then be left when he realized I wasn't enough.

"Don't do this. Don't walk away. We'll figure it out."

"I have a plane ticket for Massachusetts. I'm leaving tonight."

He stepped toward me. "Tonight? You knew? You . . . you came here, we just . . . and you're leaving?"

I needed him. I needed the memory of us and all the love we shared. I was a coward, and even knowing that, I didn't care. Grayson Parkerson owned my heart, but it was time I owned my future.

"I know I promised you a lot and that I'm letting you down. I'm sorry. I have to go, and I have to try to find myself."

His hands balled into fists and then released. "Fine. I'm here, trying to fight to keep you when it's clear you don't want me to. I want to fight and win and keep you!"

The last sixty minutes had been the hardest time in my life. I came to tell him goodbye, and ended up in his arms, kissing, touching, making love, and that was when I knew that it had to be now.

"I guess some things just aren't meant to be won in a fight."

Neither of us had a clue what life really was or the hardships that lay ahead. Naivety is a gift for the young. We allowed it to cloak us in ignorance and make us believe things were so much easier than they really were.

Not that I feel I was ever as blissfully ignorant as the Parkersons were. They lived in their gilded castle with new cars and heat each month. Where I swept the floor and learned that duct tape really could fix anything if you tried enough and wearing layers warded off the chill.

With Grayson, though, I was never cold, and that scared

me more than anything. My mother once lived in that state of dependence.

I would not be her.

"Maybe not won, but cherished isn't such a bad thing," I say, not wanting to go back to something I can't fix.

His lip quirks, and then he stands, pulling the covers up over me. "No, it's not a bad thing." He leans in, kissing my forehead tenderly. "Rest, and if you need anything, I'm just a call away."

"Thanks for everything," I say, the sleepiness starting to creep back in, tugging at my eyelids. I slip down into the warm blankets, feeling as though I'm already asleep. "I love you, Gray. I always have." I think to myself.

"Sleep, we'll talk soon."

"Soon."

His warm breath slides across my cheek. "I always will."

Seven

GRAYSON

"Parkerson, get the hose on the first floor just for good measure," Chief yells as my crew redirects the water to where he indicated. It's been a crazy night. We had two false alarms back to back and now a structure fire.

"Jack, get it higher," I direct.

He nods, lifting the nozzle a bit more. When we got here, the fire was out of control, but after the work of my truck and two others, we've finally got it contained. Luckily, the fire alarms woke the family and everyone got out safely.

There're just a few small hot spots remaining, and I'm beat.

We work to get those out and shut the water down. Jack groans, his head falling back as he stares up. "This was a tough one."

I nod, grabbing two water bottles and tossing one to him. "No shit."

"Remind me again why I let you convince me to do this . . ."

"I think it was you who convinced me."

"Well, damn, we're fucking stupid."

"Fact."

Jack and I chug the water and then toss the empty bottles into the truck. One of the newbies gets to clean out the rig as part of their initiation.

"I'm glad we got this one under control quickly," Jack says, surveying what was left of the home.

"Yeah, no casualties is always a win."

There are two fires that I will never forget. One where we arrived and were told everyone was out, but the witnesses hadn't seen the father go back in to get their dog. It was my first call as a lieutenant three years ago, and one that has haunted me. We should've geared up to go in faster. We could've saved him, but everyone was sure the whole family was accounted for.

The other is one that I wasn't a responder for, but Jack was. It was the fire that took his mother from them.

Which is why we *always* answer the call.

Jack clears his throat. "Always a win." He leans back, stretching his arms over his head. "So, tell me about you and Jess."

I jerk my head back. "What about me and Jess?"

"I hear that you rescued her like some hero from a fairy tale, pulling her out of a perilous situation and saving her like the knight in shining armor you are."

I roll my eyes. "I didn't know you knew the word perilous."

"I know all kinds of shit."

"Well, you know nothing about this."

"Sure I don't."

Thankfully, one of my rookies comes over, sweat pouring down his face. "Captain?"

"What's up, Riggs?"

Riggs is a good kid, a bit overeager, but he's going to be a great firefighter. With a last name like that, we expect nothing less. It also doesn't hurt that his father is the chief. He has no choice but to follow in those footsteps, which I know all too well.

"Do you want me to start coiling the hose?"

"We can't since they're still using it."

"Right."

Jack snorts. "You *can* do something."

Oh, I'm sure this is going to be good.

"Anything you need, Jack."

"Don't be so eager, kid, there are too many who will take advantage of it," I warn.

"Right. Of course."

Jack shakes his head. "Just stick with me, and we'll find you something to do."

That's the worst idea ever. "For now, just make sure all the guys have water," I tell Riggs.

Riggs runs off, doing as I ask. I chug another bottle of water and nudge Jack. "Chicken shit."

"He's Chief's son, damn right I am. Where are the other rookies? We can fuck with them."

When Jack and I came up through the ranks, it was a lot worse. We were basically the entire truck's bitches, but it was how we were brought into the fold. A truck is a family. It's where we put our lives on the line for strangers, but we would die for each other.

"Not anything too bad."

"Of course not, but I do need my gear cleaned."

I do another radio check, something that helps me, once again, check that my guys are all accounted for.

Once the last one confirms, we start to break down. We work as a unit, and get it done quickly and correctly. It's something I love about it. We do it right from start to finish because, if we got another call right now, we need to be ready. Everything is about teamwork and preparation. The hoses go in the same spots each time, I can reach out blindly for an axe and know it will be there.

We don't take chances. We don't ever risk someone's life by being lazy.

It's just hitting five in the morning when Jack and I climb into the back of the truck to head back to the station, and I'm freaking beat.

"Where is Melia?" Jack asks.

"Stella's."

"I thought maybe she was somewhere else."

"Where the hell would she be? After my mother takes her pills, she wouldn't wake up if the house was crumbling."

He grins. "Maybe Jessica?"

He's such an asshole. "There is nothing going on with Jessica."

"Okay, if you say so."

I huff, frustrated because, if he's saying this to me, then someone is saying it to him. This town loves a good scandal, but they live for a happy ending. Not that there's going to be one because we're nothing.

"She needed help, Jack. I wasn't going to leave her stranded."

"For half the day?"

"Half the—" I take a deep breath. "It wasn't half the day, it was a few hours, and what would you have done?"

His shoulders lift and then fall. "Slept with her."

"I didn't do that. She was in pain, so I helped her."

"Listen, I'm not judging you, but if I'm hearing about it, then I'd bet my ass your father will."

"Fuck him."

"I'd rather not."

We both laugh. "I don't give a shit what he says. When he's done fucking his mistress, then he can give me all the shit he wants. Since we both know that's not going to happen, it really isn't my problem what he thinks. Jessica and I started dating eighteen years ago, and there's nothing going on now."

"Okay, I'll drop it."

"Thank you."

"Jennie's?" Jack asks.

"Like there was any doubt?"

We ride over and grab a booth. Jennie gets to our table. "I heard that was quite a fire today. Glad to see you both here."

Jack leans back, hands on his stomach. "Your food feeds my soul."

"Good. Here's some coffee to make sure you boys are awake. I'll bring your usual."

The place is empty other than Fred and Bill, who are here every morning at four like clockwork. They both lost their wives to cancer around the same time six years ago and started meeting here for breakfast once a week—before it turned into daily.

Fred turns, lifting his coffee cup to me. "Good job today, Grayson."

I return the gesture. "Thanks."

"You too, Jack. I heard you were the first one in."

Jack is always the first one in. It's something I have tried to prevent, but he's stubborn and refuses to let someone else risk themselves when he's there.

"Yes, sir."

"Good man," Bill says with a nod. "Your father would be proud."

"If you find him, let me know," he says under his breath.

Jack and I both have fathers who we'd rather not discuss, but the town doesn't care much about privacy and our wants and needs. After the death of his mother, his father became a drunk who took off, leaving Jack to basically raise himself. That meant he spent a lot of time with me, which is why he's like a brother.

"What was that?" Bill asks.

"I said, I'm glad you let me know that."

I laugh into my coffee cup. They turn back to their food and conversation, forgetting all about us.

"This town is hell-bent on making my father into some kind of hero," Jack grumbles.

"He was a hero. He was the mayor for fifteen years, and they all love him."

"And they just couldn't care less about the destruction he left when he walked away with his bottle of whiskey?"

I shrug, not sure what to say. "They really only care about that shit when it impacts them."

Jack looks to the door, shaking his head. "Let's talk about

happier shit."

I swear, if he brings up Jessica, I'm going to kill him. "Like?"

"What's new at the inn?"

"We got the cottage fixed up since the water pipe burst."

"Yeah? Good. Anything else?"

He's fishing. Somehow he knows that Jess is going to start working for me tomorrow, and I'm sure he has all kinds of opinions about it.

"Nope."

"You're sure?"

"Did you suffer from smoke inhalation or something?" I question.

His brow raises. "No? Why?"

"Because you're being an idiot."

"If you say so."

"I do say so."

Jennie arrives with our food, and I've never been more grateful that he'll be too busy shoveling it into his mouth to talk about Jessica and anything relating to her. It's bad enough that I'm lying to myself about why I stayed by her side, lying to everyone else is harder.

The truth is, I care about her. I always have, but seeing her again, touching her face, was like being thrust back in time when life was easy and her smile would make my entire day. She's always been completely irresistible. Now, she's grown up and it's as though nothing has changed. She's still that.

That is why I have to keep her at a distance.

When I lost her, I was miserable for a long time, and I don't need to ever feel that shit again.

Jack doesn't dig right in, though. He launches into another

bunch of shit I don't want to hear. "Look, you want to deny the fact that you have some serious unresolved feelings surrounding Jessica, then, hey, live in your lies."

"Jesus Christ, I'm not lying and pretending. I know how I feel, and while I will always care about her, there's nothing going on. She was in pain, a pain like I've never seen, and I helped her. Stella is who hired her."

"But you didn't fire her." He points the fork at me. "You allowed her to keep the job."

"Would you have fired Misty?" I bring up the only girl he's ever mentioned caring about.

"Different circumstances."

"Is it? Because I don't see it that way. You never would've let someone you have ever cared about be in pain without helping them. But when I do the same thing, suddenly I'm lying to myself."

Other than the fact that I am.

"You're right, Gray. I would help Misty, Stella, Delia— hell, I'd help anyone if they were as bad off as you say she was. But I know you. I have since we were seven years old, and you're feeding yourself a whole load of bullshit if you think that, when you see Jessica Walker, a part of you doesn't change. I've seen it. We all see it. You've always loved that girl in a way that didn't make sense to me when I was sixteen, but she's that girl for you."

I shovel a bite of pancake into my mouth, choking it down so I don't have to reply.

More people come in for breakfast, and we wave, smile, and make small talk as they pass. So many people here have police and fire scanners that it's no surprise they're all talking about the fire.

He chuckles. "Tell me this, if you saw her right now, would you react? Would your chest tighten even a little?"

I roll my eyes. "No. I feel nothing but friendship for her."

Jack nods. "Okay then." A slow grin spreads across his face. He waves at someone as they enter. "Jess is here."

I roll my eyes. He's so fucking predictable. "Sure she is. Asshole." I take another huge bite, ignoring him because he's goading me.

"Come sit with us," Jack says.

The first thing I'm doing this morning is finding a new friend. Jack is fired from the position.

When he scoots over, and Delia sits beside him, I realize I misplayed this. Slowly, I turn to face her. Her long brown hair is braided and pulled to the side, honey-colored eyes staring at me as a hesitant smile forms on her lips.

Shit.

I swallow the food and try to smile. "Jess, hey."

"Mind if I sit?"

I move as I speak. "Of course not."

"Thanks."

She plays with the end of her braid, not really meeting my eyes, and it feels just like it did a million years ago. We'd come here, sit in a booth, and both pretend we weren't falling for each other. I would try to hold her hand, but she'd always anticipate it and move. It wasn't until the game before homecoming that I finally got the balls to kiss her.

It happened right outside this very window, she was leaning against the car, my letterman jacket wrapped around her because she was cold, and I lifted her chin before brushing my lips against hers.

I lift my gaze to hers, only to find that she's staring out the window, and I wonder if she's remembering the same thing. When she smiles at me, I'm pretty sure she is.

"Hey."

She tucks her head and smiles. "Hey."

"How are you feeling?"

"Much better. No headaches, and I slept well."

"Good," I say, feeling relief. "Are you ready to start work again?"

She nods. "Yeah, I'm excited and a little nervous, but . . . mostly excited."

After her headache episode, I told Stella I wanted to start this off slow. She's working five half days this week. We'll ease her in and it gives us both the assurance she'll be able to handle it. As much as she says she'll tell me if something is wrong, I remember all too well her stubborn side.

This is a safeguard. Plus, Stella owes me a few weekends of covering the inn.

"I'm glad you're excited. Hopefully you sleep well tonight."

Jessica turns her head, but I catch the slight blush on her cheeks.

Delia grabs Jack's coffee cup and finishes it. "Speaking of sleep, I could use a week to catch up with how tired I am. But I think we're heading to your beach house this weekend, so that will help."

"Who is?"

"Stella invited us a few weeks ago," Jess says quickly. "I guess she was going with Winnie, but she ended up having to work this weekend, so she said we should go. Is that okay?"

I blink a few times, trying to shove down the lump in my throat. "Yeah. No. I didn't know."

The beach house.

"This place is beautiful, Gray." Jessica smiled as she walked around the room.

"It's private."

Her eyes met mine as she traced a finger over her collarbone. "It is, which I guess is what we both want, right?"

I just wanted her. God, I wanted her so fucking much. I didn't know how I got lucky enough to convince her to love me, but she did, and I wouldn't ever let her go. Tonight, I wanted to make her happy, give her everything, and show her how I felt.

"Jess, we don't have to," I said, praying she didn't change her mind. "We can just spend the weekend on the beach."

She moved toward me, her gown swaying with each step. "We don't have to do anything, but I really want to."

Tonight was the perfect night. We danced, laughed, and I had the most beautiful prom date in the world. Every guy there was staring at her, hating and envying me. I didn't blame them, Jessica was perfect and she was mine.

I wanted to marry her. I wanted to spend every day of my life with her because she was everything I'd ever hoped for. I had known it the first time I saw her.

Tonight, I planned to make love to her and show her just how good we were together.

I pulled her close so her delicate hands rested on my chest. "Do you feel that?"

"Your heart is beating so fast."

"Because I'm just as nervous."

Her dark lashes rested on her cheeks as she chewed on her lip. "What do you have to be nervous about?"

Everything. It was both of our first time. I didn't want to hurt her or scare her.

"Making this good for you," I confessed.

She released a shaky breath. "Everything with you is good. It's you, Grayson. It's you who makes things perfect. I love you, and I want to be with you always."

It didn't matter that I was turning eighteen tomorrow and she was only sixteen. I knew, without a shadow of a doubt, that this was the girl I was meant to be with forever. My parents met when they were fifteen, and they were still together. I knew it could happen, and it happened with her. It would always be her. I was leaving for college in a few months, and she would be at home, but we would make it through.

I leaned in, kissing her softly. "I love you. I love you so much, Jess."

Her hands moved up my chest, pushing the jacket off my shoulders so it fell to the floor. "Show me."

Jack kicks my foot under the table. "You all right there?"

"Yeah, I'm fine," I say quickly. "I just . . ." I look at Jess, who is staring at me, a faint blush on her cheeks.

"The beach house," she says.

"The beach house."

Delia or Jack clear their throats. "I take it something happened at the beach house?" Jack's voice breaks the moment.

"Oh, yeah, it's where Jess gave Grayson her V-card." Delia so helpfully informs him.

"Delia!"

"What? You did. Please, the whole school knew it. You guys came back from the beach with no tan and a lot of smiling."

Jess ducks her head. "I hate this town."

"You hate that we all knew, that's all." Delia grins.

"Anyway, enough about the beach house . . ."

Jack leans back, tossing his arm behind Delia. "We should all go."

"What?"

"Yeah, we haven't gone in a long time, and I'm sure Melia would love a trip to the beach. It'll be fun. You forced Stella to work so you could have time off. There's no reason not to head down together."

Delia glances at Jack and then nods. "Yes, it'll be like old times. The four of us, hanging out and enjoying the sun. Plus, Jess is off this weekend so this is really her only chance to do something fun."

A gnawing feeling moves through my chest. "I don't know . . ."

"Why not? Stella has work covered, you have no plans, and the weather is going to be nice."

I glare at Jack, wanting to choke him. "It won't be at all awkward, right?"

"Hell no it won't. There are four bedrooms and plenty of space."

That's it, he's dead. I'm not sure how I'm going to take him out, but it will happen. "There will be five of us."

"You and Jess can share a room."

Jessica spits out her coffee, sending it flying right into Jack's face. I get a small amount of joy from that.

"I'm sorry," she says, trying not to smile as she hands him a napkin. "I can't believe I did that."

"He deserved it."

Delia can barely contain her laughter. "Jess and I will bunk together, it'll be fine. We are all adults, and Jack is right, we used to do it all the time. Come on, Gray, it'll be fun."

Jess looks back to me. "I'm fine if you are," she assures me softly.

There's no getting out of this without looking like an asshole. "Yeah, you're right. It'll be great."

Or a complete fucking nightmare.

Eight

JESSICA

"You ready for this?" Winnie asks as we pull up to the Park Inn for my first day.

"I am."

"You took your meds?"

I nod. "Yes, Mom."

"Please, you mothered me my entire life, it's nice to be in the other seat for a change."

I had no choice but to mother her because ours was working. "Did Mom say anything about this?"

Winnie shrugs. "Who cares what she says?"

Resting my head back, I groan. I knew she would have issues with it. The Parkersons have always been nice to her, but it's been hard. My mother was once friends with Eveline Parkerson. They were on the PTA together and both helped with charity events, but then my father left, changing our en-

tire financial situation. We were no longer doing . . . well . .
. we were poor. Buying new things was no longer something
they discussed, and my mom didn't have time for lunches or
charity. She had to work, feed her kids, and Eveline didn't as-
sociate with "our kind."

"Considering I live with her—I do."

"You could always come stay with me."

Yeah, that's not happening. "The money I'm giving Mom
will help her. She wouldn't take it if I wasn't living there."

"Okay, I could use your money too," Winnie jokes.

"You're doing just fine."

Winnie got a full ride to the University of North Carolina.
She came out of college with a job and has worked her ass off
for everything she has. I'm incredibly proud of the work she
does as a director at the youth club because she's helping these
kids in a real way by making sure they have the resources to
rise up.

"I'm proud of you, Jess. I just want to say that before you
go in there."

"Proud of what?"

"You're getting out of the house again. You're working
and going to therapy. Those are all good things because, when
you first got here, you sort of closed yourself off. I'm proud of
you for taking the steps to live again."

I grab her hand, squeezing gently. "It's scary."

"I'm sure it is, but you're doing it."

"Thanks for driving me."

She smiles. "Thanks for driving me a million times when
we were kids. If it weren't for you, Jess, I wouldn't have been
able to get where I am."

My sister was an all-state softball player. She was amazingly talented, and it's what got her the scholarship, along with her straight A's.

"All right. I guess I should go in."

I exit the car, my legs feeling a little jellylike, but I stand tall. I spoke with Dr. Warvel last night, and we went over some steps to take if I feel a headache coming on. I have my medication and a plan—it's all that I can control.

When I push through the doors, Stella is there, talking to someone. She spots me and rushes over. "Jessica! You look amazing. Love your outfit."

I smooth down my pencil skirt and smile. "Thank you. I'm excited to be here and get started."

"Let me show you around the desk area and introduce you to everyone."

The staff is friendly. There is one person who is always at the front desk, answering the phones and checking people in. Stella explains how they have another person who floats and is able to fill in if there are any issues. My job will be to make sure the front desk is handling things, deal with any surprises, as well as making sure guests' requests are filled, and running reports that Stella or Grayson needs regarding occupancy.

"Do you have any questions?"

"I think I'm set, but if I have issues, who do I report to?"

"Grayson."

That's what I was worried about.

"Okay."

Stella leans against the desk. "You can always come to me if you prefer. We split the duties here and both can handle anything, but he's much better with the staff and day-to-day running of the place. I do a lot more of the recreation side."

"Meaning?"

She sighs. "I make sure there's entertainment and keep the guests happy. So, it's sort of like he handles the before part of the trip, the stocking of the inventory, staff, and maintenance stuff, and I work on the once they're here."

"I can see how that works," I say with a grin. Stella is social, fun, and loves parties. She'd be an amazing event planner. Grayson is organized and likes order and discipline.

"It's lucky for me that Grayson is who wanted to stay around here and not Oliver."

Speaking of her twin brother . . . "How is Oliver? Is he liking wherever he is now?"

"Yes. No. I mean, he wanted to go to the new property after he and his girlfriend broke up. He was in Sugarloaf, Pennsylvania for a while."

I bite my lip, wondering if I should share this. Oliver is Stella's twin, and they're very close. It could go either way, but I decide it's better to put it out there. "I actually know someone in Sugarloaf who knew Oliver."

"You do?"

I nod. "He was with a girl named Devney, right?"

"Yeah! How did you know that?"

"I'm friends with someone who lives there, and Oliver dated their now sister-in-law."

Stella grips my arms. "You know an Arrowood?"

"I do."

"Oh my God! That's right! Oh! My! God! You know Jacob!" Each of her words gets a little louder as her excitement mounts.

"Shh," I say as a few guests turn to look at us. "Jacob and I were in that plane crash together."

"And Oliver dated Devney, who I fucking *loved*."

"I haven't met her, but the entire family is super sweet and has helped me a ton."

Jacob has good people in his life. Not only is he an amazing friend but also his family did a lot to get me set up here too. Brenna, his girlfriend, referred me to Dr. Warvel. Sydney, his sister-in-law, was able to get a lawyer to help pro-bono with the legal side of trying to get a settlement for medical coverage, which the airline is fighting me on. And the others sent cards or gifts to thank me. I just did my job, but they seem to think it was more.

"Yeah, I met her when they first started dating and I visited a few times. The Arrowoods weren't there yet, I guess. I was crushed when they broke up, but"—her voice drops to a whisper—"I love my brother and all, but if I had to choose between him and Sean . . . there's no choice."

"I don't know that any woman would turn him away."

"Right?" Stella sighs dramatically. "I only loved baseball because of him."

"You like sports?"

Her face crinkles. "No. I just like *him* in sports. There's something about butts in a baseball uniform." She pushes off the ledge. "Anyway, your office is back here, I'll show you and get you set up. I know this is a lot to take in, so I'd like for you to take this week to adjust and acclimate with the staff and the inn. Then we'll work on numbers and stuff once we increase your hours next week."

"Okay."

"How is your head?" A deep voice breaks into the conversation, causing both our heads to jerk to the side.

"Grayson? What the hell are you doing here?" Stella asks.

"I work here."

"It's your day off," she says with her head cocked to the side.

His eyes narrow slightly. "Tomorrow is."

"No, I'm like, one hundred percent sure it's today since you've been off every Sunday and Monday since we started working together."

"I didn't realize it was Monday," he says, giving his sister a pointed look.

She crosses her arms and raises one brow. "Really? How funny."

Grayson's attention turns to me. "How is your head?"

"It's fine."

"No headaches?"

It's my turn to be irritated. "I'm great, but thank you for being concerned, *boss*."

I can see that calling him that bothers him. "I'm just making sure."

Stella takes a step toward him. "Why are you here?"

"I needed to check on the cottage, so I dropped Melia off at Mom's for a few hours. I figured I'd check to see how everything else was going."

"Right. Well, that was very nice of you—unnecessary, but nice."

Grayson's eyes meet mine, and my pulse accelerates. Why? Why do I feel this way when he looks at me? We're nothing anymore, and I am not staying. The minute that I can travel, drive, move around, I'm out of here. I don't want my stupid heart getting tied up with his again. It's not good for either of us.

Stella's hand taps my forearm. "Come on, we can go see a few of the rooms, each is a different theme now. A lot has changed since we were kids."

I push down the feelings regarding Grayson and think about work. I'm here for a job, one that has given me a sense of purpose and I want to keep.

We move past him, and his fingers graze mine. The moment, which is so small and seemingly insignificant, somehow isn't. It's as though my heart knows that this man is what I need and there is no going back. My throat is dry, and I feel unbalanced. It was just a split second, but felt like a lifetime passed between us.

As we exit the room, I turn back to him, and as he flexes his hand, I wonder, what the hell am I going to do about this?

Dr. Warvel is extra observant today. Not that she normally isn't, but there's something unnerving about the way she's watching me. It's as if she can see things that I don't want her to see, and I don't like it.

"And how is it working with Grayson since it's been about three days now?"

"It's fine. I said that it wasn't a big deal when I took the job."

Her head bobs. "I know that, but it's a completely different thing when it actually happens."

"I only saw him that first day."

"He isn't working?"

Oh, he's working. He has just gotten really good at avoiding where I am. "We don't cross paths very often."

She writes something down, and I want to reach over the coffee table and grab her notebook. "What are you writing?"

"Just notes and things I want to remember. It's nothing bad."

"I feel like Grayson is a big deal to you for some reason."

Dr. Warvel places the notepad down before sitting up a bit taller. "I think he's a big deal for you, Jessica. There's a reason that I bring him up, and the longer we dance around the subject, the less we'll accomplish in these sessions."

My breath leaves my chest in a rush. "I don't know what you mean."

"Let's go back to the crash."

"I would rather not."

"I know, but I think it's important. Especially before you leave for the trip this weekend, which is another thing we should discuss."

"I'm going with Delia."

She raises her brow. "And who else?"

"Gray and Jack will be there, but there's nothing to it. It's just friends, and his kid will be there."

"The crash, Jessica. What did you write down about your thoughts around Grayson?"

Grayson Parkerson is my one regret in life. I loved him so much, and I let him go. Now I'm going to die, and he'll never know.

I regret reading that fucking notebook to her more than anything.

"Yes, in that moment, I had regrets around him, but . . . it's not like that now."

"Why? What has changed?"

I huff. "There's . . . the . . . I know what . . . couch . . ." Fucking hell. It's been two days since my last stutter like this, but here I am, bumbling again.

Instead of her normal method of trying to calm me, she just waits, and I count, breathe, and close my eyes. I am okay. I can do this. I just need to relax and not get worked up. After a few minutes of deep breathing, I open my eyes.

"That was very good," she praises.

"Nothing has changed."

Her lips are soft, and there's a bit of sympathy in her eyes. "No, nothing has changed other than the fact that you're here and can face it. When we're forced to deal with a life-altering event, things sometimes become crystal clear or they turn muddy. How are you prepared to deal with your nightmares on the trip?"

This is the part that has been a problem. Delia knows about them, and when it was going to be us with Stella, I was okay with it. If they heard me cry out, it wouldn't be an issue, but with Grayson and Jack, I don't know what to do.

"I'm hoping I just don't sleep. Maybe I can nap during the day."

Dr. Warvel's lips turn down. "Jessica, that's not a plan."

"It's the best one I've got."

"Okay, what if you were honest with them, told them about the dreams? I'm sure anyone in that group would understand since it's not an uncommon occurrence after a trauma."

I'm sure that's true, and I don't think that anyone in that group would ever judge me for it. "I've already exposed my weakness with speaking, I'd like to hope that maybe my dreams won't be so bad."

"Have they lessened at all?"

I release a heavy sigh. "In some ways. I'm not waking up each night in a cold sweat. Last night, I know I dreamed it, but I don't remember the panic."

She smiles, hope alighting her face. "That's wonderful. That's a good sign."

"I still felt it."

"But not to the extent you had before, this is a good thing. By facing it, you were able to start to deal with the panic, which is why I keep pushing you on other things. Look, you could be completely over Grayson and it was some small part of your subconscious playing tricks on you or you have regrets. Only you know which one it is. However, the one thing I won't let you do is lie to yourself about how you feel, and until you face it and really dig deep, you can't answer honestly."

I flop back, feeling a million things at once. I don't want to deal with it. I don't want to care or love or miss him. "We're not the same people, and the boy I loved is gone."

I turn my head to look at her. "No, and the girl he loved isn't the same either. That doesn't mean you still don't have feelings. Considering the fact that he's come up a lot in here as well as in your dream journal, I think it's something you're going to have to think about."

She's right. I know she's right. When I see him, when I am near him, it's as if something inside me is clawing its way out. Grayson is that one guy for me. He's the person I made these plans, dreams, and hopes with. He was more than just my first love, at least I thought he was, but fear became something so much stronger than love.

"Grayson scares me," I tell her. "My heart has always been his. I never was able to give my heart to someone else because they weren't as good as him. I was so . . . sad when I ended things."

"Then why did you end things?"

I sit here, trying to make sure that the words don't jumble

in my head. "Because losing him on my terms was better than losing him any other way."

Dr. Warvel leans forward. "What if you never lost him, Jessica? What if he's been here waiting, and your heart knew it?"

Nine

GRAYSON

I am a fool for coming here. Jack knew exactly what it would be like to be at this beach house with Jessica, and the asshole backed me into it.

"Daddy, can we go to the ocean?" Amelia asks as I unbuckle her from her booster seat.

"We can go tomorrow, but today, we have to open up the place."

"What does that mean?"

"It means we have to get the house cleaned up and ready for all our friends who are coming."

Melia's smile is wide. "Is Uncle Jack coming?"

"He is." I crouch so we're eye level. "Also, two friends named Delia and Jessica are coming. Do you remember at the store when I helped my friend who was sick?"

She nods enthusiastically.

"Her name is Jessica."

"Is she your girlfriend?"

"No, but she was a very, very long time ago, though."

I'm not sure how the hell to navigate this conversation, but I figure honesty is a good thing. We're never going to be more than friends, and Amelia is sometimes too smart for her own good.

"And Delia?"

Now that is funny. "No, Delia is in love with someone else. We're all just friends." That someone else being my older brother.

My phone rings, and I have to laugh when Josh's name flashes on the screen.

"What's up, big brother?"

"Not much. Just checking in to see how things are going."

"Who is it?" Amelia asks.

"Uncle Josh."

"Is that my little princess?" Josh's voice is loud enough that she can hear it.

"It is! It is!"

I laugh as the tone sounds to switch to a video call. Once I accept, my brother's ugly mug fills the screen.

"Uncle Josh! I have missed you so much." Amelia grabs the phone and gives her best pouty lip.

"I miss you too, Princess. I was thinking about coming to visit you in a few weeks. Do you have plans?"

She shakes her head. "Nope. We are at the beach."

"Oh?"

I pull Amelia up into my arms so I can see as well. "We came down to the Cape house."

Josh grins. "Fun. I bet you two will have a great weekend."

"Daddy has his friends coming."

"Oh? Who?"

Amelia answers before I can. "Uncle Jack is coming and so is daddy's girlfriend."

"I told you she's not my girlfriend, Melia."

My brother's jaw drops before his lips stretch into a shit-eating grin. "Oh? Girlfriend. What's her name, Melia?"

"Jessica."

Josh's eyes go wide, and there's nothing I can say now. "Jessica as in Jessica Walker?"

"The same one. But as I said, she's a friend and was hurt, so she's in Willow Creek until she gets on her feet."

"Or on her back," Josh so unhelpfully adds.

"Can I go see the sand, Daddy?" Amelia asks, and I put her down.

"Just stay close to the porch."

She runs off, leaving me stuck on the video call with my brother. Yeah, this will go well.

"There is nothing going on," I tell him before he can say anything.

Joshua doesn't look convinced. I watch the thoughts turn in his head as he cocks his head to the side. "Right."

"There's not."

Josh smirks. "Nope. Nothing. It's just a trip to the beach, right?"

I glare at my oldest brother, knowing that this flippant shit is just that . . . shit. He doesn't believe a word of it any more than he believes me. "It's just a trip to the beach, Josh."

He purses his lips, and I know that it's coming. He is teetering on the need to be right and let me know it. "It sounds like it'll be good for you guys to all get away. That house is a special place where things happen for you."

I might kill him. I groan, needing this back and forth to be over so I can prove my point. "Just say it."

"I have nothing to say but that, truly, I like Jess, I always have. Dad and Mom will not be happy, but then again, who fucking cares what they think?"

"There's nothing to think because we're just friends—sort of. I don't know what we are, civil ex-lovers?"

He laughs at that. "Who happen to be vacationing on the beach. Yeah, what could happen?"

"Anyway, you didn't really call to check in, did you?"

"Did Dad call you?"

My father has called me six times, and I've ignored all of them. I prefer communicating with him via email so I have a record of what was said.

"I haven't answered."

We all have a very complicated relationship with our parents. Josh, however, hates the man. He wants nothing to do with him and has been trying to buy out our father's portion of the inn Josh runs, but my father won't even entertain it. There's something going on that Josh won't tell us about that has him so adamant he needs to leave the family business.

At the age of twenty-five, each of us were gifted with shares of the company. We have enough to have a say, but not enough to actually override him. Each year, he does give us another slice, but is always careful to keep the balance in his favor. The five of us combined own forty-nine percent of the company though. It's enough to make him sweat.

"I haven't either. I just wanted to see if you knew what he wanted."

"I'm sure when I get back to Willow Creek, Mom will let

me know."

He laughs once. "If it's anything to do with him, she won't."

"You're right. Hey, listen, I need to get the house opened up before Jack and the girls get here. I'll talk to you soon."

"All right. Be smart and wrap it up. You don't need another kid." He hangs up before I can say anything.

I go to the front porch and see Melia sitting in the sand, her brown hair blowing softly in the salty air. He may be right that I don't need another kid, but I'm sure glad I have this one. Yvonne gave me something that she'll never know the true joy of.

"Ready to help?" I ask, causing her to jump.

"Okay!"

We enter the house, which has been vacant for months. It was never like this when I was a kid because we were always coming here, the five of us running around like lunatics, playing in the pool or the ocean. Then, as we got older, we stopped coming. The trips here were then, just with Mom. Dad was gone a lot, Mom was alone, and it's when we started to realize just how fucked up our parents' relationship was.

Amelia and I move from room to room, pulling off sheets, opening windows, and getting the place cleaned up a little. She laughs as I chase her with the sheet, covering her and then spinning her around.

When I turn the last time, Jessica is there, watching us spin.

Her smile is bright as she leans against the doorjamb. "Hi."

I take the sheet off Amelia, who is squirming. "Hey."

Amelia looks over. "I'm Amelia Jane Parkerson. Are you Delia or Jessica?"

Jess moves closer. "I'm Jessica. It's very nice to meet you,

Amelia."

"You were Daddy's girlfriend."

Jessica's eyes move to mine quickly, and I laugh. "I told Amelia that we were friends, and she thought it meant something else, which led to me having to explain."

She nods. "Ahh, I see. Well, a long time ago I was."

"He doesn't have a girlfriend now," Amelia explains.

"That's too bad because your dad is a pretty nice guy."

Amelia beams. "He's the best. He saves people."

"He sure does." She clears her throat and then returns her attention to Amelia. "Is this your room?"

"I hope so. It's pink and pretty and I love it."

I put her down after giving her a quick kiss on her nose. "You can stay in here if you want."

"Yay!"

"Is that Melia I hear?" Jack calls from the hallway, and before I can turn, Amelia is rushing out.

"She loves Jack," I explain.

"Most do. He's like a giant child."

She's definitely right about that. He's also going to pay for this weekend in so many ways. After a moment, Jessica rocks back on her feet and starts to move around the room.

"God, it's been so long since I've been anywhere close to here."

"You didn't travel to the beach?" I ask.

"I did, but not this beach."

I haven't either. It's been almost fifteen years since I stepped foot here. After we broke up, I tried, but the memories are everywhere. My siblings would come, and I'd have some reason to avoid it. Most of the time, the excuse was valid, but the truth was that it was too difficult.

"Why not? This house is . . ."

"Ours." The word slips out, but I should've kept my damn mouth shut. It's just that being here, standing in this place that we would sneak away to when life was too much, is making me remember.

Jessica stares at me, her chest rising and falling in a steady rhythm. "I was going to say special."

"It is special."

"Gray . . ."

Amelia rushes in, holding Jack's hand and pulling him along. "Hey, you two."

"Uncle Jack, this is my room."

He grins at his goddaughter. "It's a pretty awesome one. I wanted the pink room, though."

She giggles. "No, silly, you can sleep in the room with the bunk beds."

"Bunk beds?" Jack looks affronted. "Who is going to sleep in the bottom bunk?"

"Daddy!"

"You have it all worked out, huh?" I ask her.

She nods once, walks over to Jessica, and directs her to the bed. "You and Uncle Jack can sleep in the bunk beds, and that way, Miss Jessica and Miss Delia get their own rooms. It's what the boys should do."

Jess grins as she looks at my daughter. "I think that's a great idea. You are a very smart little girl."

"I know. My daddy says I'm like Auntie Stella."

A laugh escapes her lips. "Then you are going to be a hand-ful."

"What's a handful mean?"

"It means that you're perfect and are going to make life

very fun for your daddy," Jessica explains.

"I like you."

"I like you too."

Amelia turns to me. "You can marry her, Daddy."

I nearly choke while Jack breaks out in laughter and Jess's eyes go wide. "I didn't . . . she has these . . ." I search for the words and then give up. "No one is getting married. Let's get the house done so we can go swim, how does that sound?"

She jumps off the bed and places her hand in Jessica's. "Come on, Miss Jessica, I'll show you the house."

Jessica knows this house better than anyone. Amelia has never even been here, but Jess goes along, letting Amelia pull her around. Jack claps his hand on my shoulder.

"You are so fucked, my friend. So fucked."

Yeah, no shit. My daughter has decided I'm allowed to marry the girl I always wished I had.

Ten

JESSICA

Amelia is the cutest, most precocious kid I've ever met. She loves to talk and explore. She has also latched on to me. We're building a sand-house because castles are for little girls, and she is most definitely not little.

"And Daddy says that having a prince rescue you is only in fairy tales."

Sounds like good advice. "I see, but your daddy rescues people, right?"

She purses her lips, staring over at where Grayson is standing with his feet in the water. "Yes, but that's in an emergency."

"Totally different," I say in agreement.

"But I don't want a prince, I am going to marry Uncle Jack or Uncle Oliver."

"They're a bit old for you, don't you think?"

Amelia shrugs. "Uncle Oliver is the same age as Auntie."

"Yes, this is true, but maybe you'll meet a boy your age."

Her head tilts to the side as she watches me. "Is Daddy your age?"

"He's two years older than I am. We met when he was a junior in high school and I was a freshman."

"Uncle Oliver is a lot older."

I laugh softly. "Yes, and Uncle Jack is even older than him."

She seems to agree, and we go back to sculpting the house. She's so much like her father it's crazy. He always knew what he wanted and how to achieve it. Amelia is much the same way. The entire house is already drawn in her head, all the pieces fitting together in just the right way.

"Did you know my mom?"

My heart jolts, and I shake my head. "I didn't."

"Her name is Yvonne, and she's an opera singer in Paris."

I really want off this topic. "Have you been to Paris?"

Amelia sighs dramatically. "No, and I never will. Well, not until I'm much older and I can go by myself."

"No?"

That's strange. Why wouldn't she go see her mother?

"Yvonne didn't want kids so she gave me to Daddy."

My hands stop moving. My God. Who could ever not want this little girl? I school my face, making sure I don't give anything away because I know nothing other than what a four-year-old is telling me.

"You're very lucky to have such a great daddy."

"He's my favorite person. I would marry him, but he says it's illegal and I wouldn't get a mommy if he did that."

I try not to laugh, but her logic is so innocent and sweet.

She looks toward her dad, and even though his back is to

us, there's a sense of protection emanating from him. He always had this sense of duty and devotion to those who needed it. When we were in school, he volunteered every week to work with kids with disabilities. Grayson formed an entire team of athletes who gave their time to help those who couldn't play competitively.

He said it was unfair that they had to sit on the sidelines because of something they couldn't control. He wanted to give them the experience of hearing a crowd cheering for them and the thrill that came with playing a sport.

Amelia goes back to the task but then frowns and asks, "Jessica? Can you put more sand here?" When I reach for the bucket, she stops me. "It has to be very wet sand from the ocean."

"Okay," I say with a grin. "I'll go get the very wet sand."

I walk over to Grayson, who's just staring out at the expanse of the ocean.

"Having fun?"

I bend over, scooping the sand into the bucket. "I am. Your daughter is really wonderful."

He glances over at her. "I don't know what I would do without her." There are so many questions I want to ask about her mother, but I'm not sure we're at that point in this new friendship. "What made you venture down to the ocean?" he asks. "If I remember, you don't *do* ocean water."

I get back up and turn to face him. "I don't, you can't see your feet." I shudder. I can't stand not seeing what's lurking around you. "She's given me very specific instructions on what kind of sand she wants, so I'm here to do her bidding."

He grins. "She's very demanding when working on a task."

"Much like her father."

"I like to get things done," he says with amusement.

"You are a task master."

"We had fun too. It wasn't always tasks."

My eyes widen, and I shake my head. "You were *not* fun. You were a pain in the ass who demanded we do it your way because it was the only way to do it."

"You're making me sound like a dictator." Grayson's voice is laced with mock indignation.

I cross my arms and give him a wry smile. "You were."

"That is untrue, and you were just being a baby who didn't like following perfectly normal directions."

He's crazy and completely wrong. "You made Kate Murphy cry because she didn't use the right paint on the senior rock."

He huffs and mimics my pose. "It was all laid out, the freaking paint was numbered. If she had just followed what I . . ."

"What you said?" I finish for him.

"She went rogue. I dealt with it."

We both start to laugh, and I find we're somehow closer than we had been a moment ago. "That wasn't the only time."

Gray's lips turn into a flat line. "You're exaggerating."

It seems he needs to be reminded a bit more. "And what about when Stephen Dettler vetoed your senior prank?"

"He was an idiot, and again, I was showing him the error of his ways."

"I'm not denying that, but you were none too happy."

He moves just a bit closer. "You were there to calm me."

"I did that a lot," I add on, nudging him playfully.

"You made things better."

"So did you," I say, my voice barely a whisper.

There were many nights that I would sneak out and meet Grayson by the overlook point. It was nestled back in the woods between our houses where the rich met the poor and we were in the middle. There were no houses around it, and it gave us a view of the world that couldn't see us. We were equals there, and we could see the stars that felt so close we could just reach out and grab them.

Grayson would go there when he needed to be himself, and I would go when I needed to escape my family.

We were just two kids who needed each other.

"Jessica!" Amelia calls out, making me turn.

"I'll be right there," I say as I wave.

The moment we were sharing seems to pass, and I wish I had been brave before and told him the truth.

But it won't change anything.

Grayson and I will always be the past, and that's part of what I'm mourning. The girl who had big dreams and loved the sky before everything crashed.

"I should go." My voice cracks a little.

He nods. "She likes you."

"I like her too. She's great, and I'm happy for you, Gray. I'm happy that you have her and she has you."

Grayson reaches up and catches a piece of hair that has blown in my face, tucking it behind my ear. "And what about you, Jess? Are you happy with how things turned out?"

No. Not even a little. I miss you, and I hate that I do. I thought of you when I thought I was dying.

"Things are how I hoped," I lie, not willing to make things awkward for us.

"Good. You better get back with the very wet sand because Melia is eyeing us, and that's never a good thing."

I turn to her, my legs feeling unsteady as I walk away from him. I fight every look back at him, to see if he's watching me, and I keep my eyes forward because no matter how much I may wish I could go back, I can't. I need to remember that.

"Is Amelia asleep?" Delia asks Grayson from where she's cuddled up with Jack on the couch. His arm draped around her shoulders as she rests her head on his chest.

The two of them baffle me. Neither feel anything for each other than friendship, but you'd swear they were more. He says that Delia is just a girl who he likes being around and there is nothing but a sense of comfort. There's always been something about him, though, something that says there's someone who he's not willing to admit feelings for.

But, then again, that was a long time ago, and I don't know this new Jack very well.

Grayson looks at them and then to the only spot for him to sit—beside me. He nods. "She's out like a light. She had a busy day."

Jack laughs. "Yeah, the sea air and building an entire village of sand castles and houses will do that."

"We did very well, thank you," I chime in.

"You did. I am impressed."

"I just executed her vision."

Delia sighs deeply. "I love kids. I really thought we'd all be married and working on babies by now."

Jack shudders. "Not me."

"Please, you were the one who wanted to be married even more than those two," Delia points at me and Grayson.

I bristle. "Grayson and I didn't plan to get married."

"We didn't?"

I turn to him. "When did we plan it?"

"I don't know . . . the ten thousand times we talked about life?"

"Those were just dreams not plans."

Grayson's eyes darken, and he clenches his fists before releasing them. "Right. I guess I was mistaken."

Jack sits up, forcing Delia to do the same. "And I thought you guys were totally over everything. You know, that shit was all in the past."

"It is," Grayson says with a clipped tone.

"Yeah, totally appears that way," Delia adds on. I turn to my best friend, a little miffed that she's encouraging this. "What?"

Jack stands, offering his hand to her. "Why don't we take a walk, Deals?"

She follows him, turning back to me and mouthing, *sorry*.

Great. Now we're alone in this house with his daughter sleeping in the next room, both of us on edge after what Jack said. What could possibly go wrong?

Once they're gone, I turn to Gray, wanting to smooth this over. Today has been a great day. I had so much fun, and I don't think my words were jumbled once. It's the best I've felt in the last month and a half since the crash.

"I'm sorry. I didn't mean to downplay anything we shared."

He sighs. "You didn't. It's just this house."

I understand that more than anything. It's filled with us, the good and bad, which is probably why I haven't been *in* the room I was assigned. It's the master bedroom, and it's exactly what I remember.

Just opening the door I felt as if I had been hit in the chest and it made it impossible for me to take a step inside it.

So, my bags sit just on the inside of the door. I'm such a coward that I changed in the bathroom down the hall.

I don't want to be afraid, but I don't know if I can tell him everything, so I start where it feels safest. "Even when we forget things or make ourselves try, it's like the world won't ever really release it. After we broke up, there were times when I'd hear a song and I was back to a moment we shared. Or I'd hear a laugh, and I'd swear it was you."

"Did you want it to be?"

I swallow and look away. "Sometimes I . . . I was sad when it ended."

Grayson shifts so his hand rests on my thigh. "Answer the question, Jess. Did you want it to be me?"

The heat from his touch, the way I feel it all the way in my marrow, makes it hard to think. My brain, it's scrambling, I can feel the words. "You. We. Jump."

He touches my chin, turning it gently toward him. I can see the questions swimming in those blue eyes. I would know that unique color anywhere. If I were to close my eyes, I would be able to draw them perfectly. The deep blue in the center that lightens as it goes, and the specks of green that fray right at the edges. So perfectly him.

"Take a second. Breathe," he coaxes.

I do. I focus, allowing the thoughts to form more concretely. My lashes lift, and his face is so close it makes my chest ache. Instead of speaking, we move at the same time, and his lips are on mine or mine are on his.

The past flows around us, cocooning us in this house where we made love more times than I can count. I feel it moving between each breath, reminding me of all that we were—the promises, the hopes, the dreams. This kiss is different from the ones that came before it. It's rougher, more urgent and demanding. I feel the search for questions as his tongue touches mine.

God, it's different and yet the same.

He's still Grayson. *My* Grayson. The boy who stole my heart and gave me hope that maybe not all men would be like my father. It was a time when we were more than two kids, we grew together, found each other, and then I let go.

My lips break away, turning my head as I gasp for air.

"Jessica . . ."

"Please," I say, because I can't get anything more than that out.

He shifts a little away, allowing some much-needed distance. I keep my gaze down, knowing if I look at him, I will lose myself again. "I can't kiss you," I say.

"Okay."

"Because I like you. I have always liked you. I always will."

"And that's why you can't kiss me?"

I clasp my hands together, wringing them as I try to explain. "I can't kiss you because I can't be who I was before."

Grayson moves, sitting on the table in front of me. "I don't know what that was, Jess, but I don't regret kissing you."

I look up at him, regretting it instantly. "I kissed you."

He laughs. "Are you sure?"

I smile. "Fine, we kissed each other."

"Look, we're in this house and talking about old shit, it was nostalgia. I promise I won't let you kiss me anymore."

"Well, that's reassuring."

I lean forward, and Grayson takes my hands in his. "Have I ever broken a promise to you?"

"Not once."

"Good, then we'll be fine."

Yeah, completely fine. I won't kiss him. He won't kiss me. And in a few weeks, I'll find a way out of this town and move on just like I did before.

Eleven

JESSICA

My heart is pounding, and I can feel the sweat trick-
ling down my face as I thrash from side to side.
It's happening. No, I can't do this.

Wake up, wake up, wake up!

I yell at myself, knowing how this ends. It's never going to
stop and I don't want to feel it again. I don't want to live this
now, in this house, in this bed.

The sounds start first, filling my ears with the unmistakable
scraping of branches against the hull of the plane. The sound
of glass shattering, and the groaning from the metal bending.
The pilots are yelling and issuing orders. Elliot is telling us
that it's coming now and to be ready.

Jacob Arrowood, the most unlikely friend I'd ever make,
terrified but doing a good job concealing it. Just as I am. But,
God, pretending is a hard thing when I also know, most likely,

we won't survive. No one survives a plane crash.

The fear I'm working so hard to push down is clawing its way up my throat, making me want to scream because I'm going to die. All the things I never said and never will because this will be it. There's a reason they train us but not many live to explain how it really goes.

More banging noises are heard. I keep my eyes on Jacob's and force myself to do my job.

With a strangled voice I tell him the last words I'll ever speak. "Brace, brace, brace."

"Jessica, Jess, wake up." I hear Grayson's voice beside me. Feel his hands shaking my shoulders. "Jess."

My eyes open, and tears flood my vision. God, this happened again. It was bad. I was there, on the edge of being awake, but couldn't stop it. I must've been yelling loud enough for him to rush in.

Without thinking, I grab on to him, holding on to him, seeking comfort.

Grayson's hand cradles my head against his chest. The steady sound of his heartbeat is what I focus on. I breathe with it, using the thrum under my ear to measure my own, and allow it to coax my own into slowing. "It's okay, Jess. You're safe. It's okay."

I clutch the fabric of his shirt, fingers wrapping with all their strength to stay tethered to something real and steady.

He settles beside me, pulling me even closer. "You're okay," Grayson reassures me over and over.

I am okay. I know this, but the dreams, they don't allow for rationalization. As I come back to myself, relaxing a little more with each breath, shame and embarrassment wash over me.

Here I am, lying in this bed, holding on to Grayson for dear life.

My fingers relax, and I attempt to push myself up, but he doesn't relinquish his hold. "I'm okay now," I say.

His arms loosen enough that I can sit up. "You were screaming." His voice is layered with concern.

"I have this dream. Well, more like a nightmare."

"The crash?"

"Yes."

He sits up, back resting against the headboard as I tuck my legs under me. "Do you want to talk about it?" he asks.

Why is this man so damn sweet? Why couldn't he be an asshole who hates me? It would be so much easier. Yet, he heard me crying out, and he came. He stayed, and even now, he's being kind.

"Not really," I admit. "Thank you for coming and waking me."

He laughs once. "Did you think I wouldn't?"

"I hoped I wouldn't dream."

Grayson shifts and clears his throat. "How often do they happen?"

Even though he probably can't see my face well, I turn away, shielding myself from his view. "Every. Single. Night."

I feel the bed move, and then his hand is on my back. He moves it up to my shoulder, squeezing gently before pulling me against his chest. My need for this man knows no bounds. I should push him away, tell him I'm fine, and read until the sun comes up. Instead, I lean into his body and let his strong arms wrap around me.

"What can I do?"

I bury my head in his chest, inhaling his musky soap scent. "This is enough."

This is everything.

I have my mother, but she stopped coming in weeks ago to wake me. It did no good, and I was still so angry then. I would wail at her, scream about how unfair this is. There's Dr. Warvel, but no amount of talking has kept the dreams away.

In Grayson's arms, it feels as though I'm protected from it, which is absolutely ridiculous because . . . we're nothing.

"Do you want me to stay?" he asks.

I tip my head back to look at him. "Stay?"

"With you . . . tonight. I can . . . I mean . . . we can just . . . sleep."

Each muscle in my body locks, and I push myself up. "That would be . . ." This time, it's not my brain that won't allow the words to come, it's my heart.

I want to say yes. To feel him hold me tight and chase the dream away, but I kissed him today. Being close to him is messing with my head and all I can hear is my therapist talking about how Grayson and I have unresolved issues.

It would be incredibly stupid to do this.

"Yeah," Grayson finishes. "You being in here is hard enough. I don't think I could do it."

"I tried to switch with Delia."

"I think they're trying to fuck with us."

I softly laugh. "I'm sure of it."

Grayson clears his throat. "If you need me . . ."

"You're just down the hall," I say with a grin. "I swear I've heard that before."

"Hey, I was a gentleman the last time we came here."

"You were. You gave me this room and said if I wanted

you, I just had to come and knock."

Grayson shakes his head. "I waited up all night, just in case you did."

"I didn't even knock once before you opened the door," I tease him.

"I heard your footsteps."

It took me two full hours to work up the nerve. It didn't matter that we'd slept together already, I was nervous. We spent prom weekend here, learning how to love and what it meant to give yourself to another. Then, we went home, where the world—more specifically, his parents—didn't want us to be together. For weeks, we were both thrown into events, parties, school functions that kept us apart.

We tried to sneak off, but we were so damn tired from running all day that we never made it to the lookout.

Then Grayson and I came back here, but there was a wall that had been erected and we had to break it down.

"I loved you, Gray. I really did."

He pushes my hair back from my face, cupping my cheek. "I know."

"Leaving you wasn't easy."

"Losing you was harder," he admits.

My hand wraps around his wrist, holding on when I should be pushing him away. "You found someone else."

His hand drops, and I feel cold. "I didn't. I found what my parents wanted me to find."

"You can talk to me . . . if you want."

He cracks his neck and there's a tenseness in his voice. "Yvonne was everything they hoped for. She was wealthy, smart, talented, and selfish beyond measure. Although, I didn't really care about that. I was angry with you, and being with her was . . . I don't fucking know, it was just dumb. We met in grad school. I was being groomed to take over the Park Inn and she was singing. My whole goal was to be better than my father. To make more, have a better wife, family, job. It was all I cared about. Yvonne fit because she was like me."

"How so?"

He turns his head, looking out the window. "She had horrible parents and told me how she wanted to prove them wrong. So, we dated, it was about two years in, and it was time."

"Time to get married?" I ask.

Grayson's eyes meet mine, the moonlight making them appear almost gray and hollow. "Yes, but we didn't have plans, Jess. We didn't lie in bed, her in my arms as I traced patterns on her back, dreaming of the life we'd have. I didn't talk about kids and hopes with her. We talked about money and material things she wanted."

My heart drops to my stomach because that was what we did. For hours, we'd hide ourselves away and tell the universe what life we wanted because then it could be true.

And I denied that earlier.

"Then why did you want to marry her?"

"Because if I wasn't going to marry the woman I loved, I might as well marry the one who wanted to marry me."

The ache in my chest is throbbing. "That's . . ."

"The truth, Jess. However, I was prepared to start my life because you weren't coming back. You were flying around the world and enjoying life. I was in Willow Creek, living the life that was demanded of me. But Yvonne, she wasn't horrible, not until we found out she was pregnant."

I stay quiet, trying to keep my breathing silent, already knowing this part of the story ends with Grayson being a single father.

Grayson doesn't say anything, so I reach out, resting my hand on his. "You don't have to say anything more."

His eyes close as he leans over, kissing the side of my head. "We all suffer with different forms of nightmares. Yours haunt your dreams, and mine lives in Paris." He stands, his tall frame blocking the moonlight, but I can feel his gaze. "We both need to sleep." He pulls back the covers, holding them up so I can get underneath.

I'm not sure what possesses me to obey his silent command, but I do. I get in, and he pulls the covers around me.

"Arms in or out?"

"In." He starts to tuck the blankets in around me, starting at my legs and moving up until I'm in a cocoon. "Snug as a bug in a rug," I say, hoping to lighten the mood.

He laughs. "I've learned that girls like to be held tight, and since it's a bad idea to sleep in here, this is the next best thing."

"Thank you again," I say, my arms unable to move a smidge.

Grayson doesn't acknowledge it. He just presses his lips to my forehead, and I wish it was my lips. "I mean it, if you need me, I'm right down the hall."

And I'll be forcing myself to stay right here.

Delia and I are walking arm and arm down the shoreline. I couldn't be in the house anymore. Everyone was still asleep when I snuck into her room, waking her and forcing her to come with me.

"So, the nightmare was bad?"

I nod. "It was like I was on the outside of it though."

"Is that normal?"

"Not even a little."

"Okay, why do you think it was different then?"

"I kissed Grayson," I admit.

Delia stops in her tracks, causing me to jerk back. "You what?"

I get her moving again as I fill her in on all the things that happened once she and Jack took off.

"As your best friend, I feel it's my duty to tell you that you're a goddamn idiot."

"Well, thanks. I already knew this."

Delia huffs and then pulls my arm to stop me. "No, not because you kissed him, but because the two of you are so damn obvious about what you feel for each other. Grayson stares at you all the damn time. When you move, it's like he subconsciously tracks you, always watching, which is how it was when we were kids."

"It wasn't like that."

"Okay, if you say so."

I try to think back, but I don't remember us being that intense.

"We spent two years apart," I remind her. "We weren't like that then."

Delia laughs while shaking her head. "The hell you weren't. If anything, it was even worse. You were in school, and he would come home every weekend. I would lose you because, if Gray was around, you most definitely were not. If he didn't come home, you were at his dorm."

"Yes, but we weren't like . . . in sync."

"You two were like magnets moving in unison. It was really amazing if I'm honest about it. It's why so many people were in shock when you ended things. But the bigger question is, what does it mean for you now? You're both older, lived a lot, and are single."

With maturity and age also comes the need to be honest about it too. "I'm not going to play games with him."

"I'm not telling you to."

"How is it that I'm thirty-two years old, unmarried, no kids, and I am a fucking mess? Shouldn't this have been how it was for me in my twenties?"

Delia laughs. "Well, I'm in the similar but slightly more pathetic boat as you. I'm thirty-two and have never been in a real relationship because I'm in love with a man who lives two states away and doesn't even know I exist. Oh, and it's been four years since I got laid."

"You are pathetic."

She nudges me as we both giggle. "How long has it been for you?"

"Oh, I'm pretty sure I'm a virgin again."

"That long?"

I nod. "I was sort of dating the pilot, Elliot, a few years back. We would hook up when we were on a flight together, but it stopped when he realized I was never going to be more than casual. He recently moved in with his girlfriend, and she's fantastic."

We are about to reach the beach house when Delia's hand grips my arm. "Jess, you and Gray . . . you were always what people hoped to find for themselves. You loved each other in a really raw and honest way. Do you think that being back here is some kind of sign? Could you give yourself the opportunity at love again?"

I look up at the deck in time to see Melia open the door and rush out, waving her hand at us. I lift mine and allow the unwanted images of a possible future to rush forward. Grayson, Amelia, and I vacationing here. Another comes of us at a school play or hiking to show her the lookout we made ours so many years ago.

He emerges, a coffee cup in his hand, staring at me with such intensity it's as though he can see into my head.

But the truth comes back, reminding me that this is temporary. I don't want to live here—ever. Grayson and I have ghosts that will never go away, and I've seen firsthand what those do to men.

It causes them to leave.

I look back at Delia, disappointed that wanting something so much doesn't make it possible. "Yes. No. I don't know. It's not a matter of giving myself a chance to love again." I watch him, hating the words. "It's that I don't want to stay here. I want to go back to my life in California. I want to fly again and travel. The real question is, could I give up everything for a *chance*? And the answer is . . . I don't know."

Twelve

GRAYSON

"Yaya, you have to meet my new friend Miss Jessica?"

I really wish the babysitter—also known as my mother—wouldn't insist on dropping off Melia an hour before I have to leave the inn. It's the busiest time of day for me, and my daughter does not understand what working means. Also, I haven't told my mother about Jessica working here.

"Jessica? Who is she?"

"The new front desk manager," I say.

Amelia grabs her hand. "She's pretty and smart and she and Daddy were in love once."

My mother's face pales. "Jessica Walker?"

"The same one."

Her lips part and she sucks in a breath. "Grayson, why? Why would you do that?"

"Do what?"

"Hire that girl," she says through clenched teeth.

One day, I may see my parents as the kind, loving people who didn't place value on material things that they once were, but today wasn't going to be that day. My mother ignores my father's indiscretions providing he keeps her dripping in diamonds and labels. After each of his "business trips," he returns with some ridiculous gift that she fawns over and uses to prove to her friends how wonderful her marriage is.

It's all fucking bullshit.

Dad fucks around. Mom drinks and pretends she's the queen while my siblings and I watch in disgust.

The worst part of Eveline Parkerson is the way she looks down her nose at others.

"I don't see why you care."

"Her mother was once my friend, that's why."

"Yes, she was, and then she wasn't, why is that?"

Mom clears her throat and looks around. "Is her mother still working here as well?"

She knows damn well that Jessica's mother doesn't. She quit around the time Jessica left.

"I don't see why that's your concern. You don't work here anymore either."

Amelia tugs on her hand. "Yaya, can we go see?"

For all the faults my mother has, and there is a list the size of Texas, she's a wonderful grandmother to Amelia. She watches her three times a week for me, not because she has to but because she loves her and she's the only grandchild.

"I would love to, Princess, but Yaya needs to get to work."

Melia's eyes squint. "You work?"

"Well, I help a lot of organizations in Willow Creek, and in

two days, we're having a dinner to help with the youth organization that helps people get their lives together." My mother's eyes meet mine. "We know people who have needed that,
don't we?"

She means Jess. "Thank God for the people who can help
those when they need it," I reply.

My mother stands a bit taller, pushing her shoulders back.
"Yes, well, I guess you get your charitable side from me."

"There's no charity in work."

Not that my mother knows much about working. She
helped my father design this place and bought everything to
outfit it, but that's where it ended. Being a trophy wife was my
mother's aspiration in life, and she wears it well.

Just then, Jessica emerges from the front office, carrying
papers, and Amelia rushes to her. "Jessica!"

"Amelia." She smiles at my little girl and then leans down
to give her a hug. "You look very pretty today."

"So do you! Yaya took me shopping today and bought me
this pretty dress since Grandpa is away again."

"Who is Yaya?" Jessica looks a little confused, but then
spots my mother and rises. "Mrs. Parkerson."

"Hello, Jessica. It's been a very long time."

Jess puts a smile on her face, but I can see it's not real.
"Yes, it has. It's nice to see you again."

My mother turns her face just slightly. "You're the help
now?"

"The what?"

"You work here, for my family."

"Mother," I say in a warning.

Jessica doesn't seem fazed. "Yes, I just started, actually."

"Funny how your mother started working here after her

failed marriage, and now you're here after your failed career."

"You. I . . . that . . . crash."

That one strikes exactly where it was meant to, and I won't let Jessica be upset and stutter in front of her. "And you're leaving," I say, placing my hand on her back. "I know you have a very busy day and need to prepare to be charitable. I'm sure the effort you'll need to do that is far too important to waste here."

My mother pats my cheek. "I'll let you be, and . . . not waste more time. Your father returns tomorrow from visiting Oliver, please come by around six. We'll be having dinner and he needs to speak with you and Stella."

There's no getting out of this dinner. My father won't accept any excuse and will show up at the worst time to make a scene if I choose not to attend. "Fine. I'll have Melia."

She leans down, kissing her on the cheek. "Be a good girl."

"Always, Yaya."

My mother turns, starting to walk away before stopping. "Jessica, do stop by the house sometime this week, I think I have a check for your mother's wages she never collected." She walks out, and I've never hated the woman more.

Jessica stands there, her eyes filled with pain and rage. My need to fix it is too great to stay away from her, which is what I've done the last three days.

I turn to Amelia. "Why don't you head into the kitchen and grab some cookies and then find Auntie Stella and bring her some."

Her face brightens. "Okay, Daddy!"

Once she's gone, I turn to see Jessica still standing there. The look on her face makes me want to slay dragons. "Jess . . ."

She shakes her head, snapping out of the trance. "It's fine. It's fine. I knew it."

"No, it's absolutely not fine."

"I should've—" She breathes deeply through her nose. "Said something cutting."

I want to laugh because Jessica isn't built that way. She never was, and being rude and mean-spirited has never been her thing. Not to mention, there is no one as good at being horrible as my mother.

"What would you have said?" I ask as I make my way closer to her.

"Something about her hair."

I fight back a grin. "She would've hated that."

The color is back in her face, and she lets out a deep sigh. "I don't know why she upsets me so much."

"Because she's a horrible person and has always treated you like shit."

"How did you come from her? You, your brothers, and sister are all wonderful and kind."

I rest against the wall so I'm close to her but not so close that she doesn't have space. "My grandmother was a saint, and she was around when we were little."

She worries her lower lip. "I remember you talking about her."

It hurts to think of her. Love wasn't a weapon with Nana. She was warm when my parents were cold and always pointed out the reasons they were great parents. "When my parents were first married, back when they could actually be tolerant of each other, Nana lived with us. She was my mother's mother and loved her grandchildren more than anything. She would spend hours with each of us, trying to shield us from the hatred she saw coming from my parents and giving us a better model to follow."

There were so many times my grandmother would just talk about love and acceptance. We were learning from her, even when we didn't know it.

"She did a good job of it."

I smile wistfully. "Yeah, I hope she'd be happy with how we turned out."

Jessica walks toward me, her fingers grip my forearm. "She would."

"I'm sorry that, once again, my mother acted that way to you."

Jess steps back, her eyes turning away. "I don't know why she still hates me. I'm not staying in town, and you and I aren't . . ."

"No, we're not." I remind myself more than anything.

We're nothing. We are just two old friends who loved each other once. Who also happened to kiss a few days ago, and I stayed up praying she would come to my bed.

"So, why she is worried? I have no idea."

Because I'm crazy about you, and she knows it.

"Yeah, I'm not sure why. Maybe it was because Melia was so excited about you."

Jessica's demeanor softens. "At least she loves her."

"That is the only reason she's allowed near her. As much of a horrific mother as she was, she's nothing like that with Amelia. She's kind and loving. They bake cookies—well, the cook prepares the dough and they put them on the sheet, but the point is that my mother tries with her."

"I guess that's all you can ask for."

The other desk attendant walks over. "Sorry I took a few

extra minutes, I hope I'm not in trouble," Marie says.

"Not at all," Jessica says. "I was actually going back in the office to review this report. Thank you, Mr. Parkerson, for being so kind."

I push off the wall with a nod. "Of course. I'll see you tomorrow."

Marie looks between us and then starts to work on the computer, ignoring the awkwardness. As Jess heads back to the office, I wonder if the problem with Jessica and me is that neither one of us ever asks for more.

Thirteen

JESSICA

I'm standing in front of the mirror, feeling awkward and stupid in this dress. I rub the satin material, trying to calm myself.

"You look gorgeous," Winnie says as she enters my room.

"I look like I'm going to prom."

She laughs. "Well, it was your senior prom dress."

How I ever let my sister talk me into this charity dinner is beyond me. All of it is for her organization, and her date bailed on her. Since she's one of the main reasons the event is being held, she begged me to go with her. Also, after I told her about the run-in with Eveline, she was damn near insisting I don't back down since she mentioned to her I was attending.

"Of all the dresses that Mom kept, why this one? I was so stupid my senior year."

The cut is not ugly, but the color is hideous. It's one of

those things that, when I was young, I thought matching my eyes would be a great idea, but now, looking at it, not so much.

"Who knows why she kept any of our shit, but it works, and the fact that you fit into a dress you wore when you were seventeen makes me hate you just a little."

I grin. "It's very tight, and I will probably rip the seam if I breathe too deeply."

"Good. You can hold your breath all night for all I care. I have two pairs of Spanx on and can't breathe. It can be our theme."

I look at my sister in an emerald-green gown. Her sweetheart neckline drops deep into her cleavage, and the dress hugs her curves before flaring out slightly at the bottom. If I had a dress like that, I would wear two pairs too.

"If I had known about the event, I could've found a dress that was like yours."

Winnie shrugs. "I think you look amazing." My sister gives me a kiss on the cheek. "Let's go. We have schmoozing and checks to cash in our future."

When we get downstairs, my mother looks up, and a wide smile crosses her face. "Well, if you two aren't the most beautiful things I've ever seen . . ."

"Thanks, Mom." Winnie beams. "You're sure you don't want to come? I bet there's another prom dress in that closet. Lord knows Jessica went to enough of them."

She waves her hand dismissively. "Oh, posh. You don't want an old lady ruining your good time. It's nice that you're both going, and that I kept that dress." Her brows rise as she smiles.

"Yes, your hoarding tendencies did us well this time," I say.

"It's called being thrifty, Jessica. One does what we must when we need to."

Instead of fighting her, I walk over and kiss her cheek. "I'm glad you saved it. Even if I can't breathe."

She laughs softly. "A woman who wants to be beautiful usually must suffer for it."

"This is true," Winnie agrees. "I will either pee my pants or hold it all night because none of this can be adjusted."

I roll my eyes at my sister, who is a far cry from heavy.

"Be home by midnight," Mom says, causing us to turn and look at her. "Oh, sorry, old habits."

We giggle and head out to Winnie's car, which thankfully, has the top up already. I look at the seat, wondering if I should sit.

Winnie does the same, her gaze meeting mine above the roof. "If we bust a gut now, at least we'll have an excuse not to go."

"If we bust a gut, I may cry."

"On the count of three?"

I nod.

"One," she starts.

"Two."

We watch each other, and then she says the final count. "Three."

Slowly, we get into our seats without any incident. However, breathing is damn near impossible. The problem isn't so much the waist area as it is the chest. I was not as . . . endowed at seventeen as I am now.

Everything in town is about fifteen minutes away, so breathing shallowly is doable. Winnie and I don't say much, probably because neither of us can move without fear of tear-ing something or want to waste what little air we can pull in, and when we get out of the car at the Park Inn, I feel dizzy.

"Winnie . . ."

She left out the part about it being held here. How I missed it on the event calendar, I don't know. I've been off the last two days and all that was there on this day was: family party.

I should've known.

"It's the nicest place in the county, Jess. Where do you think Eveline would host it?"

"I wasn't thinking."

She comes around to my side of the car. "Look, I know she's a vile bitch, but she has money, and my charity needs it. You're not with Grayson anymore, so there's no reason for her to be a bitch. Not to mention, Stella won't hesitate to say something."

"Is Gray going to be here?"

She shrugs. "I doubt it. He never comes to stuff like this. Why? Do you want him to be?"

I give her a look that clearly says I want to kill her. "I'm wearing the dress I wore to the last event we attended together. No, I don't want him to be."

Winnie laughs. "If it was the dress you wore the first time you put out, would you want a repeat?"

Yes.

"No."

Her hand rests on my forearm. "I know you're nervous, but he shouldn't be here. Grayson avoids his mother as much as possible."

"Because she's a horrible person, and she's going to make me feel stupid."

"Jessica, she can't make you feel stupid. You're not the

same person anymore. Listen, tonight will be fun. We'll go in, eat fancy food, dance, drink—well, you can't have alcohol but I will—and have a good time on their dime. Okay?"

When did my little sister, who used to steal my clothes and rat me out for sneaking Grayson into the house, become this wise woman?

"Okay."

"That's my girl. Also, who cares what she thinks? She's miserable and inconsequential in our lives."

Winnie is right. There's nothing that Eveline can say or do at this point that would really matter. I'm not a young girl, wishing her boyfriend's mother would like me even after she'd made it abundantly clear it would never happen.

"I know, but there's this young girl inside me who hasn't figured that out yet."

"I'm happy to kick her ass." She winks and then loops her arm in mine.

Winnie and I were never close as kids. The relationship was always me taking care of her, not getting to be her friend, and then I left Willow Creek. I turned away from the people I loved as a way to protect myself from everyone. I won't be that selfish now.

My sister asked me to come. She wanted me to see this— see her. I don't care if I have to walk on glass, I'm going to stand beside her.

"I'm proud of you, Win."

Her head tilts back. "Why?"

"Because you're you."

She smiles, a bit of moisture gathers in her eyes. "I missed you, Jess."

I gather my sister in my arms. The crash may have destroyed and taken so much from me, but it also gave me gifts. My sister. My mother. Forgiveness between people I never thought possible.

I've gained too, and Winnie is right, Eveline Parkerson can't take anything away if I don't let her.

"Okay, enough of this," Winnie says as she dabs at her eyes. "I'm going to be splotchy and I need to be stunning."

"Don't worry, you're stunning."

Arm in arm, we walk into the lion's den. The Park Inn has always been beautiful, but tonight, it sparkles. There are crystals hung around the entrance of the lobby with tons of candles strategically placed. I haven't been to a wedding here in forever, but that's what I'm reminded of.

When we get into the sitting room area, it's been converted into a bar area, and one of the front desk staff is working to pour drinks and fill orders. She waves, and I do the same.

Winnie says hello to a few of her work friends and introduces me. I can feel my stress-level rising, but I stay calm and focus on keeping my answers short.

When we enter the main event room, which was a huge addition built after I left town, I can't stop the smile that forms when I see an old friend.

"If my eyes are playing tricks on me, it's the best one yet," Alex says as he pulls me into his arms.

"You are the same as ever."

He lifts one shoulder and kisses my cheek. "I heard you were back and looking even hotter than when we were kids."

"I am—back, that is," I add on.

Alex wraps his arm around me, holding me to his side. "And I also heard you're working here."

"Right again," I say.

He shakes his head. "I'm sure that's . . . fun."

"That's one word for it."

Alex takes a step back, tugging me gently to let someone pass. "I won't say the word I'd use for being summoned back here by my asshole father and my viper of a mother."

"Fun?" I offer.

He drains the amber liquid in his glass. "Definitely not. This fucking place makes my skin crawl."

"So, you're glad you're not here?"

He laughs. "Sweetheart, I would've burned the fucking place down if I had to stay."

I don't remember Alex being openly hostile about his parents when he was a kid. None of them were ever openly loving, but neither did they seem hostile—well, except Josh. He was the first sibling to take off to another location, which coincided with a certain incident with my best friend.

"I take it things in the Parkerson house are tense?"

Alex waves over someone from the waitstaff I don't know, requesting another whiskey neat.

"They're always tense. I don't know how Grayson and Stella do it."

I look around the room and spot another Parkerson. God, I hope Delia isn't here, or this will be bad for everyone. "Are you all here tonight?"

Alex laughs once. "You mean is Grayson here tonight?"

"I didn't ask that. I just saw Josh."

The waiter is back, giving him another drink. He puts his glass down on the table, looking around the room. "We're all in town. Oliver is leaving tonight, so you might get to see him before he goes. Josh and I are gone first thing in the morning."

"Did you see Delia?"

"She's here."

"Great," I mutter.

"Yeah, she saw Josh already and then told me she had to make a phone call." Alex and Delia's relationship went from best friends to estranged after Josh left. Alex and Josh look the most alike, and I didn't think she could take it.

"I should go find her."

He nods, grabs his drink, and takes a long sip. "I'm going to get another drink and avoid my parents as much as possible. It was good to see you, Jess."

I give him another hug. "It's always good to see you."

He leaves, and I realize he didn't say anything about Grayson. Not that it matters, but when I know I'm going to see him, there's a level of preparation I feel is healthy.

I walk the room, talking to a few people from town I haven't seen since I've been back. I focus a lot on breathing and keeping calm. It's been the key to speaking without any missteps, and the more in control I am, the better.

"Jessica, I wasn't sure you'd show," Eveline says. She is gorgeous in a black cocktail dress. Of all the insults one could wield against her, her beauty isn't one.

"Winnie is my sister and I wouldn't miss this for her."

She smiles at someone behind me. "We don't normally allow staff here, but I guess it's fine since it's family and all. You're not senior enough to attend otherwise."

I bite my tongue, knowing that if I cause a scene it would be bad for me. The time I've worked at this job has helped me tremendously. It's like physical therapy for my brain, and I won't lose it unless it's on my terms.

"Of course." She clears her throat, obviously hoping I would've given her a different answer. I use her momentary discomfort for my benefit. "You look lovely, Mrs. Parkerson. Truly. As does the inn. I'm sure you'll raise a lot of money for the charity."

My mother always said the best way to beat a bully was with kindness. We'll find out here.

Her eyelashes bat a few times, and she takes a sip of her champagne. "Yes, well, I appreciate the compliment. It's a great organization."

Stella approaches, looking like a younger version of the woman in front of me. How she's single is a mystery to me. "Mother, I was looking for you." Her smile is there, but her eyes are apologetic as they dart my way. "Dad is in the office and really needs to make an appearance."

Eveline shakes her head and then straightens her back. "I'll handle him."

"Thank you," Stella says with a grin. Without another word, Eveline leaves. "I'm so sorry, I didn't see her near you or I would've gotten here faster."

I always loved Stella. "You're fine. It wasn't a big deal."

She grabs my arm and steps back, looking over my dress. "Please tell me that is not your prom dress."

I groan. "You remember my prom dress?"

Stella covers her mouth, smothering a laugh. "That photo of you and Gray was in his room. Of course I remember."

"I promise, it was not by choice."

"Stop it, you look amazing. I'm more impressed that you fit in it."

"Anyway," I say, hoping we can stop talking about it. "Have you seen Delia?"

Stella's eyes move over to another side of the room. "Yeah, she's doing her best to ignore Josh. Last I saw she was out by the lookout."

"I'm going to find her. Thank you for saving me."

"Any time."

The air is a little cooler than when we arrived, and I rub my hands up and down my arms to create some warmth. It was stupid of me not to bring a coat.

I somehow navigate my way to the lookout without breaking an ankle, but Delia isn't here.

But I don't turn to leave, too caught up in gazing at the moon that shines so big and bright. It's incredible, and I can't look away.

"There you are!" Delia's voice breaks the silence of the night.

"Hey. I was looking for you."

Her head drops back, and she drains the entire glass of wine in one gulp. Oh, God. This is what I was afraid of. "Why would you care about me? He doesn't."

"You saw Josh?"

She laughs once and tosses the glass off the side of the cliff. "I sure did. Bastard pretends like we're nothing."

"Did more happen that you never told me about?" I ask, suddenly feeling like I'm missing something because one kiss almost twenty years ago doesn't really scream committed relationship.

She laughs. "You mean did we have sex? No. We've gotten close, but in the last two years, he's done nothing but push me away."

Oh, this is bad. "Delia, you guys . . ."

Her eyes are filled with tears. "I've been in love with him my entire life, and all he does is look at me like I'm some stupid little girl. Do I look like a little girl anymore?"

"No," I say carefully. "But you are getting a bit too close to the edge there."

Her eyes dart to the side, and she steps toward me. That's at least a good sign. "All he cares about is work and . . . he doesn't care. He doesn't see that I love him. I love him, Jess. Not like you love Grayson, but like, I would die for him."

"Yes, but I'd rather you didn't do that." The wind whips around me, causing my hair to fly in my face and a shiver to crawl over my skin. "Come on, let's go inside and get you some water."

"No," Delia says with defiance. "I'm not going back in there so he can pat me on the head again."

"He patted you on the head?"

She nods. "Like I was the same age as Amelia." Her voice breaks at the end, and she crumples in my arms.

I hold my friend, hating that she's in pain. "You may love him, but why?"

She sniffs and then looks back at the event room. "Because he's everything I want. Because he made me feel beautiful, special, and he talked to me for hours that night we kissed. It was like the world was right and it's never been the same since then."

I pull her along with me, guiding her back to the warmth of the building. "He doesn't deserve you if he doesn't see you for the woman you are now."

"Tell my heart that."

I pull her in for a hug, both of our teeth chattering from the cold. "I know better than anyone that our hearts don't listen to our heads."

"And what does your heart cry out for?" Delia asks.

Grayson. Always Grayson.

"Something I can't have."

Fourteen

JESSICA

My phone pings with a text, and I grin.

Jacob: So, how is my favorite headcase?

Me: Good! No headaches in a week!

Jacob: That's great. How about the nightmares?

Yeah, that part is no different.

Me: Same.

My phone rings and Jacob's face fills the screen.
"Hey."
"Hey. So, the nightmares are still bad?" he asks.
Jacob, Elliot, and Jose are the only people who can really

understand what I'm dealing with. We lived it together and had to come out on the other side. I don't remember that much after I bashed my head, but I do know that, if it weren't for those three men, I would've died. And for that, I owe them and am always honest about what's going on.

"Yeah, but my doctor thinks it's normal, and they're not getting worse, at least."

"Still."

"Yeah, still."

"What's new in Willow Creek?" he asks.

I fill him in on the job, the beach trip, and the charity dinner that Grayson didn't attend. Jacob listens, asking a few questions here and there. Mostly, we discuss how I had to practically carry Delia out of there and have Alex drive us home.

For hours, she alternated between crying in my arms and getting sick from drinking too much. I hated seeing her like that. She was so sad and I wished I could make it better.

"How about in Sugarloaf?"

"We decided that I'm going to stay here."

"I knew you would."

He chuckles. "Well, I'm going to surprise Brenna by renovating the house. Melanie needs her own bathroom, and I know Brenna would like a bigger bedroom."

"That's sweet."

"The things we do for the people we love, right?"

"And the pain we suffer . . ."

Jacob goes quiet for a minute. "Are you suffering?"

I shift in my seat. "No. I'm fine. Everything is how it should be. Things are looking up now that I'm working, and my stuttering is so much less. I even endured a party without one slip up."

I'm really proud of that. I've been working a lot on focus and I think that's really helping. The doctors said it's a muscle that needed not only to heal but also be trained on how to function again. With the help of my neurologist and Dr. Warvel, I've been treating both sides.

"I'm really glad it's working." I can hear the happiness in his voice. "Listen, I wanted to ask you something."

"You can ask me anything."

He sighs. "Okay, my premiere is in about two months and I'd like for you guys to all be there. My family is going, and I'm planning something huge for Brenna."

I grin, knowing exactly what he's planning. "You're going to propose?"

"Yes."

"Good! The way you did it the first time was an epic failure."

"No shit," he agrees.

Jacob asked her the night after he returned or something ridiculous. Brenna, being a therapist, asked him to wait on it. I was incredibly proud of her for not just going with it. Although, anyone who turns down Jacob Arrowood has to be a little crazy because he's Hollywood's most beloved actor.

"Are you going all out?"

"Yes, I want to give her a proposal she'll remember."

"Brenna is a lucky girl," I tell him.

"When do you go back to the neurologist?"

"You know that I am not your responsibility, right?"

He chuckles. "Yes, but I'm worried about you."

"I appreciate that. However, you don't need to be. I'm a big girl and can take care of myself."

"You're also stubborn as fuck and don't want to accept

help."

I can't deny that. "Yes, I went a week ago and there's no change. I still have residual issues, especially with my peripheral vision. I'm not cleared to drive yet, and I won't be playing sports anytime soon. She's hopeful though, I'm making improvements, which is a good sign."

"Good."

"Can you explain to me why I haven't gotten a bill yet?" I ask, knowing he's already handled it. My doctor's office wouldn't even speak to me about it other than to say that all charges had been handled in advance.

No one else could've been behind it.

"Not a clue."

"Now we're lying to each other?"

"No, I'm merely acting, which is my job."

I glance over at the clock and sigh. "I wish I could talk more, but I have to get ready for work and call Winnie to make sure she actually shows up since she drank her weight in champagne."

"All right. I'll send you all the details about the premiere."

"Jacob?" There's a hesitation in my voice, but it is something I need to say.

"Yeah?"

"Thank you. For everything. You saved my life that day, and I know you handled my medical expenses, which would've bankrupted me by now. You've been a great friend, and I just want you to know that there's no one else in the world I would've rathered almost died with."

He lets out a deep laugh. "Same. You saved me as much as I saved you."

"I don't think that's true, but I appreciate it all the same."

"Listen, you've been through hell, and you're still dealing with it in ways that Elliot, Jose, and I aren't, but we were given a chance, Jess. A chance to make things right and do the things we want."

I lie back on the bed, feeling a bit dazed and lost. "It's complicated."

"Brenna would tell you that life is complicated."

"Brenna is a wise woman."

"Let's keep that to ourselves," Jacob says with a chuckle.

"I don't know, Jacob, it's like being here is being in the past, but that's not reality. Things have stayed still since I left."

If anyone could understand what I mean, it would be him. He left the town he's from and vowed never to return but was forced to because of his father's will.

"Believe me, I get it, but coming back home doesn't mean a death sentence. My brothers and I are proof of that. If my father didn't force our hands, we would've all been living very sad and lonely lives. Now look at the Arrowood brothers. We're all in very different places."

"But is it the place you would've chosen?" I ask.

"No, because I didn't know this place existed."

Pushing aside the branches and overgrown brush, I walk deeper into the woods. It's crazy that I remember how to get here. It's been so long, but the path is etched in my mind. I walk a little to the right, avoiding a rock that looks like it fell from the cliff above.

Today was a hard day. I had a migraine that left me feeling nauseous and then ended up having to call out of work. Then

Winnie called to tell me she has to go out of town for her job, which means I'm unable to get anywhere unless Delia or my mother can drive me.

I slept the entire morning and afternoon, so now, it's almost dusk, and I am wide awake.

Hence the hike.

This overlook was one of my favorite spots, not just because it was something I shared with Grayson but because it was a safe place. Somewhere that was untouched by the outside world and was a piece of Earth that was just mine.

I climb up the side with a grin on my face because I know that, once I get around this curve, it'll have a small open space where two people can fit without anyone being able to see them.

One more step up and two twists and I'll be in the clearing. There's a sliver of my heart that wants him to be here, waiting like he was all those times. I'm clearly a freaking fool.

When I see my spot, a part of me weeps because he's not here and another part weeps because it's everything that I remember.

The ground is covered in soft moss, the mountain carved out on both sides gives a feeling of a cocoon, and the view . . . the view is breathtaking.

As many times as I once dreamed of this, it didn't come close.

There is a town over on the right, and I can just make out a few lights. Over to the left is nothing but trees and mountain tops.

The sounds of nature are all around—an owl hooting, trees rustling in the breeze, and frogs croaking. I pull out my blanket, place it on the ground, and lie down, just breathing.

Minutes pass as I sink into the peace of this place. For the first time in a long time, the sky is my friend and I feel safe.

Until I hear the crunching of branches.

My heart picks up, and I sit upright, which has my head throbbing from the quick motion.

Relax, Jessica, no one can see you here. You're protected.

I repeat this over and over.

The sound stops, and I release a deep breath. "It was probably a deer," I say under my breath.

But before I can lie back down, something catches my eye, and then I know it. I'm not alone.

I'm not safe.

Someone else is here.

GRAYSON

As though I conjured her from my mind, Jessica is sitting on a blanket in front of me. Only, instead of smiling at me, her arms are wrapped around her legs and there is fear in her eyes.

"You're here," I say and watch her shoulders drop.

"Grayson. Jesus. You scared the shit out of me."

She shouldn't even be here. She should be at home—resting. She called out of work because of a headache, which had me concerned. When I left the inn, I drove to her house, but I ended up turning around before I got there because she's not mine anymore.

Stella came by and offered to take Melia for the night as a thank you for saving her ass with Mom over a misunderstanding at dinner.

So, I found myself worried and stuck in the house.

Instead of sitting alone for the night, I came here, needing to be close to Jessica but not near her. That didn't exactly work out.

"Me? What are you doing here?" I ask.

She shifts onto her knees, moving a backpack to the side. "My headache is gone, and I needed to . . . I don't know . . . be out of my mother's house."

I move deeper into the space. "I needed to be out of my house too."

"Where is Melia?"

"With Stella."

She nods. "So, the single dad has the night off and doesn't know what to do?"

More like the man who keeps trying to avoid kissing the girl he loved once is going out of his mind. "Something like that." I walk over to where she's sitting. "Is there room for me?"

Jessica scoots a bit. "Always." I take the spot next to her and pull my blanket out as well. We can use it if the temperature drops more. "It seems we were both drawn to a familiar hideout."

"Well, I've been here the entire time."

"You weren't here when I got here, and it doesn't look like you've been in a while."

She's got me there. "It's been a bit."

Jess grins as though she knew it. "How long?"

"Since before Melia was born."

The truth is, I can't remember the last time I came out here. Like the beach house, it's something that belonged to the two of us. This was where *we* were lost and found together.

"Does it feel different to you?" she asks.

"I think everything is different."

She looks out at the horizon. "It is, but being here doesn't feel that way, does it? When I got here, it was like this sense of belonging filled me. Almost as though the spot has been here, waiting for us. Everything is the same as it was—well, other than the house I passed that wasn't here years ago."

I lean back on my elbows, looking at her in the moonlight as the stars begin to show themselves. Sometimes I feel as if everything has been waiting for her. It's why I needed to pretend I didn't care.

Why everything in my life has been about moving forward and not looking back.

She's my past, but I always thought she'd be my future.

I'll never understand how two kids managed to fall so hard for each other that, after all this time, it still feels as strong. It all came back the day she did.

"Yeah, it's a few years old."

"Hopefully, the owners have never found this spot."

I grin. "From the overgrowth, I'd guess not."

No, it doesn't look like anyone at all has been here.

"I hope they don't mind us being here."

I shrug. "I'm not worried."

Jess shifts her weight, bumping into me. "You were always able to get out of trouble."

"I'm a likable guy."

"You're something, all right." Jess's smile is warm, and I want to kiss her so much it hurts.

"What else do you have in there?" I ask, looking at the bag.

She opens it up, pulling out a water bottle, a pillow, a bag of snacks, and her phone, which is comical because there's no reception over here.

"Were you planning on sleeping here?"

"No," she says slowly. "I just wasn't sure I'd find it, and I swear it was you who told me to always be prepared in case I got lost or hurt."

"That I did."

She leans back on her elbows, mimicking my pose, and I grab at the snack bag.

"Hey! Bring your own snacks," she says with a laugh.

"I like yours better."

I open the bag of crackers and pop one into my mouth. She rolls her eyes and rests her head on the pillow. I hate that I still find her irresistible.

I look out at the view, focusing on the stars instead of how beautiful she is. Her long brown hair is pulled up in one of those buns that make zero sense, and she's wearing leggings and an off-the-shoulder sweatshirt that shows off her tattoo. "What does that say?" I ask, avoiding the complexity of my thoughts around her.

Her head turns to me, eyes filled with confusion. "What?"

"Your tattoo."

"Oh," she says with a grin, "It's Latin for: strength isn't measurable."

"That's very true."

"I sometimes have to remind myself that we aren't born with a finite amount of strength because there's always more when we need it. We have to harness it, use it, refill it once it's depleted."

"Look at you," I say, nudging her softly. "A philosopher."

She shakes her head. "Far from it. I just have thoughts about certain things in life."

"What do you think about this moment then? The two of

us, finding each other in a place that has gone untouched for years."

Jessica stares at me for a beat before turning away, resting her hand along the column of her neck. "I don't know. What do you think?"

I shift so I can gauge her reaction. "I think it means we were meant to be here."

"Why?"

"I don't know. Why did you come here? Honestly."

Her breathing grows a bit faster, her eyes searching mine. "I needed to feel alive again."

"And this place is where you felt it?"

Jessica shakes her head.

"No?" I ask, confused as to why she'd walk out here.

"I felt it with you."

The pounding in my chest gets louder as indecision wrestles within my head. I want her. I've always wanted her. I need her, and yet, I know I will never have her. Jessica can't be caught, and that was my biggest mistake before. She can't be caged, and any man who tries to contain her will fail.

This time is different. I know I can't keep her, but maybe I can hold her for just a while.

The two of us watch each other, waiting for the other to make a move. This time, I will tumble over the side.

I reach my hand out slowly, my thumb brushing her cheek. I move at a pace that gives her every opportunity to push me away.

"I felt safe with you," I say as I inch nearer to her lips. "I shouldn't, but you're the one thing that I can't seem to let go of."

A tremble runs through her body, and she places her hand

over my racing heart. "What are we doing?"

"Whatever we want. Do you want me?"

Her eyes, which are a rich amber color that is rimmed with a thick line of black, move to my lips. "I told you I can't kiss you."

I move a bit more, our mouths just barely a whisper apart. "Then I'll just have to kiss you."

I don't wait for her to answer, I kiss her. My lips meld to hers as though we were made to fit this way. She tilts her head, and I take advantage of it, deepening the kiss. Jessica's arm wraps around me as she clings to me, and I lay her down.

The moan that escapes her runs through my bones, and I want to hear it again and again. Her lips part, and then our tongues slide along each other's. I'm so fucking done. I hold her head steady, controlling the kiss, needing to fucking take anything she'll give me.

She makes soft noises, clutching my back as I roll atop her. "Jess," I say her name into the silent air.

"Kiss me, Gray. Please don't stop."

I do as she asks, my hand running down her side as my mouth stays fused to hers. She's everything I remember but better. I've kissed this girl over a thousand times. I've felt her love, passion, and body so many times, but this is like something new.

We're new.

This isn't the old Grayson and Jessica, this is something new.

I never should've kissed her. I should stop, but there's not a chance in hell of that happening.

My hand is moving back up her body, and I cup her breast, moving my thumb over her nipple.

She grips my back, trying to pull me tighter.

"Tell me to stop," I say against her mouth.

Her eyes find mine, blazing with passion and desire. "I don't want you to."

"Jess . . ."

"Grayson, it's you. You're why I came here."

"Christ," I say before I kiss her harder and with everything inside me. She's why I'm here.

I hoped that I'd find her here, and when I saw her, it was as though all the questions surrounding what we should be disappeared.

This may never work, but I can't resist her.

I graze the skin where her shirt has lifted, moving my hand under the fabric. I push under the wire of her bra, letting the weight of her breast fill my hand perfectly.

She moans as I knead and rub her nipple. Her head moves to the side. "God, yes."

I kiss down her neck, nipping at the skin right where it meets her shoulder before my tongue licks over that spot.

Her hips lift slightly, and I shift, needing to see her. "You're so beautiful. Laying here in the spot where I fell in love with you. Your lips are swollen from my kiss."

"And look at you . . ." Her eyes move over my face. "Your hair is mussed. Your eyes can't move off me, and you . . . you found me."

"I've been searching for you for years."

Jess's brows scrunch slightly. "What do you mean?"

Shit. I shouldn't have said anything. "Nothing."

Jessica sits up. "That's not nothing, Gray."

"I just mean that you're the girl who I have never really forgotten. I've tried, fucking hell, I've tried. You're everywhere, and I can't forget, Jess. I can't pretend that I don't want you and us and . . ."

Her hand moves to my lips. "I tried too. And then my life literally came crashing down around me. Do you know what I thought of when that plane was falling?"

I wait, the masochist in me wanting her to say it was me. The realist keeping that side in check.

"Your life. Your family."

"The man I let go," Jess answers. "I thought about you and how I missed you."

"You had a head injury."

She laughs softly. "Or maybe I just finally had some sense knocked into me. You're why I'm here. Yes, I needed to recover, but I couldn't keep living this way. I had to see you . . . to know if how I feel is real or not."

"And now that you're here, what? Are you going to stay here and not leave if we try this?" I ask, already knowing the answer.

The crestfallen look on her face says everything. "I . . . I . . . we . . . the . . ." Her eyes fill with tears.

"Don't, Jess. Don't get upset." A tear falls down her cheek, and I wipe it away. "Loving you has never been a question, but keeping you has always been our downfall. I can't leave here and you won't stay."

She lets out a deep breath and then speaks. "It's not that way."

"But it is. I'm stuck here whether I like it or not. I have Amelia to think about, the inn, and my family, even though they are a pain in my ass."

"So, what if we try?"

"And I end up with a heartbroken little girl and my own

pain?"

She chews on her lower lip. "You can't tell me what I'm going to want, Grayson. I've left you and know how that feels. If we try, and I love you like I . . . and it all . . ."

I lean in, pressing my lips to hers, refusing to hear the end of that. "If we fail," I say softly, "I won't hurt my daughter by allowing her to watch another woman walk away."

I have to protect Amelia and myself because Jessica doesn't belong here, just like Yvonne didn't.

Sixteen

JESSICA

"So, you decided not to reconcile. How did he take it?" Dr. Warvel asks from where she sits with her legs crossed, writing in that fucking notebook.

"Badly."

It's the day of one-word answers, and I don't care.

"You're clearly agitated," she muses.

"Yup."

"Do you want to tell me why?"

I look away. "Nope."

"Okay." Her voice is even as she leans back in her chair. "I think you're upset because you allowed yourself to be vulnerable and you're hurt."

I huff. She got all that from just a few words. Wow, she's a goddamn genius. I cross my arms, wanting to build a fortress around myself to stop her words from entering.

I'm not upset because I'm hurt. I'm upset because I was stupid. I lied to myself and thought I could have it all.

What a bunch of shit. No one gets it all.

I clench my teeth together to stop from saying it to her. I don't want to be here, but my mother took off work so I couldn't skip. I'm here, but I'm done talking about Grayson Parkerson and my stupid feelings about him.

"Can we not?" My tone is clipped.

"We could, but then this session will leave you exactly where you started."

"I'm not going to feel better recounting it."

"Maybe not," she agrees. "Or maybe you'll get to the root of why you're pissed at the world."

I don't know how Jacob lives with a shrink. I would kill someone if they kept poking and prodding. I don't want to talk. I don't want to feel better because pain is the only thing that reminds me that life sucks.

"I'm good."

Dr. Warvel nods once and then gets to her feet. "Okay, you have about thirty minutes left in the session, so you're welcome to stay here or, if you want, you can leave, that's fine too. I'm going to catch up on some things."

She walks over to her desk, grabs her iPad, and starts tapping away.

Great, I'm not only angry, broken, and a damn mess, I'm also wasting Jacob's money.

Could I feel any worse? No. I don't think that's possible.

I'm being a baby. That's the truth of it. "I told him I wanted to try," I say softly, but I know she heard.

Dr. Warvel sets the iPad down and heads back to the seat she usually occupies. "And he rejected you?"

I nod. "He said he knows I won't stay and he has to protect his daughter."

"Sounds like he's a great dad."

"Far better than mine ever was."

She inclines her head. "Maybe he was protecting you by not giving you a choice."

"Or himself."

Dr. Warvel doesn't say a word, she just watches me, and I start to fidget.

"What?"

"We often create truths from the experiences we have as children. They aren't true all the time, but our minds deem them to be so. For example, your father left you, therefore you believe that people leave, which is why you left Grayson, right?"

"I guess."

She clasps her hands in front of her, leaning forward. "Jessica, why did you leave him?"

"Because I wanted to . . ."

I wanted to protect myself. I wanted to leave him before he could leave me and I wouldn't be hurt and broken. He was the one thing in the world I didn't want to lose, so I gave him away.

My eyes open wider, and my breath hitches.

"Tell me," she urges. I feel the moisture running down my cheeks as I say that entire thought aloud. Dr. Warvel extends the box of tissues. "It's not easy to work through our pasts and change the way we think, but Grayson has endured people he loves leaving him too."

His father in a sense, me, Yvonne . . . we all left him.

"I don't want to hurt him. I still love him."

She gives me a sad smile. "Love is a gift when given free-ly, but it can also be painful when taken back. You both have to have trust and openness. If your headaches were gone and you were cleared to fly, would you take flight or stay grounded beside him?"

Two parts of my soul start playing tug of war. "I don't know."

"And that's the answer that scares him."

It also terrifies me.

Stella rushes into my office. "Oh, good! You're here. Thank God."

"What's wrong?"

"I *need* you to help me."

I get to my feet. "Of course, what's up?"

Stella swallows deeply. "I have to watch Amelia tonight, but something has come up . . . an emergency with an old friend, but she has dance tonight and can't miss it."

"Okay . . ."

"I promise, I wouldn't ask you this if there were any way around it. If there was another option, I swear, Jess, I wouldn't do this. But I'm desperate, and I have to leave right away. I know it's a lot, but can you please take her for me?"

I'm not sure that's such a good idea. I don't know much about other people's kids, but your ex-girlfriend who you made out with a few days ago and then rejected probably isn't very high on your list of babysitters.

"Where is Grayson?"

"We had a huge issue out in Wyoming with Oliver's property, and he flew out first thing this morning."

"Oh."

She smiles tightly. "Look, I know it's a big ask, and I wouldn't ask if I hadn't already cleared it with Grayson and he said it was fine if I had no other options, and I don't."

"What about Winnie?"

My sister loves Amelia and has watched her before.

"Winnie said she's bogged down at work."

A sense of dread fills my chest, weighing me down. I love Amelia, but she's Grayson's daughter.

"You really have no one else?" I ask.

"I promise, I wouldn't ask if I did. I swear, if I didn't need to leave within the hour, I wouldn't do this."

"I can't drive," I remind her.

"I know. It's fine. I will drive you to my place and you can hang out with Melia there since it's in town a block or two away from her dance studio." Which means it's walkable. "She has her own bedroom, and there's a guest room, so you'll be completely comfortable. *Please*." She begs with her hands in front of her chest. "If you say no, I'll have to take her, and she'll be crushed."

Ahh, the Parkerson guilt trip. I've missed it. Still, I have nothing else to do, and it would be helping Stella, who has done a lot to help me.

"I guess, but I still get nightmares and don't want to scare her."

"You won't. I promise. She would sleep through an entire army marching through her room."

I release a heavy sigh. That was my last excuse. "All right. As long as you swear Grayson is fine with it."

She grabs her phone, types something out, and then waits.

Her foot tapping.

Then my phone pings with a North Carolina area code.

Unknown: It's Gray. I swear it's fine, just don't listen to her if she says she's allowed to eat KitKats for dinner.

Me: I am not that gullible.

Grayson: She's just that convincing.

Stella clears her throat. "Okay?"

"Okay."

"Good. Let's go."

I grab my bag, and we leave to pick up Amelia from the daycare before heading to Stella's. She chats a mile a minute, telling us all about her day, what she ate—where she mentions KitKats—and how excited she is that I'm going to be watching her.

Stella shows me around her loft, pointing out a few key things, and then gives me her cell number before leaving.

Amelia plops herself on the couch, grabbing the remote. "Auntie Stella lets me watch cartoons."

I am so out of my element. After the texting with Grayson, I'm not sure how much I should believe from her. "Yeah? Which ones?"

"Not scary ones."

"How about we watch it together?" I offer.

Melia pats the seat beside her. "I like the funny one with the singing cat."

Singing cats sound like a safe territory. Although, Tom and Jerry weren't exactly the model we should've followed regarding how to treat others.

Once I'm seated, Melia scoots closer, snuggling into my

side. She's such a sweet kid.

"We only have about twenty minutes before we head to your dance class."

She grins. "I love dance. Daddy says I'm the best in the class."

"I'm sure you are."

"Mrs. Butler isn't a nice teacher."

"I had Mrs. Butler when I was a little girl." She was a horrible woman then, so I'm not surprised she still sucks.

How she's still in business is a mystery. Then again, it's not like there are any other options in town.

"Did she smile then?"

I laugh. "Not once."

Melia changes the channels until she finds her show. "This is the singing cat. His name is Winston, and he's afraid of spiders."

"That makes two of us."

"I don't like them either, but Daddy isn't afraid. He's not afraid of anything."

Except me.

I smile at her. "He has to be afraid of something."

She shakes her head. "Nope."

"Not even snakes?"

Amelia grins. "Nope."

"What about fire?"

"He's a firefighter, silly."

"Oh, that's right," I say, trying to appear pensive. "What about . . . storms?"

Amelia gets up on her knees. "No way, storms aren't scary, they're fun."

"Fun?"

"Daddy and I go on the deck to watch them."

Grayson and I used to do that as well. We would go in the back of his truck, watching the electric storms on the other side of the mountains. I had a ridiculous sense of false security because he convinced me that the tires would prevent us from being electrocuted, ignoring the fact we were in the metal truck bed.

"There has to be something," I tell her.

Amelia taps her finger on her lips and it's so easy to forget she's only four years old. "I know!"

"You do?"

"He's afraid of me."

"Oh? Are you *scary*?" I ask with my voice dramatic at the end.

"Yes! Look!" She lifts her little fingers and growls. The laughter is instantaneous, and I grab her, tickling her sides.

I get why he will give up his own happiness for her. You protect the ones you love. You protect your child, even if it means cutting out your own heart.

Seventeen

GRAYSON

Everything at this property is a mess.

It's in the middle of nowhere, smells distinctly like cow shit no matter where you are, and needs to be completely gutted.

"How the hell did Dad think this was a great investment?"

Oliver shrugs. "The fuck if I know."

"Why did you agree to come here?"

"Do any of us have a damn choice? He said he bought land and said I should go. After the breakup with Devney, I was all too happy to leave Sugarloaf."

I know that feeling all too well. If Jessica had stayed in Willow Creek, I would've begged to take one of these locations, even if it meant I lived in cow pie hell.

"Jessica knows his brother," I tell him.

"I'm aware, she was in the crash with him."

It seems that everyone was aware of that except for me. "Have you spoken to her?"

"Jessica? Yeah, she was at the party last week. The one you somehow got out of."

I didn't get out of it, I just didn't go. There's absolutely no reason I need to pretend we're this idyllic family to keep my mother happy. She doesn't give a shit about any of us or what we want. It's about appearances and status. Two things I give zero fucks about.

"I had plans."

He smirks. "Sure you did."

"I had no idea she was going," I say as we enter the lobby area.

"Would that have changed your plans?" my little brother asks, and I have the urge to put him in a headlock.

"No."

"Liar."

I flip him off. "Let's see what you screwed up and needed me to come out and fix."

He groans but leads the way back into the office.

If I thought there was a mess before, I was sorely mistaken. This is next level. The office is small, but there's spray paint on the walls, papers strewn around, and the desk light is shattered on the ground. This person was out for something.

"Did you call the cops?"

Oliver shakes his head. "I'm pretty sure that's who did this."

Okay, now I'm confused. "You think the cops destroyed your office? Were you fucking the lieutenant's daughter?"

He releases a heavy breath and walks over to the desk area. "I wasn't, but I think another member of the Parkerson family was."

"Fuck," I say, taking the note from his hand.

There in black and white is what my brother feared.

"You disgust me. You're a liar and I never want to see you again. You said you weren't married, and then I saw the photos!"

"Did you, by chance, marry someone and not tell us?"

Oliver laughs without humor. "Nope."

"So, you think one of his side pieces in the area found out and wrecked the place?"

"Well, the charity dinner was newsworthy, and I'm going to assume our mother wanted to bask in her glory, which means press was there. It doesn't take a rocket scientist to figure out why this happened now."

"Jesus. You'd think . . ."

"What? That he wasn't this way anymore? Come on, Grayson. You're not a fucking idiot. Well, you are, but not that way. Look at all of us. Five kids. Five, and we're all like this. We date people who will never be more than casual. We fight back against anything that feels real. I dated Devney for years, knowing the entire time that she was in love with her best friend. I couldn't even manage to be pissed about it when I found out she kissed him."

"I would've married Yvonne," I say, needing to prove him wrong. We can't all be fucked up. There has to be at least one of us that has hope.

"Yeah, and that was a healthy relationship?"

No, it wasn't. It was toxic and I'm glad I didn't marry her, but really, none of us are the models of healthy relationships. I think about each of my siblings, trying to see where our parents may not have totally ruined us, and I feel like total shit.

Stella has never really dated anyone. She's had short-lived bursts of something, but she always walks away at the first sign of anything deep. Josh has been denying his feelings for Delia for as long as I can remember, trying to say he's "too old" for her. Alex is the happiest, loneliest person I know. He has zero intentions of marrying, and we know Ollie is a mess.

God, this is a sad group.

"It was what I needed at the time," I say honestly.

"And that's what Devney was for me. I would've married her. I planned on asking her, even though a part of me was hesitant. I don't doubt that I loved her, but how fucked up is it that I would've married her, knowing that she loved another dude?"

I clasp his shoulder, squeezing tight. "At least you're not in love with the girl who broke your heart, showed up again, made out with twice, and then pushed away."

"I see you're the healthy one out of us."

"Far fucking from it."

"What's the issue with her? Why are you pushing her away?"

I glance at the mess around me, feeling like this room looks. "Because of this."

"What?" He pulls his head back and quirks his lip.

"This is what happens. Things are destroyed when it doesn't work out."

Oliver doesn't say anything as he leans down, gathering the papers and putting them in a box. He lifts it and then hands it to me. "And then there's this."

Now it's my turn to be confused. "A box?"

"No, it's cleaned up. I keep thinking how we're all making these mistakes by trying to not make them."

"Oliver, I have no clue what the hell you're saying."

He sighs deeply. "So what if there's a mess at the end? Who gives a shit if things don't work out or we aren't getting what we want at the finish line? We can pick the pieces up and pack them away. Isn't it supposed to be about the journey? I'm tired of living this way, Grayson. I want to get married and have kids. I want to be fucking happy. When I was back home last week, all I could see were people who didn't have money or hated their jobs, but they looked happy because they weren't alone."

"I see it every day."

"And you don't want that?"

He has no fucking idea. "I built a house because I hoped someone would live in it with me," I remind him.

"Yeah, and now she's back and you're afraid."

"Damn right I'm afraid!" I yell, tossing the box on the floor. "I know what it feels like to lose her."

Oliver nods slowly. "You also know what it's like to love her. I guess the question is, which one is worth more?"

I'm done with this conversation. "Let's clean this up," I suggest sternly. "Then we'll call him and let him know about the damage."

Thankfully, he takes the hint and we start working on cleaning up the messes we can.

Eighteen

JESSICA

"**A**re you sure you don't mind?" Stella asks as I push the phone to my ear.

What am I supposed to say? No. I can't because Amelia is four and can't exactly stay home alone. So, here I am, packing up her stuff to head to Grayson's house and spend another night with her.

"It's fine."

She sighs with relief. "You're the best. Truly. I thought I could get back, but the storm is bad, and I can't see with the sheeting rain."

"I understand."

Even if I hate the idea of sleeping at his place, Amelia needs clean clothes and she's bored here.

"Thank you, Jess. I know this isn't easy for you since you and Gray have history, but . . ."

"It's really okay. We're friends, and this is what friends do."

The thunder echoes in the background, punctuating that thought. "I have to go."

"Be safe, we'll see you tomorrow."

Amelia comes rushing in, a big smile on her face. "Are we going to my house?"

"We are."

"Yay!" She jumps up and down. "I can show you all my toys. I have a lot of them because Daddy says I'm cute."

And she is. Just then a horn honks, and I grab our bags and hold out my hand. "Ready to go?"

Delia, the lifesaver she is, came to drive us over so we didn't have to walk. We get in the car, and I strap Amelia into her booster seat. When I climb into the front, Delia is staring at me, giving me a dubious look.

"Don't say a word," I warn.

She grins. "What would I even say?"

"Nothing."

"Nope. Nothing. I have nothing to say about this."

"Good. Then say nothing."

Delia looks in the rearview mirror. "Do you have anything to say, Melia?"

Melia smiles. "I love dolls."

"Yes, it's fun to pretend, isn't it, Jessica?"

I grit my teeth. "Yes."

She continues on. "I like to pretend that my best friend is going to find her prince someday. He's tall, has dark hair, and the bluest eyes."

Amelia perks up. "My daddy has blue eyes."

Delia gasps. "He does?"

"And he's tall."

"Look at that."

"So much for not a word," I say out of the corner of my mouth.

She ignores me, making a right onto Grayson's street. "Do you think my friend should tell him she loves him?"

Amelia nods vigorously. "And she should kiss him!"

"She should?"

I want to throw myself from this car. "Kissing boys isn't a good idea," I try to inject some reasoning into this asinine conversation.

"That's true," Delia agrees. "I think she might love him, though, and if she does, she should kiss him before his evil mother gives her poison."

"Oh Jesus," I mutter.

"She has to have a kiss!" Amelia agrees.

"Yes, because then, maybe my friend will wake up and see what's really happening."

Blessedly, we pull into his driveway and Delia parks. I don't say anything because I won't give this conversation another second of my time. I'm not sleeping. I'm fully awake and aware of the truth. This isn't a fairy tale, and the happy ending isn't coming my way.

I look at the log cabin in front of me and try not to think about how I'm going into *his* home. It's two floors with huge windows and a wraparound porch on the front. There's a black tin roof, which I imagine makes rainy nights sound like a lullaby. On the front door, there are three white papers with drawings on them, obviously Amelia's handiwork.

I make my way closer with my heart in my throat because this is their life and I'm walking into it.

Amelia, having the attention span of a four-year-old, rushes to the door, busy telling Delia about her dance class. "And then Mrs. Butler said I have to move my right foot to be in second position, but I don't like it. Fourth is my favorite, so I wanted to stay there."

Delia and I did ballet for years, which is how we became best friends. We both sucked—horribly.

"You should tell her that you want to wear a purple leotard."

"Are you trying to get her thrown out?" I ask.

"I'm hoping maybe I can drive Mrs. Butler to finally retire."

I roll my eyes, find the spare key where Grayson told me it would be, and open the door. "You wear your pink tights and black leotard and don't listen to a word Delia says."

Amelia shrugs and rushes off to what I assume is her room. I take a second and look around. This is his home, where he's raising a little girl on his own.

The house is exactly like what we always dreamed of when we looked out at the mountains. It's a beautiful log cabin with a lot of open space and a huge loft on the second floor. The back wall, though, it's—incredible. Floor-to-ceiling windows that give you the perfect view of the mountains. Why the hell he came out to our spot I'll never understand. Here, standing in the middle of the room, I can see the same view.

Over to the right is the town that is the only light we can see from the lookout. And then, to the left is the mountain peak that looks like a pencil.

I feel the air leave my lungs in a rush.

"It's one hell of a view." Delia stands beside me.

There are tears forming in my eyes, the moisture threatening to spill over, and I turn so no one will see. He bought a house on the same side of the mountain, looking out at the view we always loved.

Then something starts to niggle in the back of my mind. "Delia?"

"What?"

"This house . . . has it always been Grayson's?"

"Yeah, he had it built. He bought the land years ago, but didn't do anything with it, then when he and"—she looks around for Melia—"her mother were a thing, he put it on the market but kept rejecting the offers. He built the house right after Amelia was born and *she* left."

I can feel my breathing growing labored. Oh, God. He bought the land. He owns this plot and he owns our spot. "Oh."

That's all I can say as I stare out the windows.

"Why?"

I shake my head. "Nothing, it's just a great view."

"Yeah, must be nice to be a Parkerson and buy part of a mountain."

I take another few steps, my heart pounding as I get closer. It's all here. Everything that we shared, the memories, the hopes and dreams whispered into the air—they are all right here. Another tear falls down my cheek as another part of my heart realizes just how much I'm in love with him.

"Jess," Grayson's deep voice sounds so far away even though he's right here in my arms.

I don't want to be woken from this dream.

Grayson's scent is around me, his lips are on mine. We're

in our spot where nothing can touch us.

"Jessica." His voice is low and sultry. "Love."

When he uses the term of endearment, I break. I grab for him, reaching, but he's not there. I groan, trying to bring him to me. "Gray, please," I beg. "Please, don't leave me."

I can feel the hesitation raging between us. "Fuck," he curses, rubbing his nose against mine.

So close.

He's right here.

"I need you," I confess.

He lets out a low grumble that comes from his chest as his forehead rests on mine. "You're killing me."

I run my hands along the stubble on his cheek. "Love me," I plead.

"I always have."

I smile, loving how he makes me feel. "I've always loved you, but I was afraid."

Grayson's fingers run down my jaw before brushing my lips. "Afraid of what?"

In my dream, I am not afraid to tell him. I close my eyes and the heat of him surrounds me. "Losing you. I never want to lose you." He lets out a heavy sigh as though I've just said something that hurt him. I feel him pulling away, and I clutch at him. "Don't."

"Wake up, love. Wake up."

My throat goes dry, and my eyes fly open. He's there, hovering over me. I'm . . . in a bed that's not mine.

Because it's his. I'm in his bed, and he's in it too.

I gasp, and he moves to the side. "I was dreaming?"

Grayson grips the back of his neck. "Yeah."

"Oh, God." I clasp my hand over my mouth.

"Yeah."

"Oh, God," I say again, realizing that I was dreaming of . . . him and not the crash. I sit up, my heart pounding. "Do you know what this means?"

He rubs his forehead and then pinches the bridge of his nose. "That I'm going to be taking a very long, very cold shower after hearing all that?"

"No! It means I was dreaming of *you*. Of us. Not the crash. It means that, for the first time in two months, I didn't have the same horrific nightmare."

Happiness feels as though it's exploding from my body. This is what I imagine a miracle would feel like.

"You were dreaming when I got in."

I move close to him, feeling alive and happy. "Yeah, but I wasn't dying. I wasn't literally shaking and hurtling toward the ground at a speed that meant I would never see you . . ."

His eyes, so close and open, stare into mine, and my heart begins to race. "Is that what you fear?"

I can feel the heat flame my cheeks, and I nod. Dr. Warvel wanted me to be honest, well, here it goes. "Yes. Even now, you're here, and I feel like I'm still falling from the sky when we're close."

"You're not the only one."

His confession stuns me. "We're only going to hurt each other," I tell him.

"We're doing that now anyway."

He's right. This push and pull isn't good for either of us. We're lying to ourselves if we think we can keep going in this circle. It's madness, and we're failing.

I scoot closer. "Grayson . . . this house."

The sun is rising, bathing the room in beautiful rays of

light. On our mountain, nothing can hurt us—at least, that's what I always believed.

He closes his eyes and turns away. "I couldn't let it go, Jess."

"Why?"

He laughs once, turning back to me. "Why do you think?"

"Why didn't you tell me?" I ask.

Grayson's hand runs through the thick brown locks as he lets out a low groan. "You hadn't been back here in how long? I thought that seeing you wouldn't matter. If I could spend every fucking day looking out my windows and be okay, then it was fine, right?"

I'm not sure what he's saying, but I don't interrupt.

"And then you come back. You show up here, broken, beautiful, and not mine to love anymore. You *left* me. *You* fucking left *me,* and I needed to get over you. Now the tree line that stopped hurting years ago is like tiny needles to my heart. The pencil mountain is sharper, mocking me as I look out. The people, the ones we gave fake lives to, are living our future while I sit here, pretending that you being right across the tracks doesn't matter. I bought this land because it was ours. The memories, the path to that spot, the entire thing was ours."

I lift my hand, bringing it to rest on his arm, needing to touch him. "I left you and could never say your name again. I left you and forbid myself to talk about you because, each time I did, it felt like my heart was dying."

His hand covers mine, and a million questions dance in his beautiful eyes. I want him to kiss me.

It took one night in his house to chase the nightmares away. All of it because of him.

After another minute of silence, his thumb glides along my

palm. "You know, we keep ending up in bed or alone. I have always wanted you, Jess. My resistance isn't this strong."

"Maybe we should stop resisting."

I do everything I said I wouldn't but wanted to. I kiss him. Grayson responds immediately, pushing me to the bed, kissing me back while his hands hold my face. He rolls us so I'm on top, and I don't waste a second. Who knows when one of us will come to our senses or remember that the reason we pull back is because this is stupid.

I will leave.

He will stay.

We will break. That's the reality.

However, this kiss is the dream, and I don't want to wake up.

He built a house in the place we fell in love, and right now, there's no way I will pull back from him.

I moan against his lips and kiss the stubble along his strong jawline. He's so damn sexy like this. Not perfectly put together, just a man—a very sexy one.

I nip at his ear and then go back to his mouth. He was my first kiss. My first lover. My first love, and while I've spent a good portion of my adult life pretending we were nothing, my body remembers otherwise.

His deep voice vibrates through me. "You drive me insane. Your mouth, your fucking mouth is everything I remember."

He threads his fingers through my hair, tugging our mouths back together. I kiss him, letting my body mold against his.

"No stopping," I say.

"No stopping. I'm going to love you again."

I love him now. My legs straddle him, feeling his erection hard between us. I've missed this, the way he touches me, bringing me to life in a way only he can.

My shirt lifts, his rough calluses touching the skin on my back as he pulls it up over my head. The fabric falls to the floor, and then he pulls my sports bra down, palming my breast. God, this feels too good. It's so right, and I want nothing more than to feel him inside me, filling me with everything I've been missing.

Him.

My head tips back when his tongue runs around my nipple before he takes it in his mouth. Grayson flicks it a few times, causing the moan coming from my throat to be low and husky.

"You feel so good," I say quietly.

"You feel so right."

I look down at him, his wording making my breath hitch. "Gray."

"Don't tell me to stop."

I shake my head. "Not this time."

If we were somewhere else, I might have the strength, but not here. His bed faces the windows looking out at the vista, and I wonder how he did it. It would've destroyed me to be here. Just two seconds was enough to have me crumbling inside. Instead of pretending we never were, Grayson lived in it, surrounding himself in our past.

He rolls us again, staring at me as he pulls his shirt over his head. "Do you know how many times I wished for this? How often I rolled over, wishing I'd find you next to me? Can you even fathom how looking out at that view every morning drove me crazy? And then you came back. You came here, and fuck, Jess, I can't push you away again."

The deep emotion in his voice breaks me. I want to speak, but I know I can't because my head is spinning.

I reach up, pressing my palm to his chest. "Love. We. I. Sorry."

What I want to say is: I love you. I'm sorry I left you. I need you, and this is what we always should've been—together.

He leans down. "Don't say anything. I don't need the words, love."

A tear falls down my face as I nod. He kisses me tenderly, and I pray he can feel everything I wish I could express.

He pulls back, wiping it away. "Tell me we're not dreaming."

I smile up at him. "We're not. I would know."

The crinkle around his eyes softens as his lips turn up. "You would?"

I nod. "Kiss me."

Right as his lips near mine, a soft sound causes us both to turn our heads. The door creaks open, and then a soft, sleepy voice calls out. "Daddy?"

Before I can do anything, Grayson turns to the side and I go tumbling to the floor.

Nineteen

GRAYSON

S hit. Fuck. Shit.

Okay, stay calm. First rule of your daughter walking in when you're about to have sex is don't freak out, just be cool. "Amelia, you're awake." My voice is a bit too high-pitched, so I clear my throat to cover it. "Hi, sweetheart."

She rubs her eyes. "You're home!"

I grab my shirt, throwing it on quickly and glance down at Jessica, who is doing the same. "I just got here."

"Where's Jessica?" she asks.

Jessica pops up, pulling her hair into a tie. "I'm here. Hi, Melia. Did you sleep well?"

Her lips are just the right amount of swollen, and she looks to me nervously, as though I have a clue what to do. This is all new territory for me. The only women who have ever been in this house are my mother and Stella.

"Why were you on the floor?" Melia asks with her head tilted.

"She was having a bad dream," I explain stupidly.

My very intelligent daughter narrows her eyes. "Did you sleep on the floor?"

Jessica clears her throat. "When I have bad dreams, sometimes I fall off the bed."

Amelia rushes to Jessica. "Are you okay? I have bad dreams too, and Daddy always helps. I don't fall off the bed, though."

Jessica smiles at her and looks to me as I adjust my very uncomfortable erection. "I think I'll be better soon."

I sure as fuck hope *soon* means tonight when I send Amelia somewhere and don't have to think about anyone walking in when we pick up where we left off.

She hops onto the bed, holding her very worn bear by the neck. "You can have Mr. Snuggles."

"I can?"

Melia grins. "I got him when I was just a baby, and he keeps all the bad monsters away."

"Well, I couldn't take him from you then."

"We can share him," she offers.

"That's very sweet of you," Jessica says as she taps her on the nose. "I'm finding that my dreams aren't so bad anymore."

Amelia looks to me. "Did you help Jessica with her bad dream?"

I want to laugh, but I don't. "I think so."

"Maybe Jessica should sleep in my room, and you can chase the monsters away for her at night."

My sweet kid has no idea what I want to do to Jessica at night.

I change the conversation, thinking of anything other than Jessica, a bed, kissing, or breathing as I keep a pillow very strategically placed.

"Why don't you head downstairs and see what I left on the counter," I suggest.

Amelia's eyes pop wide. "Did you bring me a present?"

"Uncle Alex sent something for you from Savannah, but there's also something you may want to eat."

"Donuts?"

I grin. "You will have to go find out."

There's nothing this kid loves more than donuts, and I thank God I had the forethought to get them. She's gone in the blink of an eye, leaving Jessica and I alone.

I reach out, wrapping my hand around her wrist and pulling her back up onto the bed. A soft laugh escapes her before the moment shifts. I need to kiss her, to know that what we shared wasn't nothing.

"Tonight, I'm sending her to my sister's and then I am going to make love to you," I tell her.

Her finger slips against my lips. "Is that so?"

I raise one brow, challenging her to rebuke me. "Is that a no?"

"What about Amelia? About all the reasons we have?" she asks.

What Oliver said about which one being worth more is ringing in my head. I'll lose her again, but isn't loving her again, no matter the time I get, worth it? Looking at her, there's no question anymore.

"This is between us. I know it's not forever, so we have to be careful."

"We don't have to tell anyone," she agrees.

"This is just for us. We'll take what we can, and no one will ever know."

She watches me, looking for something, and then nods. "Okay. Tonight."

My lips touch hers, and I can't remember the last time I looked forward to the night.

"You owe me," I tell Stella as she moves around her loft, putting things away.

"My debts are all paid up to you, dear brother. I can't take her tonight because I'm busy avoiding your father."

Yeah, sure, he's my father.

"Stella, I swear to God, I ask you for nothing, but I'm asking now."

"You ask me for shit all the time," she points out.

I was banking on her helping me. She always helps, especially when it comes to Melia. Of course, the one time I decide to throw caution to the wind and let my dick decide the direction, this happens.

"Okay, but you bailed on her the other night."

She drops the shirt she was folding, glaring at me. "Are you kidding? I was stuck in a storm! I didn't bail on her, and I swear to God, Grayson Parkerson, if you even insinuated that to her, I'll beat you to within an inch of your life."

My sister, who weighs a whole buck twenty, couldn't do anything, but the look she's giving me does inject a healthy dose of fear.

"I would never."

Her heavy breath falls from her lips in a rush. "Good. I'm

sorry I can't take her. You know I love having her."

"What plans do you have?" I ask.

"None of your business. What plans do you have?"

"None of your business," I echo.

Stella turns, eyes assessing me in a way that makes me feel as if she could read my mind. "How did things go with Jessica and Amelia?"

Oh, how I hate siblings. "Fine."

"That's good. Anything happen?"

"Nope."

We kissed, we got interrupted, and we aren't telling anyone that.

"That's good. I'm thinking of inviting her to come tonight."

I clench my jaw and refuse to say anything. My sister is goading me, and I have to play the part right. "I'm sure she'd like that."

She nods. "Yeah, she hasn't really gotten to go out much or meet anyone. I can't imagine she has much of a dating life."

"I didn't know you were so interested in her love life."

Stella grins. "I'm not, but us girls in these small towns have to help one another out."

"Is that what your plans are tonight?" I ask.

My sister stands and grabs my face in her hands. "I love you, but it's none of your business."

My grandmother used to squish my damn cheeks, which is who she learned it from, and I still hate it. "One night. I'm just asking you this once." She breathes heavily through her nose, and I know I'm going to have to give her something. "Jess and I . . . well, we need to talk."

"Talk?"

"Yes." There will be talking, lots of dirty talk as I strip her naked.

"Fine. I'll cancel my plans and watch my niece." I go to say something, but she points her finger in my face. "But I don't want to hear shit when I ask for a favor in return."

I raise my hands. "Fine, fine. I won't give you crap later on."

"I regret this already. You're the worst of the Parkerson boys. You could talk a penguin into buying snow."

"You're the best sister I have."

"I'm the *only* sister you have."

I head to the front door and she follows. I'm standing on the other side of the threshold, ever so grateful that my parents didn't stop at Alexander and gave us Oliver and Stella.

I kiss her temple. "Which makes you the best."

"Yeah, yeah, go away so I can call this guy and not get laid tonight."

My big brother instincts kick in, and I glare at her. "Who is he?"

"Stop it. I'm thirty, and I am definitely not a virgin, so spare me the Neanderthal routine." She takes a few steps toward me. "Plus, it's not like I'm an idiot and don't know exactly how little talking you plan on doing tonight." She closes the door before I can reply, and I don't even care that she guessed it.

Twenty

JESSICA

My leg won't stop bouncing, and the smile I'm trying to smother keeps appearing.

"Are you going to tell me what has you so overwhelmed with emotions?" Dr. Warvel asks.

"Huh? Oh. It's just . . . a lot."

"Are you stumbling over the words or was that you're not able to voice them?"

I lace my fingers together and hold my hands in my lap. "No, that wasn't a stutter, it was more a jumbling of thoughts."

"I thought so." She smiles softly. "Do you want to discuss it?"

She's my safe place, and talking to her is really what I should do, but I sort of like the idea of whatever Grayson and I are starting will be only ours. It doesn't matter what anyone thinks about it. It's what we both want.

"I'm not sure."

"That's fair. I want to remind you that there are no judgments here. My goal is to help you work through things."

"And you have helped," I assure her.

"I'm glad. You've made great progress in your time with me. It's clear that your brain is healing, and with the techniques we've been able to implement, you're able to handle most situations."

"Except for one," I murmur.

Dr. Warvel tilts her head to the side. "Which would that be?"

"Grayson."

"He's the one topic you've tried to deny."

I love my therapist, but I hate when she calls me to the carpet. In my heart, I haven't denied anything. I know what I feel, I always have, I just haven't wanted to deal with it. Those are two very different things.

"I don't think that's possible anymore."

"Did something happen?"

I may as well tell her. I need to be honest and work this out. Tonight, something will change simply because it's not possible for two people who love each other this way to have sex and not alter their relationship.

Not that I'm sure how we'd define this anyway.

Friends? Friends who loved? Friends who are denying this is going to change everything?

As the breath leaves my lungs, the words follow as well. I tell her everything from my time with Amelia, how he bought our spot and built a house there, and then the dream. That is the pivotal moment for me.

"How could you not share that?" Dr. Warvel asks with a

smile. "You didn't have your nightmare."

"I know. I think I'm still not sure though."

"That you didn't have the dream?"

I nod. "Maybe I did and then this was just another dream."

"For argument's sake, let's assume you had the nightmare. What does it matter? You didn't wake up with your heart racing and covered in sweat. Your mind allowed you to rest through it, to get through the dream without forcing you to live it again. So, my question is, so what if the dream about Grayson came after?"

I lean back, processing what she said. Maybe it's not the nightmare that scares me, then. If I don't remember it but still had it without waking up terrified, does that mean it's still an issue?

"I guess it's more that I don't want it to be a fluke."

I see from the shift in her gaze that I hit the nail on the head. "And also the fact that there are some variables that are different."

"Like I was sleeping in his bed, surrounded by all his things."

"In a world you gave up," she adds on.

Therapy is not always fun. "Which I have struggled with."

She rests her forearms on her knees. "Let's use this time to think about it, Jessica. If you want to meet Grayson tonight and let go of it all, then you should. If you want to run away and marry him, then that's your choice. I just want you to be self-aware enough to know why you're choosing what you are. Is it because, when he's around, you feel safe? And if you only feel safe with Grayson, why? There is no right or wrong answer, just the truth."

I look up at her, my heart pounding. "The truth is that I

love him and I feel safe with him because he doesn't want to hurt me."

"That's good."

"I want to meet him tonight because I can't imagine not having whatever parts of himself he's willing to share."

Dr. Warvel sits tall and crosses her legs at the ankle. "And the question is, are either of you really giving up or are you sharing with the other as a gift?"

I've washed, scrubbed, and shaved every part that needed some TLC. After leaving therapy, I felt good. I know what my limits are and what I need to do to continue being honest with myself and also what Grayson is asking us to do.

We're not going to be serious. This is two people who have feelings for each other but also know the outcome. At least, that's what I think it is.

Dr. Warvel suggested we talk about it to set the boundaries and expectations.

I just really want him naked.

However, she's right, and so, I'm standing in my room an hour before he's supposed to pick me up—with a long text unsent.

Me: I know what we're doing is very adult, but there's still a girl inside me who will always think of you differently. I want to make sure that when we do this very adult thing (which I really want to do) that neither of us thinks it means something more or less to the other. So, this is me, asking you . . . what does this mean?

I hover over the send button. Talking myself in and out of it on repeat.

"Send it, Jessica. Just send it," I tell myself. "What's the worst that happens? You don't have sex?"

That would be a tragedy. It's been a very long time since I've had an orgasm that wasn't self-induced.

I close my eyes, deciding to let fate take over, and press the general vicinity of the send button. Either it'll go or it won't, but I won't have to see.

The whoosh sound plays, and my heart drops to my stomach.

It's sent.

Now I have to wait for a reply.

This is why I avoided dating all these years. Nothing good comes of it. I never understood my friends who loved this part. The will-they or won't-they part of the beginning of something. I hated it. Give me a man who will be like, "You, there, I will love you so all this time we're going to spend together will matter."

That sounds like a much better plan than this.

My phone pings, and I want to vomit as I open it.

Grayson: It means whatever we want it to mean.

I roll my eyes. That doesn't help.

Me: That cleared it all up.
Grayson: What does it mean to you?

Now I want to throw myself out of my window. I don't

want to be vulnerable, damn it. I want him to be first to clarify so that, when I say what it means to me, I don't feel stupid. However, I'm not sixteen and I'm a grown-up who needs to be honest.

I'm also quitting therapy because it's making me deal with shit I'd rather not.

Me: It means a lot. It means that, even if we're not telling people, I'll know, and it matters to me.

I wait for those little dots to show up on the screen, letting me know he's at least typing, but there's nothing.

Great. I followed my stupid feelings and was honest, and look where it's gotten me. I could've been having sex tonight. With a great guy who I could be naked with and would've left me very, very happy.

Now, I'm pacing because I went and listened to my shrink and tried to define what this is to keep myself from getting hurt.

I start to wonder if maybe I should text back and say I was just kidding and that I'm naked and waiting, but that seems ridiculous.

This is all so damn complicated. Why do I have to love this man? Why couldn't it be Jack or someone I don't have a past with who wants to meet up tonight?

The reason it's not anyone else is because there is no one else. And that's the saddest part of it all.

Fifteen minutes pass without Grayson responding, and I sink onto my bed, rejected and embarrassed. I let out a long sigh and debate changing back into my sweatpants and removing this rather uncomfortable lace bra and underwear.

Once I stand, I hear something tapping my window. The smile forms before I even have to look because there's only one person who has ever done this. I rush over, push it open, and find him looking up at me.

I rest my elbows on the sill, smiling like a lovesick teenager. Grayson turns me into this. A hopeful girl who doesn't think life is full of nightmares. "What are you doing?"

"Come down so I can show you."

"You didn't answer my text," I tell him with my heart pounding.

His lips turn to a playful smirk before he reaches into his back pocket and takes out his phone. After a few seconds, I hear the chirp behind me.

"I'll be right back, I just got a text." I practically dive for the phone to see what he said.

Grayson: *It means something to me.*

I clutch the phone to my chest, fighting back the urge to run to him, but I think about what Dr. Warvel said about expectations. It will mean something to both of us, which means we will both end up hurt. Then again, isn't that the truth with anything in life? We take risks, we put our hearts out there, and sometimes, we don't come out unscathed.

I don't want the rest of my life to be filled with regrets regarding him.

He bought the land, built a house, and a part of me—the very stupid part—wants to think it's because he's been waiting for me.

I head back to the window, looking at him with fingers hovering over the phone, knowing I need to reply.

Me: I don't want to get hurt, and I don't want to hurt you.

He looks up at me and then back to the phone.

Grayson: Then don't make me scale your house. Come down here, Jessica.
Me: Okay.

There was never really any doubt I would.

My feet move quickly, taking the stairs two at a time to get to him. I reach the front door, my breath is coming in short bursts as I throw the door open.

He's standing there—waiting.

But it's as though all the patience we had is gone in that single instant. The time that we've allowed to pass is used up and one more second will kill us.

Grayson's hands move quickly, capturing my face, and then his lips are on me. There's desperation, desire, and determination that encapsulates us. I hold him tight, letting him kiss me, kissing him back.

He walks us inside, his mouth not leaving mine until I kick the door closed, causing us both to jump. "Your mother?"

"Work," is the only word I can get out before his mouth returns to mine. He lifts me up, my legs wrapping around his middle as he carries us back upstairs. "Third door on the . . ."

"I remember."

I grin, running my fingers through his thick, brown hair. I want to ask him questions, ask him where we go from this, but I want him more than I care about any of it.

Nothing will stop me from having him again.

We enter my room, and he pushes me against the door. His hands on each side of my head as he cages me in. "I want you so badly."

"Yeah?"

"Oh, yeah."

"I want you too."

Grayson's lips move to my ear. "I'm going to have you here because I can't . . . I can't fucking wait."

My eyes flutter closed as the deep timbre of his voice goes through me. The blood pumping through me warms every part of my limbs. "And then?" I ask.

"Then I'm taking you to my place where we'll do it again." He kisses my neck. "And again." Another kiss, this one lower by the hull of my throat. "And again."

"That's a lot of stamina," I manage to get out, sounding breathless.

"For you, love, I plan to go all night."

If his body weren't pressed against mine, I would've sunk to the floor. Holy hell.

As if to seal his promise, he kisses me again, hands moving almost frantically to get me out of my clothes. Grayson pulls my shirt off as I scramble for his belt.

There is nothing about this that's sexy and slow. It's two people who can't wait another minute to feel each other. I fumble with the button on his jeans as he takes my nipple in his mouth, sucking hard.

He grips my wrists, pinning them over my head. "Stay like that," he commands. "Don't move."

"But . . ."

"Don't move, or I'll stop, and trust me, you won't want me to stop."

Oh, God. My back is against the cold door, and I'd swear I was on fire. Everything is burning around me as he pulls my pants down and drops to his knees.

"Gray."

"Not a muscle," he says again as a warning.

I'm trembling as his eyes travel up my body, causing my breathing to labor even more.

"I've dreamed of you for years." His husky voice is low as his fingers just barely touch my skin. "They were so intense, I'd swear I could feel you." Slowly, he drifts them higher up my leg. "I'd think about how you tasted, sounded, and felt in my arms." My head falls back against the solid wood as a soft sound escapes my lips. "Have you thought about me, Jessica? Have you wondered what it would feel like again? How good I could make you feel?"

"Yes," I admit as a whimper, needing more.

"Good," he says, and then he lifts one leg, putting it over his shoulder as his mouth finds my center.

I know I'm not supposed to move, but my hands drop to his hair, fisting the strands, needing to hold on to him in some way as his tongue presses against my clit. He pulls back, eyes unfocused as he breathes hard.

"Hands," he says, and I want to cry out as I try to return them to their position.

He doesn't make me wait, he goes back in, licking, sucking, and swirling his tongue in the best way, holding my body up as he drives me crazy.

"Grayson, please," I beg, not knowing what I'm asking for but needing it all the same. It's so close.

He spreads my legs wider, his tongue entering me, fucking me with his mouth. He goes back to my clit, pushing a finger into me, and I swear I may pass out.

I scream as the most intense orgasm of my life hits me fast and hard. I feel myself sagging down, legs no longer able to bear any weight, but Grayson is there, making sure I'm safe.

When I can open my eyes again, he's over me, his pants gone, and he's opening his wallet.

"This is going to be fast," he warns as he slips the condom on. "It's been a long time, but I promise, I'll make it up to you."

"I need you," I tell him. "I need you now. I don't care about anything else."

His breathing is unsteady as I feel him start to enter me. Grayson's eyes close as he inches in a little. "Please tell me this is real."

I bring my fingers to his face. "Look at me." He does. "It's real. Make love to me, Grayson. Make it be us again."

He pushes deeper, seating himself fully inside me, our eyes never leaving each other. "It's always been us," he says and then no more words are spoken because our bodies say everything.

Twenty-One

JESSICA

I'm lying in his arms, a blanket wrapped around us as we look out of the massive wall of windows, staring at our view.

"You bought our mountain," I say, resting my cheek against his chest.

"Not the whole thing."

I grin. "Enough of it."

"I bought the part that mattered."

I turn my head, wanting to look at him when I ask this. "When?"

He swallows and shifts, moving me a bit so we both have to sit up. "When, what?"

"You know what I'm asking."

Grayson looks uncomfortable, and I wish I had kept my mouth shut. Tonight has been . . . well, nothing short of amazing. We made love the minute we entered his house, tossing our clothes all over as he chased me into his room. Then he came into the shower where we had to wash ourselves again afterward.

It's been heaven. It's been everything, and I never want this to end.

Now, the sun is rising, breaking the spell of the night and forcing us back to reality.

"I bought it two months after we broke up."

"Why?"

"Would you believe me if I said I didn't know?"

I move toward him, giving him a soft kiss and then nestle against him. "After we broke up, and I started working for the private airline, I bought a black 2000 Ford F-150," I confess.

"You what?"

I look up at him through my lashes, hoping it shields some of my emotions. "I . . . I needed something that was you."

Grayson drove that truck. It was all I could do to feel like maybe, somewhere, we were both sitting in the same vehicle at the same time. It was so stupid, and I felt ridiculous, but after college, when I moved to California, I could feel a little of Carolina—a little of him.

He pushes up, leaving the bed, and goes to the window. I can feel the distance growing between us. And here is exactly what I worried about before he came over. We have issues that need to be resolved, and now it's more complicated because we've crossed a line we can't turn back from.

"Why didn't you call?" Grayson asks.

"It would've changed nothing."

"You don't know that."

I get to my feet, pulling the sheet and wrapping it around

me. I walk over to where he stands. "At the time, it was what I believed. I was young, stupid, scared of loving you and ending up like my mother, and then there was your family. I don't know what to say other than I regret it. I wish I could go back and be brave enough to tell you how I felt and give you the opportunity to tell me how you felt. All I can do is be honest with you now."

He cups my cheek, leaning down so we're breathing each other in. "And what's honest?"

"That I have always loved you. That I don't know what this means for us going forward, but I know that I don't want it to stop."

Grayson's forehead rests against mine as his arms wrap around me, holding me close. "I don't want it to stop either. Even if it means I watch you walk away again."

"I don't want to think about leaving."

"Think about staying, Jess. Think about what we could have."

Our lips touch, and in this moment the idea of leaving him again seems impossible. I know that I've never had dreams of settling down here, but with Grayson, it doesn't feel like I'd be giving anything up.

I would have him.

I would have us.

I would have everything.

Delia, Stella, and Winnie keep giving each other weird looks as we eat at Jennie's diner. I've been quiet, smiling and basking in the sense of calm I have.

"What?" I finally ask after another glance between them.

"You look different," my sister notes.

"She looks happy," Delia states.

"I'm just quiet."

Winnie eyes me curiously. "Yeah, but you have this glow."

I shrug. Earlier this morning, Grayson dropped me off at home, giving me a sweet kiss before telling me we'd talk later. He plans to spend the day with Melia, and then he and Jack are heading out for some training thing with the fire department.

As far as anyone knows, I was at home last night.

These three are nosy, though, so I need to give them something. "I guess I slept well."

And then Stella groans. "Oh, God. You slept with Grayson! That's why I had to keep Melia last night!"

I drop my sandwich, eyes wide and my cheeks on fire. "Shh! Are you crazy yelling that?"

"Well, did you?"

"I . . . what . . . I—" I am seriously the worst liar, and now there's no way I can hide it.

"I knew it!" Stella says, slapping her hand on the table. "I knew it."

Of course, the people in here heard her and are all staring at me. Mrs. Pruitt gives me a horrified look while covering her daughter's ears as though it wasn't already said. Fred, who is a permanent fixture on the end stool, laughs once before saying something that sounds like, "About damn time." And then there's a face I would've cut my arm off if it meant the person wouldn't be standing there. Mr. Parkerson.

My eyes close, and I'm sure my face is beet red. Maybe he has headphones in and didn't hear his daughter proclaim my sexual activity with his son last night. Maybe there's not a chance in hell because he's staring at me.

"What's wrong?" Delia asks, and then she turns, seeing what I see. "Fuck. Stella, your dad is here."

Her lips part as she reaches her hand out to me. "I'm *so* sorry. I'll fix it. I just got excited, but I'll handle him, I promise. Maybe he won't come over."

Yeah, right. He doesn't leave because my luck is crap. Instead of walking out the door, he comes to the table. "Hi, girls."

All four of us look up.

Stella is the first to say something. "Hello, Father."

"Having a nice lunch?" he asks.

Stella smiles demurely. "We are. How long before you leave town to go see another"—her fingers make air quotes—"property?"

He bristles. "I was planning to go in a few days to check on Oliver, but maybe I'll stick around for a bit."

Great. The Parkersons have never hidden what they think of me or my dating Grayson. If they think there's even a possibility of it, I have no doubts they'll do what they can to thwart it.

Stella sits back, crossing her arms over her chest. "I see, so you heard about the damage there?"

He nods. "It's a shame about the vandalism. The town seemed so safe. But your brother is handling it well from what I can see."

"Yes, I guess it's not safe from lies though."

He continues as though her last statement wasn't spoken. "No reason to go out there when the flagship may need me."

At that, I see the first flash of emotion in her. Her lips are tight, eyes unwavering as she says, "We're doing better than any other. I'm sure the other locations will have more of a need for you."

He looks at me. "How are things with the front office, Jessica?"

"Good," I manage to say without issue. I don't know what it is about these people that makes me feel insignificant. Here I am, a grown woman who has accomplished goals that no one thought I could, and one look from them makes all of that irrelevant. I'm back to being the poor girl who was after the Parkerson fortune.

It was never true. I would've loved Grayson no matter where he came from.

"Anything new that I should know about?"

Stella clears her throat. "I'm her supervisor. If you need to ask questions, please feel free to come to me."

Mr. Parkerson smirks. "As the owner, I'll ask whomever I want, and it seems Jessica might have some news."

I count to five before opening my mouth. I will not stutter before him. Of all the times I need to keep calm and focused, this is it. "There's nothing new, Mr. Parkerson. If there were . . . I . . . ." No, please no. I feel Winnie's hand touch my leg, and I pull myself back in. "I would tell my supervisor."

I finish, my heart pounding so loud that I'm sure everyone can hear it. My sister's hand relaxes, and Stella smiles. I was able to get through it, even though it's the first time in over a week that I've had even the slightest stumble.

"Well, you girls enjoy your lunch. I'm heading to the Park Inn to see Grayson." His eyes dart to me and then back to his daughter. "To check on things with him."

"I'm sure you are," Stella says dismissively.

"I'll see you for dinner this Friday."

Stella lifts her hand, waving fingers. "Bye, bye."

The second he's out the door, Stella groans. "I'm sorry, Jess. I didn't know he was here, and I guess I got a little loud."

"Yeah, I'm sure the entire town heard," Delia snorts.

My head drops onto my arms. "This is what we were afraid of."

"What? My father?"

I lift my chin. "And everyone else."

She waves dismissively. "Please, he has zero room to talk. His last mistress literally vandalized the B&B that Oliver is running. Grayson had to go help clean it up."

"That didn't stop your parents from making things hard for us before."

"Grayson isn't a kid anymore. They don't make decisions in his life, and I promise, he doesn't give two shits about what they think."

"Is there an *us*?" Winnie asks. "Are you guys together or . . ."

I let out a deep sigh. There were no intentions of telling anyone, let alone discussing this with them. "We're taking things slow."

"Clearly not," Delia says with a snort. "I said you should kiss him, not sleep with him."

"Yes, and I was clearly taking all your advice."

She shrugs. "It was a foregone conclusion anyway."

"What was?" I ask.

"You and Gray," Stella cuts in.

Winnie nods. "Yeah, I mean, I had you holding out at least another week. Stella, what did you have?"

"I thought they'd have done it much earlier, I'm actually impressed with her."

Delia puts a twenty on the table. "I said she wouldn't do it at all and that she'd heal and leave. You win, Winnie."

Winnie takes the twenty and then extends her hand to Stella. "Pay up, bitch."

I stare at these people like they have four heads. "You bet on us?" No one looks the least bit apologetic. "And what exactly was the point?"

Stella rolls her eyes. "Listen, you and Grayson may want to pretend that you were going to be friends and whatnot, but we saw it. Grayson bought that freaking plot of land that was special to you guys and then refused to sell it. After you got back, I can't tell you how many times I would find him standing at those windows, staring out. He's loved you forever, and I'm pretty sure the same goes for you."

"We're taking things slow," I say again.

Winnie gives me a soft smile. "Yeah, whatever you both need to tell yourselves."

Delia puts another twenty down. "Twenty bucks says they're engaged before the end of the year."

"I'll see your twenty and raise you ten that it's in the next two months."

I lean back in my seat, knowing they're both wrong because it's just a matter of time before I'm cleared to leave, and then, I'll have to make a decision that I really don't want to make.

Twenty-Two

GRAYSON

"Uncle Jack!" Amelia rushes to the door, launching herself into his waiting arms. "You were gone *forever*!"

"Hello there, princess." He hugs her tight, groaning and rocking her.

"It's a bear hug!"

"It sure is, am I scary?"

He loosens his grip, and she looks at him with her eyes slightly narrowed, seeming to ponder whether he is or isn't scary. "Not really. But you're scratchy."

Jack laughs, rubbing his camping beard on her cheek. "I was in the wilderness, searching for dinner."

"Did you find any?" Amelia asks.

He turns, grabbing a pizza box. "This is all I caught."

She giggles and then turns to me. "Can I have a piece?"

"One and then it's bedtime. I know you can't resist pizza,"
I tell her.

We head into the kitchen, and I set Amelia up with a small
slice. "How did camping go?"

Jack rolls his eyes. "I swear, these girls are absolutely ridiculous."

About three years ago, Jack quit his very successful job
as an accountant and decided that the mountains of North
Carolina would be an ideal place to teach survival skills for
the . . . random idiots willing to pay him to keep them safe. Not
that there isn't danger out here, but we're not in an area where
hikers go missing.

This trip, he was gone for almost two weeks, showing them
how to fend off any animals and find food sources. It sounds
like complete fucking hell to me, but he loves it.

"Was it another bachelorette party?"

"No, thank God. Those girls were another level of insan-
ity."

"You did sleep with the maid of honor," I remind him.

A sly grin forms, and he looks lost in the memory. "She
was a gift from the heavens. Mouth like—"

"I get it."

"Like what?" Amelia asks.

"Nothing, Princess." Jack shrugs and grabs a slice of pizza. "No, it was a company retreat, a lot of bonding and in ways
I don't think they anticipated."

"You mean they didn't like taking a shit with their boss
behind a bush?"

He laughs. "No, they most certainly did not. I think they
thought we'd be camping and a lot less of the down and dirty."

"Yet another reason I said no when you asked me to come

work with you."

"Chicken shit."

I couldn't care less if he thinks that. I like being outdoors, but some of the crap he tells me about, I'm totally fine with skipping. Not that my life would allow for it anyway. I couldn't spend nights on end on the mountain and away from Amelia.

"That's enough about me, tell me what's new here."

"Not a thing." Other than the last few weeks have been fucking fantastic.

Jessica was here two nights ago, and last night, we had some pretty amazing sex over video. Sometimes, modern technology is a goddamn gift.

"No? Because I got back into town and heard some pretty interesting stories."

"You haven't even been back two hours."

"Funny how much people talk. Especially when it's juicy gossip." He uses the pizza as though it's a finger, pointing it at me.

"What are people saying?" Amelia asks.

I smile over at her. "Just that I'm the best tickle monster in the world."

"Daddy . . ."

I grin, stalking over to her slowly, each step taking a few seconds as she scrambles away. "I feel the need to tickle something."

"The tickle monster doesn't like little girls," Amelia says.

Jack grins and goes around to the other side of the table. "But his best friend, the tickle king, does."

We grab for her, and she squeals, laughter filling the room as we chase her around. Amelia goes in circles around the table and Jack and I crash into each other dramatically before falling to the floor as though we can't get up.

She runs into her room, closes the door, and yells, "You can't get me here! I put a potion on my door that won't let you tickle."

Jack chuckles. "What do we do?" he asks me.

"I don't know. I guess we just have to tuck her in. But only if she opens the door."

Amelia barely inches her door open enough for her little blue eye to see through the crack. "If you tickle me after you enter, then your hands will fall off."

I widen my eyes and look to Jack. "That would be terrible."

"It sure would," he agrees. "It looks like we'll have to behave."

She opens the door another few inches. "Don't lose your hands, you need them."

I lift my palm. "I swear I won't tickle."

Amelia glances to Jack, who follows my vow. "I swear it too."

The door pushes open. "Then I will disable the potion."

I get Amelia ready for bed, which takes almost thirty minutes since she won't stop talking to Jack about anything he'll listen to. Once she's settled, music and stars on, I head back out, rubbing the back of my neck.

"Everything okay?" he asks, holding a beer he helped himself to.

"Yeah, she should be passed out soon."

I grab another slice of pizza and pop the top of my own beer as Jack finds the football game on television. "Carolina sucks this year."

"Well, our defense sucks," I say, sitting next to him on the couch.

"No shit."

"So, about that rumor . . ." Jack says after a few minutes.

"I can only imagine."

Mostly because I've heard it a few times. Thanks to my sister's big mouth, the whole town is talking about Jessica and me.

"Is it true?" Jack asks.

"It's mostly true. God only knows what embellishments have formed to make it sound worse."

"So, you and Jessica had sex a few weeks ago and she's moving in?"

Jack has been my best friend since we were seven. There's nothing he doesn't know about my life, but for some reason, I don't want to tell him about her. What we're doing, it's just ours. Well, it was supposed to be.

"She's not moving in, Jesus. Is that what they're saying?"

"That, and how the two of you have been spending a lot of time together. Apparently, you were spotted driving her home very early in the morning the other night when your daughter was at a sleepover."

"This town needs a hobby."

Jack shrugs. "They have one. Talking about you and Jess."

"We're taking it slow."

He laughs. "You two don't know the definition of slow."

I drain my beer. "I don't want a lecture."

"I'm not giving you one. I'm just saying that *slow* would've been a date, then another, then after like three weeks of coming home, jerking off thinking of her, maybe she lets you diddle a little."

"Did you just say *diddle*?"

He smirks. "That's all you'd get to do. But no, you guys skipped all that and went headfirst."

I huff, not really giving a shit about what he thinks. "We're not jumping in."

"Gray, you want to fool yourself, then have at it, but we both know the truth."

"Whatever."

"I don't blame you," he adds after a minute of silence. "You loved her. You always have. It's not like we all didn't see it coming."

"She's going to leave," I say because it needs to be said. "She's gone as soon as the doctor clears her."

"And you're okay with it?"

"Of course I'm not."

He shifts in his seat, tossing the remote onto the ottoman. "What are you going to do about it?"

"I don't know."

And that's the thing, I don't know how to hold on to someone who wants to be free.

"Then, take my advice, Gray, life is about moments. I know we all want the endings to be great, but the end is . . . well, it's hell. It's knowing you can't have what you want. It's seeing all that could've been but watching it slip away. The end is not what you want. Trust me. So, don't go for the ending, go for what you can have now. Date her, love her, try to hold her or let her go because, if you do none of that, you'll regret it." Jack takes a long, slow pull of his beer, draining it. "Now, enough talking about this shit, let's watch the game."

I stare at my best friend, who just gave what was probably the longest speech he's ever given about something non-sports related, and think about how right he is.

I may not get the ending I want, but I can live the story now.

"See, going slow has its merits," I tell her as I push the hair off her face. Her breathing is ragged as she turns and bites my chest. "Hey!"

"That was for not listening when I said it was too much."

I laugh, pulling her tighter. "I wanted to set a record."

Three orgasms were achieved, and I feel like a fucking stud. I don't know if sex has ever been this good. It sure as hell wasn't like this when we were kids. Not that it was ever bad, but this is out of this damn world.

"You broke me," Jess says, turning to lie facing the ceiling.

"I feel no remorse."

She turns her head, a smile on her lips. "What time do you have to pick up Melia?"

I glance over at the clock. "The sitter can keep her until six."

"We should probably get dressed then."

"I'd rather we stay naked."

Jessica laughs. "That would be the talk of the town."

"We're already that."

Since my sister announced that Jessica and I slept together, it's been question after question. We've done a good job of avoiding committing to anything, mostly because neither one of us can really answer it anyway.

Are you guys back together? Did you tell her you love her? Does she love you? Have you convinced her to stay this time? What does all this mean? What happens when she is cleared to leave again?

None of those questions are things she and I are ready to face yet. Regarding how I feel, there's nothing about what I want that is slow.

It's as though I want it all—now, which is fucking stupid.

Jessica sits up, her dark hair falling down, creating a curtain around her face. "I hate this town. Why can't we just . . . be?"

"Because they're rooting for us."

She laughs once. "Not everyone."

No, not my parents. "The people who matter are."

Jess turns her head, eyes filled with a myriad of emotions. "You don't care about what your parents think? Not even a little?"

"Not even in the slightest."

"So, if they were to cut you off and fire you from the inn, that wouldn't matter?"

Little does she know that's exactly what Friday night's dinner conversation was. Mom going on and on about appearances. Dad talking about the family money and how he'd do everything in his power to make sure that it was protected. Stella and I sat there—stunned.

Not that I should've been. My parents are both assholes.

Still, to be so openly hostile about her, after all this time, it was ridiculous.

After I finished my salad, I stood and walked out. Stella sent me a text after fifteen minutes, thinking I just went to get fresh air, but I left. I'm not a kid and I won't listen to it.

"Would it matter? I guess. It would be hard for Stella and my brothers to have to pick a side. It would make it financially difficult, but if we were more than whatever this is then, no, it wouldn't matter. I'd find a way."

Jess tucks her hair behind her ear. "This is insane, you know that? We're adults, and I am not a bad person. I don't get it. I don't understand why your parents hate me so much. I was poor, oh well."

There's a reason, and it's one that I will never tell her. Jessica's mother and mine were once friends, there's a reason they're not anymore. My father tried to start something with her mom, but she turned him down. However, my mother doesn't believe her and, to this day, thinks that she left with him.

"It doesn't matter. It wouldn't matter to me. I guess that's what I'm saying."

"Do you want . . . more?" Her voice is small, the vulnerability breaking me.

"What do you think?"

Her hand lifts, touching my cheek. "I think we are fools who are pretending we're not already more."

I wrap my fingers around her small wrist, bringing her palm to my lips. "I won't beg you to stay. It has to be your choice. I'm here. I'm not going anywhere."

Tears fill her eyes. "I knew that all it would take would be one look in your blue-green eyes and I'd be done for. I knew that I would fall right back in love with you. It's why I stayed away."

"And now?"

Her head shakes gently. "Now I'm afraid there's no hope."

"There's always hope, Jess."

She leans down, her hands on my chest. "Not at keeping my heart from being yours."

"Good."

"Good?"

I nod and bring her lips to mine. "Good because I have no intention of letting you leave without a fight."

Twenty-Three

JESSICA

I open the door to see the most handsome man standing there. "Well, aren't you spiffy," I say.

Grayson pulls flowers from behind his back and extends them to me. "Spiffy?"

I shrug. "I have a brain injury, blame that. Or that you're so hot I couldn't think straight."

He laughs and then gives me a soft kiss. "You look gorgeous."

"Thank you."

I'm wearing a pair of jeggings with a halter tunic. It's comfortable but still cute since I have no idea what we're doing.

"You ready?" he asks.

When I get to the car, Melia waves frantically. "Hi, Miss Jessica."

"Hello, Melia," I say with a bit of confusion.

"We are kidnapping you!" she exclaims with a grin.

"Well, this is a very well executed plan then."

Grayson looks back at her. "Remember what I said?"

She nods. "No telling her."

"No telling me what?" I ask.

"Where we are taking you!" Her giggle is adorable and loud as she covers her mouth. "Daddy said it has to be a surprise."

I turn, dropping my voice to be conspiratorial. "You can tell me, I won't let him know."

Her gaze shifts to him. "He can hear everything."

"Everything?"

"He said it's a Daddy superpower."

I can't stop the smile that grows. "Oh, well, then we have to be super careful around him."

Melia beams. "That's what Auntie says too. She says that she has superpowers too."

"Your family is very special," I agree.

"Auntie can block Daddy's hearing."

I had no idea that our date out was going to be with his daughter, but I couldn't be happier. She's the sweetest kid, and I love being around her. The other morning, she woke up to find me on the couch, feigning sleep, and we made pancakes and bacon to wake Grayson up.

It was the most fun I've had in a very long time.

When Gray drove me to work, he asked if I would go out with him tomorrow so he could show me something. I assumed that it was another way to get me in bed, but it turns out, he was serious.

"I like her powers," I tell Amelia.

Grayson snorts. "I am the most powerful because I can

take her powers away."

Amelia looks horrified for a second and then laughs. "You're silly, Daddy."

"I am not."

"Yes you are!"

Seeing him like this still takes my breath away. I always knew he'd be a great father, but actually witnessing it is something else. He loves her with a ferocity that makes my heart grow each time I see them interact.

It's clear that Amelia thinks he walks on water.

"So," I say, clapping my hands together, "where are we going?"

Grayson tilts his head my way while giving me a wry smile. "You'll have to wait and find out."

We drive thirty minutes outside of Willow Creek Valley before he pulls onto a dirt road that has a no trespassing sign at the front.

"Did you bring me out to the middle of nowhere for a reason? If you break out a shovel, I'm going to hit you with it first."

He chuckles. "Come on."

We get out, and Amelia rushes over and takes my hand. "You have to see the lake!"

"A lake?"

"It's called Melia Lake." The pride in her voice rings through the air.

I look over at Grayson, who is smiling at us. "Go ahead. I'll bring the food."

She pulls me along a well-worn path and then we exit to a breathtaking sight. It's a gorgeous lake that is surrounded by lush trees and birds flying overhead. The sky is a beautiful light blue with just a few fluffy clouds overhead. Over to the right, there's a short fishing dock with a small skiff moored to the post.

We move a little deeper, and I inhale a deep breath of the pine-scented fresh air. It's a place where a person could be both lost and found at the same time.

"Wow," I say, taking it all in.

"It's my secret place," she tells me.

"Why is that?"

"Daddy doesn't want anyone to know about it. It's where we come when we want to hide away."

"So, no one else has been here? Not Auntie Stella or Grandma?"

"Nope."

"What about Uncle Alex or Uncle Joshua?"

Grayson's voice cuts in, causing me to jump a little. "No, just Melia, and now . . . you."

I turn, my chest tight as emotions swirl inside me. He brought me to a place that matters to him. He's sharing something he's never shown anyone else.

"Not even Uncle Jack knows!" Melia informs me as she spins in circles.

"Why. You. Place." I release a shaky breath, feeling so overwhelmed I can't get the words out.

Grayson reaches for my hand, lacing our fingers together. "Easy, Jess."

Nothing about this is easy. He's letting me into his life, his heart, and something that he and his daughter shared.

I want so badly to ask him why, but I already know why. Because it's us.

He and I have always been this way. We don't know how

to love with reservations. The day I fell in love with Grayson Parkerson, he stole every part of me. He loved me so wholly that there wasn't a chance of anyone else being able to hold my heart in its completion.

"You really suck at this slow thing."

He grins. "I don't know how much time I have, so here's my warning, love, I'm not holding back."

Before I can respond, Amelia rushes back to us. "Come on! I have to show you the boat."

I walk away with her, looking back at Grayson, already feeling like I'm up to my neck in water.

"Will you come to my recital?" Melia asks while we're floating in the boat—if one can call it that.

"When is it?"

"Next month."

"I would love to," I tell her.

"Daddy, do we have enough tickets?"

He nods. "I got extra."

Grayson is rowing us out toward the other side of the lake as Melia and I lounge at the front under a blanket.

The boat, which I swore I would not get in, has no bench in the front, forcing us to lie down. Melia thinks it's great since we made a makeshift bed and we have snacks. I feel much too close to the water and the lapping sounds make it seem as if I'm about to get soaked at any second.

After a few more minutes pass, I start to relax a bit more, and Melia and I decide to find shapes in the clouds.

"That looks like a castle."

"It does."

She keeps searching. "And that looks like a caterpillar."

I grin. "I think it could be a worm."

"Or maybe it's a pencil!" Amelia moves quickly, causing the boat to rock.

"Easy, Monkey, or we'll be going swimming, which is not in our plans."

She lies back down carefully. "Sorry, Daddy."

"It's okay, just go slow."

I instantly look up at him, smiling. "Yes, we should all go slow."

"Only when safety is involved." He gives me a wink.

I roll my eyes at the playful banter we tend to have. Grayson brings out the carefree side of me, and I love every second of it.

He rows a few more times, and then I see the dock on the other side. "I'll tie us off and then get you girls out."

Melia and I sit patiently as Grayson handles it. Then he reaches down, hoisting Melia out in one pull. "Go over and wait by the big tree," he tells her.

She rushes off and then he helps me out. His strong arms wrap around my waist, steadying me because it still feels as if I'm rocking.

"You feel good here," Grayson says with a slight tremble in his voice.

"What do you mean?"

"This place, it's more than just this."

I look around, trying to understand his words. "I don't . . ."

His lips are flat except for the slight curve at the ends. "I want to show you something." Gray steps back, stretching his hand out. "Will you come with me?"

If he only knew just how much he'd already shown me. He's reminded me that his love is beautiful and I want nothing more than to live in it.

Leaving him, it would be . . . stupid.

How have I let this happen? How did I fail to guard myself, even when I kept saying I was going to?

Instead of saying no or asking to leave, I take his outstretched hand and let him guide the way.

We climb, Melia running beside us, holding my other hand. We go up a set of old stairs made of wood that look like they've been here since the mountain formed. And then, there's a clearing.

How I didn't see it from the other side of the lake, I don't know. But a very old, very sturdy-looking home sits here.

Instinctively, I walk toward it, almost as though it calls to me.

"Grayson," I say, my breath leaving my lungs in a gush. "It's incredible."

"It needs a ton of work."

"But the bones are good, right?"

He nods. "It's structurally sound."

I think about the house he built on our mountain. "Why didn't you fix this house?"

Grayson looks at Melia and smiles. "This isn't where I want to live."

"No?"

He lifts up his daughter, holding her tight. "It's where I plan to work."

It's dark, everything feels as if it's on the periphery and the fog is thick. I can see it, but I can't touch it.

The sounds are the same. The scraping, the bending of metal. The crunches and banging as we hit the ground, but it fades as the dream wears on.

I fight against the memories, and they start to dissipate slowly. It's as though the plane isn't hitting the ground, but hovering. I work harder to shove the dream back.

It's not real. It's not real.

I tell myself as something wraps around me tighter. I hold on to the feeling of being held together.

I can do this.

There's pressure against my neck, warm heat pushing through the ice-cold panic that the dream injects into my bones. My limbs tingle as it starts to thaw me. I can feel the muscles relaxing into the comfort.

I see the house on the lake. The way the water glints off the sunlight. This is new. This place, it's beautiful and bright. There're no planes here, just Grayson and Melia, smiling as we talk about their plans.

Yes, it's working.

It's hard to see the plane now. It's dissipating as the light—that beautiful, warm sunlight—takes over the darkness. The house is there, the clouds framing it again, and I want to weep because it's disappearing too.

I open my eyes to see Grayson looking down at me, his hand on my cheek, holding my face against his chest.

"Are you okay?" His voice is thick with concern.

Once again, Grayson chased away my nightmares, but there is a new fear gripping me. I wrap my arms around him, clutching tightly. "I'm okay."

"The dream?"

I nod against him. "Always. Well," I stop, turning my face to see him better, "when I'm with you, they're not as intense and things are changing."

By the slow grin that spreads across his face, it's clear he likes that. "Good."

"I should go back in the guest room." My arms don't move away from him though.

"You should. Amelia will be up soon."

"It's so early."

Grayson laughs and then lifts me slightly, bringing our lips together in a sweet kiss. "Trust me, I don't want to let you go either."

"I'd rather her not catch us again."

"At least we had a late dinner after the lake and could use the excuse of being too tired to drive."

"You know in, like, two years that won't fly with her," I break it to him.

"Are you planning to be around in two years?"

My heart starts to race because my initial instinct is to say yes. That I want to be here. I want to be in his bed, his life, and his heart. However, I don't know if that's the best option for me. What if I do get cleared and I can leave? While staying here has never been in my plans, everything is . . . unclear. I want things. Things that aren't centered around a life in Willow Creek Valley, but then there's Grayson and Melia. I want them. I just worry that, at some point, I'll regret not going back to the hopes and dreams I once held.

The life I was living before coming back was full of possibilities. If I didn't like where I was, it was simple to make a change.

Here there are no choices.

It's the factory, the inn, or some other shit job where I'll be working just to live.

"Hey," Grayson calls my attention as I push away. "Why are you doing that?"

"Because I don't know how to answer that in a way that doesn't hurt."

He sits up. "Then don't say anything."

I get out of the bed, getting dressed just in case Amelia wakes a bit earlier. "But that's the thing, Gray. I want to answer it. I want to tell you that I will be here—with you and Amelia. I want to be able to say yes, but there's this part of me that is screaming inside."

"Telling you to pull away," he finishes.

"And I don't want to pull away. I feel like I'm being ripped apart."

Seeing the place that Grayson wants to renovate into being his own inn was . . . too much. I still can't fully understand how he's owned this property for years and never showed anyone other than Melia.

He shakes his head, standing and pulling his shorts on. "I don't want to tear you apart, Jess. I want to be the man who keeps you together."

"Which is what you're doing, but it's terrifying."

He touches my cheek. "It's why I said slow."

I give him a sad smile. "Right. But how do I slow down what I feel? None of what we're doing is slow."

I can see the hesitation in his eyes. "I'm trying too."

"I know that, but tell me. Tell me, how do I slow my heart from calling out for you?"

"You don't."

"That doesn't freaking help!"

He sighs deeply. "Jack said some shit about life being about the moments, and he's right. We may only have months or maybe longer, but no matter how much time we get together, I want it all. I want to kiss you, make love to you, talk to you when I can because we've gone without each other."

I nod as a tear falls. "I knew that the minute I saw you again, I would be right here and I'd never want to leave. I knew that I would love you so easily because you have always been the man I wanted. I also fear what it means because I struggle to reconcile the two parts of me."

"I'm not trying to trap you, Jess. I don't want to take from you, but I won't lie to you about how I feel. I'm not going to let opportunities like this pass."

"I know. It's the fear of what it means to stay here," I tell him. "What my life would look like and what it means for you too."

His head jerks back slightly. "If you're talking about my family . . ."

"Of course I am. They hate me. Your mother has made it abundantly clear I'm not welcome. What kind of a future is that for us?"

"Why do you think that matters?"

This sweet man. He is nuts to think that none of that will affect us. We both work for the company his father still owns. It would be so easy for them to ruin everything for him just to get at me.

"Because we both know it does."

He runs his hand through his hair. The nervous habit he's had since he was a kid. "Let me worry about them."

"It's not that simple."

"Nothing is simple, but what's the alternative? We walk away from this? From us?"

I can't let myself think about that right now. Not when he makes me feel this way. Grayson is filling the holes in my heart. Each day, each kiss, each time he looks at me like I'm the reason he breathes is healing me.

Already, the idea of leaving him hurts too much.

I walk to him and press my open palm over his heart. "No, we just . . . we live in the moment, like you said. We temper our desires and be realistic about what it all means."

"I showed you the future, Jessica. I gave you everything you needed to see yesterday. The fears you have about my family aren't mine."

My breathing grows more intense as I stare up into his eyes. "So, you'd just walk away?"

"For you?"

His hand moves up my spine, sending waves of delicious heat through my limbs. "I've never stopped loving you, Jessica. Not one single day. I would tell you, but . . ."

"But what?" The dryness in my throat gets so intense that I barely manage to get the question out.

"Slow, Jess. We go slow."

There's no slowing down what I feel. I keep trying to remind myself of my plans, but I'm standing in this room, surrounded by everything that made me happy, and I can't breathe.

Grayson kisses me reverently. The emotions that were boiling from arguing are gone as his tongue strokes mine. The kiss is warm, and I want for him to lay me down and love me until I can't think anymore.

My lips press against his throat, and when I reach his ear, I let him know exactly what I want. "If Amelia wouldn't be waking up, I would beg you to take me again . . ."

Grayson's hands slide down my sides, a low groan emanating from his chest. "I see bribing my sister for another night of babysitting in my future."

"Yeah? And what would you do if we were alone?"

He leans down, his mouth grazing my ear as he speaks. "I will strip you down, kiss every single inch of you, and make you scream until you have no voice left. And then, then I plan to do it again."

God help me, I may not have the strength to leave.

Twenty-Four

GRAYSON

I wake up to the tones going out on the radio.

Shit.

I rub my eyes and get up, grabbing for my clothes I keep ready for this very reason. It's one in the morning, and the tones are just ending.

"Attention all Willow Creek Fire, we have multiple reports of an explosion and visible fire at the old railroad building. All units respond."

This means it's not just some bullshit call. I need to be there. Normally, I would call Stella and either bring Melia there or ask her to come here, but she went to visit Alex. After the last time I saw my parents, that's not an option.

My phone rings, and it's Jack. "Hey," I say, slipping my pants on.

"Hey. You going?"

"Yeah, I need to find someone to watch Amelia."

"Shit, Stella is away."

"How did you know that?" I ask.

"She mentioned it. What about Jess?"

The radio cues up, and this time it's Chief's voice.

"All units, be advised, I'm on scene. We have multiple homes burning, and I've advised dispatch to call for other towns to assist."

This is bad, and as the truck's captain, I can't bear the thought of not being there for my guys.

"I'll call her." I disconnect with Jack, and Jess answers on the first ring.

"Grayson? Is everything okay?"

"There's a fire, and I need to respond. I hate to ask this, but can you watch Amelia?"

I hear rustling behind her. "Of course. I wasn't sleeping anyway. Do you want to bring her here?"

"Can I?"

"Yeah, she can stay here until you're done. Winnie will be by to get me for work, so I'll just bring her with me."

"Thanks, Jess."

"No problem."

I grab my stuff and grab Amelia, who doesn't stir as I get her in the car. She sleeps soundly as I make my way to Jessica's house. When I pull into her driveway, she's waiting on the porch, hair a mess, and wearing a pair of shorts and tank top.

"I appreciate this," I say as I carry Amelia in.

"Bring her up to my room, she can sleep there."

As soon as I lay Melia in Jess's bed, she makes a soft noise, curls onto her side, and is out like a light.

"I envy her," Jess says with a soft laugh. "I'd give anything to sleep like that."

I kiss my daughter's head, and when we're out in the hall, I pull Jess into my arms. "I missed you."

Her breath hitches. "I missed you too."

"I have to go, but maybe tomorrow night you can sneak over to my place?"

She nods. "I'd like that. Winnie owes me a favor."

I give her a quick kiss before we head back downstairs. "There are some clothes for her in the bag, and if you need anything, I hate to say it, but call my mother. She has a full wardrobe for her, and—"

"Stop it," she cuts me off. "Go, we'll be fine. Call me when you're done."

"I will." I start to back away, not quite ready to take my eyes off her.

"Be careful, Gray. I love you," she says and then she clamps her hand over her mouth.

My heart, which had been pounding from the adrenaline, is now racing for another reason. I walk toward her, long strides eating up the distance between us. When I get to her, I take her face in my hands. "I love you too."

"I didn't mean to say it . . ."

"Did you mean it?"

"Yes," Jessica admits.

It may only have been three weeks of sneaking off with Jessica, kissing in hallways, and pretending we're not falling in love, but it's been there since the first time I kissed her at the beach.

We said slow, but it's impossible to reduce the speed of a bullet.

My heart feels like it's found the missing puzzle piece that fits perfectly.

I love this woman. I always have, and then I wonder, what if I showed her how great our life could be? Would she stay then? If I don't try, I'll never forgive myself.

"Let's go away this weekend," I say to her.

"Go away? Where?"

"The beach house." As if there were any other place for us.

"Do you really think that's a good idea?" she asks, worry in her eyes.

"Why wouldn't it be?"

She replies with one word. One word that is the only thing that could make me pause.

"Amelia."

"We spend the weekend as friends as far as Amelia sees, which I'd like to think we are. She loves you and has been asking about you nonstop. We'll go, have fun, keep it light, and just enjoy a vacation. You just admitted you love me."

"I did."

"And I love you," I tell her again.

"You do."

I kiss her again. "What do you say? Come to the beach with me and let me love you."

Her eyes are warm as she nods. "All right."

Relief spreads through me. I want to spend as much time as I can with her. When she's near me, I feel alive again. "Good. I'll pick you up Friday after work."

"We're going as friends if anyone asks, right?"

I nod. "During the day, absolutely. At night?" My voice drops. "Well, at night, you're mine, and I'm going to show you exactly what that means—repeatedly."

Jessica's lips lift as a coy smile plays on her lips. "I look forward to our first night."

"Me too, love. Me too."

"And then, my daddy said that I didn't have to wear the pink leggings, I could wear the white ones, but Mrs. Butler was so mad."

Amelia hasn't stopped talking for more than three seconds the entire ride. One hour of her peppering Jessica with stories of dance, daycare, dinners, conversations that she heard, and what she wore. How Jess hasn't thrown herself from the car yet, I'll never know.

Hell, I've debated it.

We pull into a gas station, and Jessica takes Amelia to the bathroom. I watch as the two of them walk hand in hand, smiling as though they've known each other from day one. Amelia stops at the door and then wraps her arms around Jessica's hips.

I can see it now. The future—this, her, us as a family, and it's terrifying me.

Everything feels frozen as I stare at the two people I love. Amelia is my world, and Jessica is my soul. How is this my life? How did just a few months change everything?

"You all right, son?" a voice asks from beside me.

"Huh?"

"You look a little lost," the older man says.

"No, I'm fine."

He turns, seeing where the girls just entered the store, and then looks back to me. "I see."

"See what?" I ask.

"You were standing there, looking at something, and I thought maybe you didn't know what you were looking for, but now I see I was wrong."

I grab the handle to the pump and shake my head. "No, I'm not lost."

"How long have you been married?" he asks.

"No, no, she's not my wife. I'm not . . . she's a friend."

He laughs once. "A friend, eh?"

Great, even complete strangers can see we're more than friends. "Yeah, friends."

"If you say so. You looked like part of your heart was walking away."

I clear my throat as the lever pops, letting me know I'm filled up. "The little girl is my daughter, so I guess that's partially true."

And also only partially a lie. They both hold very special parts of my heart.

This was a bad idea. The more I fall back in love with Jessica, the more this is going to be agony in the end. But Jack was right, if I were to walk away to protect myself, I'd regret that as well.

The old man puts the handle back in the slot and then tips his hat. "Good luck convincing yourself that's what you were looking at, son."

A second later, Melia comes running out of the store with Jessica. "Daddy! Guess what? Miss Jessica bought us snacks!"

Jessica gives a sheepish grin. "Sorry, she was so cute, I couldn't resist."

"It's fine," I assure her. "But we don't eat in my truck."

I hear the snort from Jess and turn. "What?"

"Oh, nothing, different truck, same rules."

Melia tugs on Jessica's arm. "He doesn't let *anyone* eat in the truck. No matter how hungry I am."

Jessica squats down. "I'll tell you a secret." She leans in so I can't hear what she says, but Melia giggles.

"Okay!"

"What did you say to her?" I can't stop the smile from forming as I look at Jess.

"Nothing."

"Liar."

"Okay, nothing that I'm going to tell you." She sticks out her tongue as she walks with Amelia to the driver's side before helping buckle my daughter in.

Once my daughter is secure, Jess straightens and looks at me from over the roof.

"You'll pay for that," I warn with a hint of amusement.

Jessica shrugs. "Or you will, we'll have to see."

We get in the car, smiling at each other as I start to plan my version of payback. She'll pay, but probably not in the way she's thinking. Or maybe it is exactly what she's thinking.

I focus on not letting my mind get too far into that or it will be a very uncomfortable drive. The next few hours pass much the same as the first one did. Amelia finding topics to discuss while I wish I brought ear plugs.

I love my kid. I love her more than anything, but she hasn't stopped.

"Why don't we be quiet for a few minutes," I suggest when we're only about twenty minutes from the beach house. Surely, she can last that long.

Jessica grins and then turns back to Amelia.

"Do you know how to play the quiet game?" Jess asks her.

"No, what are the rules?"

"They're simple, we all have to be very quiet, not make any noise, and the person who is quiet the longest, wins."

Amelia tilts her head to the side, staring at Jess. "What do I win?"

I glance at her through the rearview mirror. "What do you want? I'll pay anything."

I realize immediately that this was a bad strategy, but I'm desperate for even five seconds of peace. "I want a monkey."

"Not a chance."

"You said anything," Amelia counters.

"Yes, anything but that."

"Okay, then I want a baby elephant."

Jessica giggles. "Where would you put it?"

"The living room," Amelia answers as though it's perfectly reasonable.

"But what about when it grows?" Jess continues this line of conversation.

"Then it can go in Daddy's room, it's big."

Here I thought I might get a few minutes of quiet, not a debate over livestock and exotic animals.

"I think the elephant might be happier in the wild, don't you?" Jessica reasons with her.

"Fine. Okay, then I want a puppy. We can have a puppy because they're small and they're cute and Bryson Hewitt has one and he named it Dog."

"He named the dog, Dog?" I ask.

"He's not very smart, Daddy."

Jessica laughs and covers it with a cough. "Dog is a good name."

"Dog is a stupid name!" I protest. "It's a dog, you don't name it Dog."

She shrugs and then looks out the window, her shoulders bouncing.

Amelia raises her hand as though we're in class.

"Yes?"

"I know what we should name our puppy."

"We're not getting a puppy," I say sternly because we've rehashed this particular conversation at least once a month. Between my job and the fire department, getting a dog would be impossible. We're hardly ever home, and I can barely take care of Amelia and myself, let alone an animal.

"If we did," Amelia cuts in, "I would call him Bryson."

"What?"

"If he can name the dog, Dog, then I will name my dog Bryson. That way the dog doesn't feel sad."

Jessica and I both burst out laughing. Amelia preens in her seat, seemingly happy with her logic.

"You better get her a dog now," Jess says between her fits of giggling.

I shake my head and smile. "You can have anything that isn't an animal."

Amelia groans, her head falling to the side dramatically. Not that it matters anyway since I'm pulling in the driveway.

"Fine, then I want a new mommy."

And with that, the laughter fades, and the car falls silent.

Twenty-Five

JESSICA

Grayson and I look at each other, the awkwardness growing with each second.

I have the strangest urge to weep. As though, her answer is too profound to explain. I love this man and I love her too. In just a short period of time, Amelia has become so dear to me, and it's unfathomable how anyone wouldn't want to be her mother. How any woman could turn away from her is beyond me, and then I realize, that's exactly what I would do if I left.

I'd walk away from them both. I'd give up this . . . this wonderful little life that I could have. How has just a few months of being back home altered everything inside me? How did spending that one night in his arms make this big of a difference?

So much so that even thinking about him with another

woman makes me want to cry. The mere thought of someone else helping her into her car seat has my heart wanting to rip from my chest.

I need to get a grip.

We both said go slow and here I am, imagining becoming a family.

Grayson's eyes never leave mine, and I can see the hesitation. Neither of us knows what to say, and then he turns to her. "I don't know that you can get that from a game, but how about we go inside and you can help me with the sheets?"

Amelia claps her hands and reaches over to unbuckle herself. "Okay! And then can we build a sand town? And then go swimming? Can we have pizza for dinner?"

Oh, to be four years old and have the attention span of a goldfish.

He hops out of the car, and I follow, grabbing bags and the coolers we packed with food. Amelia rushes toward the front of the house, giving us the first bit of privacy.

"You okay?" he asks.

"Yeah, of course, why?" I ask with a squeak.

"Because Amelia just shocked the shit out of both of us."

I relax and force a smile on my face. "She's four, and I can't imagine she doesn't long for a mother."

Grayson looks away. "I hate that I can't give her that. Of all the things I can provide, I can't make her own mother want her."

The pain in his voice makes me ache. I would do anything to take it away for him. "Gray, you give her everything."

"Do I?"

"She is the happiest kid I've ever met. She adores you. You've given her a lake . . . I mean, seriously, there's nothing that you have to feel bad about."

He nods once, which I can tell he doesn't really mean, but I'm not going to press it. "Let's get the house ready and get lunch."

"Okay."

We work as a team, Melia bouncing between us as we work to uncover furniture and get the air working. It's not overly hot, but with the windows closed up the last two months, there's a slight stagnant smell.

Wow. It's been only two months since we kissed. Two months of feelings and love and fear of what all of it means.

I stand in the bedroom, my fingers just brushing against the comforter as I walk to the sliding glass door that looks out at the ocean. When I move the heavy curtains to the side, the light filters in, showing tiny flecks of dust in the air. All of it orbiting around me, small pieces, but once the dust settles, what then?

Will it get swept away and forgotten or become a piece of something greater?

I feel Grayson's presence before I hear him. Then his hands settle on my shoulders.

"What's wrong?"

"I'm in love with you," I say, not turning to him.

"And that's a problem?" There's a slight laughter in his voice.

Fragments of me are his. Parts that I will never get back, and I worry what it all means. "I don't want to leave you, Grayson."

He wraps his arms around my middle, holding me against his strong chest. "Then don't," he says. "Stay."

I tilt my head back and sink into his embrace. "Okay."

Because right now, there's nowhere else I'd rather be than with him and Amelia.

"I want to tell her about us," Grayson says while we're cuddled up in my bed. Amelia went to sleep about three hours ago, and Grayson will soon leave to sleep alone in his twin-sized bunk bed.

"Tell who?"

"Amelia."

I sit up straight. "Tell her what?"

"That we're dating. It'll make it a lot easier for us to be around each other."

I chew on my lower lip, not sure how I feel about this. Not that I don't want her to know, but after what she said earlier, she might assume certain things.

"It might not go as well as you hope."

"She adores you, Jess."

"Yes, as her daddy's old friend. It's different if she thinks I'm something more."

He tugs my arm, pulling me so I'm lying on top of him. "We don't have to do it now."

"I just, I want us to be sure when we tell her. Amelia is sweet and special, I'd like for her to be happy when we break it to her."

Grayson's fingers slide through my hair, pushing it back behind my ears. "How about we give it a week or two? Let's get through this trip and then back home so she can see us together."

I give him a quick kiss. "I think that's a good plan."

The pads of my fingers play with the skin at the hollow of his neck. "You know, I have plans too."

"You do?"

I nod. "I do. For you."

"And what might they be?"

My lips inch closer. "First, I'd like to kiss you."

"I like this plan."

"I thought you might."

Grayson chuckles. "Anything more than just kissing?"

I move my hands down his body, tugging his shirt up so I can touch him. "There could be some touching."

"Well, I like touching."

"Do you now?" I ask, playfully.

Grayson's hand finds the skin along my back where my shirt has ridden up a bit. "I definitely like touching you."

I grin against his lips. "I think I'd like to keep kissing. But not just your lips."

His dimple deepens a bit, giving him a devilish look. "What else do you want to kiss, love?"

I pull his shirt up over his head as I straddle him. He's so beautiful. I know that's not what men want to hear, but that's what he is. Perfect. Gorgeous. Still able to make my heart race with just a look.

Grayson is every fantasy in living form. He is strong, sweet, and funny. To be given another chance to love him is a gift I don't deserve.

I move down his body slowly, never allowing my lips to leave his skin. "I like this spot," I say as I swirl my tongue around his nipple. His eyes close, and I move lower. "But I think there are other spots that I'd like to kiss more."

A throaty moan falls from his lips, and I slide down farther, hooking my fingers in the waistband of his shorts, removing them as well. "Jess," he says my name, low and gruff.

"Do you want me to kiss you there?" I ask with a coy smile, staring at his thick, hard cock.

"That's like asking a dying man if he wants to draw another breath."

"Well, I wouldn't want you to stop breathing." I bring my lips to him, running my tongue around the rim. "Do you feel like you're dying?"

"You're definitely killing me."

Instead of a witty comeback, I take him deep into my mouth. His hips buck up, and then his fingers are in my hair. I bob my head, trying to take him into the back of my throat, wanting him to feel nothing but ecstasy.

His grip tightens, pulling on the strands as I move faster while cupping his balls.

"Jess, baby, stop." He barely gets the words out between breaths. "Love. I can't." The tone is clear that he's barely hanging on. But I want this.

The power to make him lose it.

The thrill of knowing I'm giving him pleasure and driving him to this point.

However, he's not having it. He grips my hips, pulling me up so fast that I gasp, and then I feel his mouth on my clit.

Grayson's tongue presses hard, circling the nub as he pushes a finger into me, causing me to almost scream.

Two can play at that. I adjust myself and take him back into my mouth. Both of us using our tongues, sucking, and driving the other to release.

His low moan against my clit causes me to tremble. I can feel my orgasm racing closer. Not just from the things he's doing but because of how much I love doing this to him. Grayson's tongue moves faster, and I can feel the edge nearing.

Then, right when I'm there, he stops.

I nearly cry out, but he turns me, lining himself up at my entrance. I don't hesitate before I sink down on him.

Our eyes meet and something so powerful passes through us that I start to cry. I am so in love with this man.

Just feeling him inside me is too much, and I fall apart and my world will never be the same again.

Twenty-Six

JESSICA

"**S**o you're staying? Like, for good?"

Delia and I are a few towns over, eating lunch.

"I mean, I think so. Grayson wants to tell Amelia about us and move forward." Not that I'm really sure what that means.

She leans back, popping a fry in her mouth. "I'm really happy for you."

"I'm happy too, which is what scares me."

"Why?"

"Because happiness fades and reality sucks."

Delia nods. "True, but you could be in love with a guy who doesn't care about you. That would really be shitty, huh?"

"Deals," I say reaching out for her, but she waves her hand dismissively.

"Don't. It's fine. I'm the idiot."

Before we can say more, Stella walks over. "Hey! I didn't know you guys were here. I thought you would be resting after three days at the beach house."

It's crazy how invested these people are in my love life. "There's no need to rest, we really took it easy."

Delia snorts. "I'm sure you did."

"What are you doing here?" I ask Stella.

Stella pulls a chair out to sit. "Where else do you think I can shop? It's not like we have stores worth a damn in Willow Creek."

"True. Story." Delia nods while eating another fry.

"So, I'm here with a new handbag and a lifelong desire to move. Anyway, how did your trip go? Did you and Grayson talk and decide what's going on with you guys?"

"Yes, we talked, and . . . I think we're going to tell Amelia next week."

She smiles brightly. "She's going to be so happy."

"You think?"

Stella's hand grips mine. "I do. She really likes you. She said you're her favorite of Grayson's friends and hopes you live with her. I'd say that's a good sign."

Amelia has become incredibly important to me. During our trip to the beach, we laughed, played games, and she cemented herself in my heart. As much as I despise the decision her biological mother made, a part of me is grateful because I'm able to spend this time with her.

"Hopefully, she takes the news that we're not just friends well."

"I'm assuming this means the two of you have really solidified your relationship then?"

"Yes," I tell her with a smile. "We have."

"That's wonderful. I always loved you with Grayson. He hasn't been this happy since, well, since before you left."

I squeeze her hand and then release it. "Thank you."

"Now, whatever bullshit you hear from others, dismiss it. What matters is you and Grayson and Amelia. That's it."

I don't need to be a genius to know who she's talking about. Grayson and I haven't discussed his parents in a few weeks. There's really nothing that either of us can say to make that front any better. The only other thing I need to decide on is my career.

While I enjoy working at the inn, it's not what I want to do.

I miss flying. I miss having a job that I love and looked forward to. Even though I was in a horrific crash, there is something about being in the air that I love. I'm not afraid of falling, I'm afraid of being told that I can't go where I want. Working at the Park Inn is a placeholder job, and I need a permanent job that fulfills me the way my last job did if I'm going to stay here.

"No matter what, since I'm staying, I don't know that I'll continue working for you guys," I tell Stella.

She grabs one of Delia's fries. "Okay . . ."

"I think it would be better for me to find my own thing and not have it tied in any way to your parents."

Delia laughs once. "What, are you going to work at the factory with me?"

"No, I don't know what I'll do, but there has to be something."

"If you find it, let me know because I hate my fucking job."

"There is going to be a job opening at the inn," I say with a smirk.

"Then maybe I'll have to apply."

Yeah, that is a disaster ready to happen. Delia and Stella are friends, but working together is a whole other type of friendship. Not to mention, Grayson will probably kill her.

Stella and I exchange a glance that lets me know we're on the same page, and then she stands. "I need to get back to work and then I have a date."

"Oh! With?"

"No one you know." Stella grins.

Delia rolls her eyes. "As if there's anyone in a twenty-mile radius that isn't connected to someone in this town . . ."

"Then I guess you'll hear about it sometime soon." She walks off, leaving Delia and I a little stunned.

"Who do you think she's dating?" she asks.

"No idea."

"Me either, especially because I'm pretty sure she has a thing for Jack."

My jaw falls slack at that proclamation. "Jack? Like, Jack O'Donnell?"

"Yup. I mean, she's never *said* anything, but I've seen her eye-fucking him a few times. Then there was this time a few years ago . . . I don't know."

"Grayson would kill him," I inform her.

"Why?"

"Stella's his baby sister. The Parkersons have always protected her in a way that is almost ridiculous."

I can't imagine a world where Stella and Jack are a couple. Not just because he's older than her but also because he's . . . Jack. He's the jokester. The one who laughs off life because he knows just how cruel it can be. He's never serious about love, not after watching his mother die and his father take off.

"She'll never do anything about it. At least, I doubt she

would because of those reasons. Also, Jack has made it abundantly clear he wants sex with zero expectations."

"Have you slept with Jack?" I ask. "When we were at the beach the first time, the two of you were gone for a very long time."

Delia snorts. "Eww! No. We kissed once when we were both drunk as hell at a party. It was fine, but also kind of like . . . weird."

Now this I want to hear. "Weird how?"

"Like, he's good at it, I guess, but it was . . . Jack. We both stopped, looked at each other, and burst out laughing. If that gives you any indication of what our passion level was."

I smile, trying to picture them together and failing to create a good image. "He deserves to be happy."

"He does, and hopefully, one day, he'll allow himself to be. He talks about this girl he loved, but she's gone and he's tormenting himself over it."

"Losing someone you love is hard."

Delia raises a brow, staring at me. "You would know."

"I would."

"It took you a long time to let yourself be happy again."

"And it's something I'm still learning to allow," I admit.

Some days, I feel as if being happy is a curse. I've felt loss, some of it was self-inflicted, but it was to protect myself from the pain of it not being on my terms. Which caused another version of suffering. All of it sucks, and thankfully, Dr. Warvel has helped me to see that.

Things happen. Life isn't easy, but the struggle allows the beauty to shine through. Without that pain, we wouldn't know what joy feels like. I'm finding ways to endure them both and not let one determine the other.

"Speaking of learning and your mental health"—Delia gets to her feet—"it's time for your first appointment of the day."

"Yes, let's go see the neurologist and hear that I still can't drive."

"I feel like a lot has been changing for you since we began," Dr. Warvel says. "It's all been happening very rapidly, which isn't a bad thing, but I'd like to gauge how you feel about it. Do you feel like things are going in the right direction?"

"Yes. I mean, it's all good things, right?"

"It sounds like it, but I sense a bit of hesitation."

"I guess I'm just scared."

"Scared of what?"

"Do you know when you get a gift that is everything you want? It's perfect and no one can tarnish this present in your mind. Then, something happens, maybe it just isn't functioning right. You still love it, but . . . there's a pause when you think about it. I worry that's how all of this, Grayson and me and being in Willow Creek, is going to go."

"How so?"

Why does she make me answer everything I don't want to? Sometimes, these sessions are insanely frustrating. I know that's the whole point but isn't there some saying about ignorance being bliss? I'd like some damn bliss please.

I sigh, which sounds more like a groan. "Because! Hasn't history shown that life . . . life doesn't get to be perfect."

Dr. Warvel studies me for a moment. "Do you think he could be worried too? Maybe not the same fears, but that you'll leave him?"

"I know he does."

He tries to pretend, but I can see it. We're waiting to tell Amelia, and there's a part of me that thinks he's hesitating just in case.

In case today goes a certain way.

In case . . .

And now the case is true.

"Well, Jessica, that's the risk we take when we allow our hearts to be vulnerable. It's scary, but it's beautiful. Life and living are beautiful." She changes topics. "Tell me about the headaches?"

"Their frequency has dropped enough that they aren't really an issue." I can see her settling in to ask the next question, which is one I wish she would just forget about.

"What about the nightmares?"

That is the one area there is very little improvement, at least, not as much as I'd hoped. There is sometimes a reprieve, but it's only on the nights when Grayson is there to keep them at bay.

"Still reoccurring."

"And still as intense?"

I nod. "Sometimes, I wake up and I can't see. Like the concussion just happened, and my sight is gone for that minute. I have to fight to stay calm because I know it's just that there's no light in the room."

"Are you still writing them down?"

"No," I admit.

Dr. Warvel purses her lips. "Okay, are you having them on the nights you're with Grayson? If so, how is he handling them?"

Well, crap. "I don't . . . well, that's to say I don't know if

I'm having them when I'm with him."

"What do you mean you don't know?"

"There are times that I don't remember if I wake up, and he doesn't tell me."

She taps her pen on the notepad. "And you don't ask him?"

"I don't want to know."

Sympathy fills her gaze. "I see."

What does she see? Because all I see is that I'm being a chicken shit. I should be dancing around the office that I'm doing better. There should be streamers and confetti instead of doom and gloom.

"I am struggling today."

"What happened?"

I was having a great day. Lunch with Delia was fantastic. And then . . .

"Today was supposed to go one way, my appointment with the neurologist didn't go as I expected."

I hear Dr. Havisham's voice from two hours ago.

"Well, it looks like everything is healing nicely," my neurologist said.

"Really?" I asked.

"Yes, you haven't had a fainting spell in over a month and your eyesight isn't an issue either."

Delia took my hand, squeezing. "What does this mean for Jessica?"

He wrote something on my chart and then looked up with a smile. "It means that she's cleared to drive and return to her normal activities. You may still struggle with headaches, but you haven't had one that has left you feeling too badly in a while. I think that, if you wanted to return to work, you could start with one short flight and see how it goes. If there aren't any problems, then you can work your way up."

"I can fly?" I asked with breathless fear and anticipation.

"I see no reason medically why you can't. Your scans look great, and you've healed wonderfully. Your restrictions are lifted, and you can resume the life you had."

I got big news—great news—and yet, I feel like I was issued a death sentence.

"What did the doctor say before you came here?"

I turn my head away, feeling stupid. "I got cleared."

"That's great, Jessica."

"Is it?"

"You're not sure," she says with understanding, causing me to look up at her.

"It means I can go. It means that . . . there's nothing making me stay anymore. It's my choice again. I didn't expect that today. I thought I'd have another month of no driving and definitely no flying ever again."

"Do you want to return to your old job?" Dr. Warvel asks.

"Yes and no. It's not that I'm eager to return to the plane. God knows, I will probably be a damn mess. I honestly don't care about that part. It's that I didn't think it was ever going to be an option, so I made peace with it because I found him again."

She nods in understanding. "Flying is what made you feel free, though. You said that a few times."

"I don't want to be free."

Dr. Warvel moves her chair a bit closer. "Explain that."

"I want to be here. I want to be with Grayson and Amelia. We are going to tell her about us and make plans."

Her eyes are soft as she stares at me. "Why do you think

that changes because you're cleared?"

Grayson has this thing about me wanting to fly and be away from Willow Creek Valley. He says how he knows I don't want to be here. How clipping my wings will break me.

He's what makes me soar, not my job.

"I just feel like he'll push me away."

She nods. "I see, and that scares you because you want . . ."

"I want him."

"Then tell him that, Jessica. Be honest and communicate because you two have been doing that very well. If you can be open and start off by saying how happy you are about being cleared but that it changes nothing about your desire to stay with him, then what can he say?"

Maybe she's right, but I don't think that's the case.

Twenty-Seven

GRAYSON

There's a knock at the door, and I'm hoping it's Jessica. It's been a rough few days. Amelia came down with some virus that had her running a fever, vomiting, and completely miserable for almost nine days.

Then I got a call from my mother, who demanded I be at dinner next weekend, a dinner in which I am forbidden to walk out on and have been ordered to bring Jessica.

I open the door, but it's not Jess, it's Jack. Normally, this wouldn't be an issue, except I can smell the whiskey coming off of him in waves.

"Did you know . . ." He slurs. "I don't even want to like her."

"Like who?"

"Her!" Jack yells and then slams his hand on the porch railing. "She's insane."

"Most women are. How much have you had to drink?"

He shrugs. "Don't matter. It's gone. She's gone."

"Are you talking about Misty?"

He shakes his head. "Not this time."

Considering my best friend hasn't dated anyone since college, I have no idea what the hell he's talking about, but it's clear he's a mess and needs to sleep.

"Did something happen?"

His eyes meet mine, and he leans against the railing, head resting on the side of the house. "Did you know that whiskey does not make you forget? I remember. I remember it all, and I remember that I shouldn't remember."

Whiskey and I were very good friends for quite a while after I found out Yvonne was pregnant. I would've done the right thing by marrying her because we were heading that way regardless.

She didn't love me enough to try.

She didn't want a family with me because of her career.

I found myself circling the drain, wondering how the fuck I kept doing this to myself.

"What do you remember?" I ask, hoping to get a semi-coherent answer from him.

Jack snorts. "Well, I wanted to forget."

Guess that's not going to happen.

"How about you come in, and we'll get you a vitamin drink and a bed? Sleep might help you forget."

"I want no bed!" he declares. "I want to forget the bed. The bed is bad."

It's clear there is a lot more to this, and I'm not going to get any of it with him drunk off his ass. "Okay, well, you can't be out here, and if you wake Melia, I'll kill you."

His face falls and then he whispers. "She's not insane."

"Who?"

"Melia. She's the best."

"Yes, and she's sleeping, so let's get you inside and cleaned up."

Jack nods, takes a step, and catches himself on the banister. "Oops. I'm falling again. I'm always falling and I never get up."

"Come on, buddy," I say as I wrap my arm around his chest, trying to steady him as we walk.

We get inside, and I take him straight to the guest room. I smile when I see Jess's over-loved and oversized sweater in the corner from the last time she stayed the night. At night, she's usually freezing and wraps herself up in it. I can't bring myself to point out that the holes don't help with warmth.

"You're always happy," Jack says as I get him to the bed.

"Yeah?"

"You have Jess. I want that. I thought . . . I thought it was possible one time."

This wasn't exactly the night I had planned, but I can't remember the last time Jack was a mess like this. Not since . . . and then it hits me.

The date.

It's the anniversary of his mother's death.

I sit beside him on the bed. "You're sure this isn't about a fire or someone you lost?"

He shakes his head. "Not this time. It's another girl and another time. Another loss."

I can usually understand Jack's ramblings, but he's got me totally lost this time. I have no idea what girl and what loss he's going on about.

"Talk to me, man. What the hell happened that caused you to drink a bottle of whiskey?"

His eyes drift open and closed and a low sigh comes from him. "She likes me still, and I don't want to like her. I can't like her. I can't be who she wants."

"Who is *she*?"

Jack flops back on the bed, his legs still hanging over the side. Then I hear a loud snore come from his mouth. Great.

I move him around so he's at least on the bed and shove some pillows under his head. I shake my head, looking at my best friend who is going to hate himself in the morning.

Once in my room, I grab my phone and video call Jess, needing to see her.

"Hey," she answers with a sleepy smile.

"Did I wake you?"

"No, no." Her voice is quiet, and it's clear I did wake her. "How is Melia?"

"Better, I think. Low fever today, but she was in a much better mood."

She smiles. "Good. I'm glad to hear it."

"But, while I got one person on the mend, another showed up on my doorstep requiring aid."

"Oh?" she asks with surprise.

"Yeah, Jack is passed out in the guest room—drunk. He kept talking about a girl, but won't say her name."

Jess's eyes widen just a touch. "That's . . . wow. Who do you think it is?"

There's something going on that people are aware of, I can feel it. The tone in her voice says she isn't telling me the truth. "Who is it, Jess?"

"I have no idea. I'm just surprised."

I lean back in bed, watching her. "Why don't I believe you?"

She rolls her eyes. "I don't know. Could it maybe be Delia? She mentioned something about him."

Now it's my turn to react. "Delia? No. Not a chance."

"I know she was meeting him tonight."

"Shit. Then maybe it is." I scratch my head. For him to be so torn up like that about her would be . . . strange. Delia has been in love with Joshua for as long as I can remember. Jack has never given any indication that he had feelings for her, but maybe it was her. If she shot him down, I could see him being pissed enough to drink a bottle.

"Well, I'll find out tomorrow when he sobers up. Anyway, how are you? I feel like we haven't had any chance to talk."

Jess smiles warmly. "You've been a bit busy."

"Are you feeling neglected?" I say with a smirk.

"No, Amelia comes first. I'm fine. Things are fine. I've been a little nauseous the last week, and I wonder if I'm not coming down with what Melia had."

"Are you okay?"

"I'm fine."

I hate that she's not feeling well. "Did you call the doctor?"

"Grayson, it's fine. I promise." Jessica's voice turns to laughter at the end.

"Speaking of the doctor, when is your next appointment?"

She smiles, but it looks a little forced. "Soon."

"How soon? If you want me to go with you, I will."

"No. You don't need to."

It's clear that she doesn't want me there and I try not to let that bother me. "Jess, I want to be there with you."

"I appreciate that," Jessica says, but her tone says otherwise. "I don't have an appointment for a bit. I'll let you know, though."

"Okay. What about things at work?"

Jessica fills me in on everything that's been going on at the Park Inn. My receptionist apparently had sex with the gardener in the shed, which was a big scandal because he was dating the cook. She found out and threatened to cleaver him. Stella and Jess were able to get her to calm down, but the gardener demanded she be fired. My sister, being all about girl power, fired him. The guests in the cottage were unhappy about the distance they had to walk, so she was able to "upgrade" another couple into switching. Mostly, it was a lot of nothing, but I listened, smiling as she told me all about it.

"And then your father came in today . . ."

The smile is gone.

"He did?"

She nods. "He was actually really nice. He asked if we'd spoken because I guess there is a dinner next weekend that you didn't tell me about."

"There is, and they'd like you to come."

"Why?"

"I have no idea, but they're evil, so I don't think we should go."

"Gray," Jess says with exasperation. "I don't know why they hate me, but if we're really going to be together, then . . . I need to deal with them. I've done nothing wrong."

"No, love, you haven't."

"Then, we'll go, and we'll endure."

I laugh because it's the same words Stella used a few months ago.

"What?" Jess asks.

"Nothing. I just love you."

"I love you too."

"Let's hope you still feel that way after dinner."

Twenty-Eight

JESSICA

"You're cleared!" Winnie says with a huge smile.

"Please don't tell anyone."

My sister's head tilts to the side and she stares at me as though I'm a zoo animal she's never seen before. "What? Why the hell are you keeping it a secret?"

"Because I am."

Winnie gets up from the kitchen table, refilling her coffee. "That makes no sense. Not to mention it was bullshit I found out from Mom."

"I have my reasons."

It's been two weeks. Fourteen whole days of keeping this to myself. The first few days, I didn't say anything because I needed to digest it. I was so sure that after being cleared, I would get a migraine or faint or some other random thing that would set me back on restrictions. Waiting felt like the right thing to do.

When I realized I was being stupid, Amelia came down with a fever and Grayson needed all his focus to be on her. Since she's still not back to a hundred percent, I'm clinging to that excuse until I can really make sense of my new life.

A life with Grayson and Amelia would be everything, so I'm not exactly sure what I have to work out.

But now that I *can* go, does it change things? I don't know.

"Do you think that Grayson isn't going to be happy?"

"I think I'm not in the mood to discuss this."

Winnie takes a sip of her drink while not taking her eyes away from me. "If you want me to keep schlepping over here to drive you, then you should get in the mood."

God save me from younger sisters. "Yes, the ten-minute drive is so inconvenient."

"I didn't say that. Jess, look, whatever it is that you're afraid of, I'm sure it's not a real thing."

"I'm not ready," I blurt out.

Winnie sits beside me. "Ready for what?"

"To deal with it. I came here with a plan, you know? I would heal and avoid all this messy stuff. Grayson was supposed to be married with a kid—"

"You made that shit up in your head."

"I know, but that was the deal I had," I explain, feeling foolish. "I got here, and a month later, that plan was obliterated. It's been so good I can't even be mad. We're happy and things are great and now everything is going to change again. I know that's life. God, I know all this, but my head and my heart won't align." I stand, needing to pace as my stomach does somersaults. I can feel myself getting worked up and queasy. "I'm not ready for it to change again."

My sister watches me move around like a caged animal. "You can't pretend, Jessica."

"I *know* that!" I say, tossing my hands in the air. "I know it all. Do you understand how freaking stupid I feel? Things don't stay the same, and they shouldn't. But here I am, a grown woman, *knowing* how dumb I am, and yet, I don't care. I want to keep this to myself for just a bit longer because there are other things that are changing and I can only take so much at once."

Winnie gets to her feet, her hands grip my shoulders, forcing me to stop moving. "Okay. We'll wait a few more days, let Grayson deal with Melia, and then we'll deal with your crazy bullshit."

I nod once, my stomach settling a bit now that I know I have a few more days. "Yes. That's a good plan."

"All right. I'll drive you tomorrow." Winnie kisses my cheek. "I love you, even when you're a lunatic."

"I know, and I love you for it."

I grimace, feeling sick again. I thought it was nerves, but maybe I'm sick. Suddenly, it's too much. I run to the bathroom, barely making it before I heave. Winnie rushes in, her hand pulling my hair back.

"Jess?"

"Damn it," I say as I grab for a towel.

"Are you all right?" she asks, handing me a glass of water.

"Yeah, I guess I really do have what Amelia has."

Winnie helps me up and then puts her wrist to my forehead. "You don't have a fever."

"I don't think she did to start with either."

"Well, drink and rest," she instructs.

"I'll be fine. I already feel better."

Maybe it was something I ate. I did have eggs this morning, so it could be that.

"Either way, you should rest."

I yawn. "I don't think there's any chance I can stay awake anyway."

We make our way to the front door. "You sure you're fine?"

"Winnie, you didn't worry this much when I had a brain injury. Go to work." I practically shove her out the door. She's already late because she had to pick me up from working the night shift. With Grayson out, we're all trying to adjust to make sure there are no gaps.

She waves as she gets into her car, and then I trudge up to bed, where I hopefully can sleep without another nightmare.

My mother and I are watching television together. She has become addicted to these cooking shows where they're forced to make strange dishes with ingredients they've never used before. I normally don't watch, but this one is crazy.

"Do you think she's going to be able to cook a squirrel?"

My stomach roils. "I am trying not to think of it."

She laughs. "You're still not feeling good?"

"I was totally fine until you forced me to watch the road kill edition of this show."

All day today, I've taken it easy and have felt fine. No fever still, and it was my day off so I've been relaxing almost all day.

"I had no idea this episode would be so gross. The last one was funny when they had to boil everything. It reminded me of the way my mother cooked. I didn't know that frying was even an option until I met your father."

I smile softly at her. "Do you regret it, Mom?"

"What?"

"Dad."

She mutes the program and turns to me. "Of course not. I was young, but I loved him very much. The life we had wasn't perfect, but it gave me you and Winnie."

I feel like that answer is very . . . kind. "You don't have to protect me."

"Is that what you think I do?"

"Don't you?"

My mother's lips form a thin line. "Maybe," she admits. "That's what a mother does. I never wanted you kids to see bad things. It was my goal to make life easier for you."

"It wasn't easy for you."

"Not always, but I was happy."

I pull the blanket tighter around me and see my mother in a different light. For so long, I felt bad for her, pitied her in some way. But she didn't need pity, not really. She did what she needed to, without complaint, for me and Winnie.

"I don't know that I've ever thanked you."

Her head jerks back. "Whatever would you thank me for?"

"Being a great mom."

Her cheeks redden a touch. "That was my pleasure, Jessica."

"Why do you think Dad left?" I ask with hesitation. "I don't want to dredge up the past, but there is so much about that time in our lives that I feel defined me. So much I don't understand."

My mother takes a sip of her tea, watching me for a moment before speaking. "If there's anything I do regret, it's that we never talked about him or what happened. I should've shown you and Winnie parts of it, maybe then you both wouldn't be so afraid to love."

"I'm not afraid . . ."

"Yes, you are. I see it now, my sweet girl. You have this wonderful man who has loved you since you were too young to know what real love was. And you haven't told him you're cleared out of fear."

I look away, not wanting her to see the shame I feel. She's right, I'm doing all of that. No matter whether I thought I had an excuse or not, it's been fear.

"I just don't want to lose him. I don't want to feel that again. When Dad left, it was horrible. He just walked away from us as though we meant nothing."

"Maybe he did feel that way, but the man I married and loved didn't feel nothing. I believe, in my heart, that he ached from it, but he didn't know how to come back. Imagine the self-reflection and guilt he would've had to endure. Not that it excuses it because, for you and Winnie, there's not a single thing I wouldn't put myself through, but that's what mothers do for their children."

"You think Dad stayed away out of shame?"

She shrugs. "I have no idea why he's done this, but he destroyed our family when he left us. I think that he couldn't handle it and took the road he could walk down."

"Leaving pain and destruction in his wake."

My mother's smile is sad. "Did he really? Look at you both. My girls are strong, independent, smart, and resilient. I had one go through a plane crash and come out okay. The other fights for children who have far less than any child should. He may have left you, but you both rose above and defied any odds. Be proud, Jessica. Be strong and don't let your past be what destroys what could be a beautiful future."

"I think you're pregnant," my stupid best friend says.

My head is resting on the wall as I try to quell the vomiting. "You're ridiculous."

"Jess, it's been almost three days of this weird puking, and you're exhausted."

I roll my eyes. "I'm exhausted because I keep puking."

She points to my stomach "Which is why I think you're pregnant."

"I'm not pregnant."

"Says the woman with a baby growing in her stomach."

"You're being an ass."

"You're in denial."

I get to my feet and grab my toothbrush. "First, I'm on the pill. Second, we always use . . ."

Oh my God.

We always use condoms, except when we were at the beach house. That night, we forgot. Maybe not forgot, but it wasn't a discussion, and . . . holy shit.

I clasp my hand over my mouth as my stomach roils again. I drop back down, feeling sick for another reason.

"Easy," Delia says as she rubs my back.

I look up at her, tears brimming in my eyes. Jesus, I could be pregnant.

"You have to go get me a test." I grip her hands, holding on for dear life as panic starts to build. "*Please*."

"What?"

"A test. I need a test so I can . . . I don't know, scare my body into sync or something." Yes, that's what will happen. I don't think I'm late yet. It's only been a few weeks. I should be starting my period any day now.

Delia raises her brows and grins. "But I thought you weren't pregnant."

"I'm probably not. But now, now I need to know because you've scared the shit out of me!"

"Oh, yes, this is totally my fault, not Grayson's."

I close my eyes, hand resting on my stomach. "I can't be pregnant. It's too soon. We have dinner tomorrow night with his parents, and I can*not* be pregnant."

"I don't think babies give a shit about any of that, but what do I know?"

"Delia, please, go to the store. If I go, within an hour, everyone in this town will be talking about how I bought a pregnancy test. I *can't* go."

She lets out a deep sigh while leaning against the doorjamb. "And my going isn't going to stir up drama?"

"Deals . . ." I say her nickname as a plea.

Delia throws up her arms. "Fine. I'll go a few towns over and get one."

"Thank you. I just need the test so I know I'm not and can move on."

She gives me the side eye and smirks. "Okay then."

Twenty-Nine

GRAYSON

"So, what do you think they'll serve for dinner?" Jessica asks while we stand in front of the large wooden double doors.

"Hopefully, they'll be eating crow."

Her hand tightens around mine. I dropped Amelia off at my sister's, refusing to bring her into this place in case things went bad. Plus, Jessica and I haven't had a night alone in two weeks, and I need her. I need to be alone with her tonight, love her, and not worry about everything around us.

"It'll be fine, Gray."

I shake my head.

God, I hate this house. All the years of happiness I had were destroyed because of the people who still live here. Now, all I see is the anger and disapproval lurking in the shadows. Bringing Jessica here goes against every protective instinct I have.

"You say that, but you don't know them."

"Oh, I think I do."

I look over at her, she's wearing a navy dress, and her hair is curled and pulled to one shoulder, allowing me to see her tattoo. Strength isn't measurable. God, how true that is because I feel like all the strength I have is being sucked away by this fucking place.

"You look beautiful," I tell her again.

"You're stalling."

"I'm just ready for this to be over already."

Jess turns, her honey-colored eyes staring into mine. "The sooner we go in, the sooner we are done. I . . . there's stuff I want to talk to you about, good things, all good things, but I want to get through this dinner so it can be just us."

I rub her cheek with my thumb. "You have me curious."

She smiles, and her fingers wrap around my hand. "Good, now let's go inside, eat, and get out of here without bloodshed."

The door is yanked open before we can say anything else, and my father is standing there. "Are you planning to come in or make us wait on you?"

And so it begins.

He takes a step back, indicating his question didn't require a response and we're to enter. We take a step forward, my hand on the small of Jessica's back, guiding her into the family room.

"Hello, Dad."

"Your mother is in a mood. A lot is going on, and . . . well, it's better we get this over with."

I have no clue what the hell that means, but he looks irate

and not just because he had to come let us in.

It's been almost fifteen years since she's been here, but the place is exactly the same. My mother had this ridiculous house built when she was pregnant with Joshua. It's exactly as she wanted it and completely over-the-top.

There is a grand staircase that can either be climbed from the right or the left with a huge open balcony that you can look down from. As we walk under those stairs, we descend the two steps into the grand family room. I don't know why we call it that since no one is ever in here, but I guess the grand part is true.

Large triangular windows allow maximum light in, and the entire back of the house is windows. The entire thing. Aside from the two front guest rooms, every room has a mountain view. Where the house is positioned there is one hundred percent privacy. My parents ensured as much.

My mother rises to her feet with the grace of a ballerina. "Hello, Grayson."

"Mother," I say as I kiss her cheek. The hair on the back of my neck stands as I look around.

"Jessica, it's lovely to see you. I'm glad you could make it."

Jessica smiles warmly. "It's nice to see you as well."

"Dinner is ready, we were hoping to have drinks first, but since you were late, we'll just have to drink during." She looks at me with obvious disappointment.

"Amelia took a bit longer to get settled with Stella."

She purses her lips. "Yes, well, I can understand that, I guess. As much as I hoped you'd bring her, it's probably best she's not here."

"Oh, good, so there will be bloodshed tonight on the

menu."

Jessica's eyes flash with anger as she looks at me. I shrug. It's true, and I'm not going to let her or my father say anything disparaging where Amelia might hear. She has no idea about my last dinner here, and I'd like to keep it that way.

"All right, let's eat," my father says as the tension builds. "Jessica, can I lead you in?" He extends his arm to Jessica, and she takes it.

I do the same for my mother.

The table is set, food already plated. Lord knows my mother had the cook prepare the meal because she hasn't made a meal in years.

We sit, my parents at the heads of the table and Jessica and I across from one another. At least I can focus on her.

My father smiles, pours us all a glass of wine, and lifts his glass. "To family and reconnections."

My mother lets out a maniacal laugh. "Oh, how fitting, Mitchell."

We all raise our glass along with him, Jess and I give each other a look.

There is an eerie silence around us. One that causes every fight or flight instinct to scream out. I don't know what's going on, why they were adamant about a dinner, but it feels . . . odd.

Jessica lifts her eyes to me a few times, giving me a look that says she's uncomfortable with it too.

I put my fork down and clear my throat. "I'm assuming you wanted us here for a reason?"

Mom pats her lips. "Yes. Your father and I want to discuss a situation."

"You mean Jessica and I?"

"Not that we have an issue with it," Dad cuts in. "I think

we just want to know what it all means. You're due to inherit your portion of the Park Inn Enterprises, and Jessica is aware of that."

"Of course I am, but that has nothing to do with why I'm with Grayson."

"They know that," I say, looking at my parents.

"Yes, none of us believe that Jessica's intentions aren't pure," Dad adds quickly. "I'm more concerned about the possibilities of complications that your relationship brings."

"You do realize I'm a grown man?"

"Yes, but that is not what I—"

I glare at my mother, silencing her. "No, I don't think you do. I'm not sure what the issue is, and honestly, I don't give a shit. I'm not a kid. I have never asked you for a damn thing. I built my home, care for Amelia, and run the damn inn while neither of you does a damn thing."

"Where do you think you procured the funds to build your house, Grayson? Let's not be ignorant. You earn a lot more money than anyone else would in your position," Dad says with a clipped tone. "You act as though you've been working at the factory and have been saving your wages. You've been given quite a bit from us."

The sympathy in Jessica's eyes crushes me. She looks over at my father. "I don't want your money. I want to be clear. I'm not unhappy with my lot in life. I've saved my own money, worked very hard, and I make significantly less money than someone else would in my position in your company. I don't complain, in fact, I'd work for free if I could because, for my entire life, I've tried to win you both over. I'm not sure what I ever did, but it really doesn't matter because you think I'm not good enough. However, your opinion isn't what counts, is it?"

Jessica asks me.

"No. It isn't."

"I'll never be liked by you, and that's okay because Grayson is who matters."

My mother volleys her gaze back and forth between us and then to my father.

"You're what matters," I assure her.

She grins. "Good." She turns back to my mother. "Then you can like me or not. You can remind me how far beneath you I am or that my mother once cleaned your toilets, and that's fine. She did. We're not ashamed of it, regardless of what you might hope."

I get to my feet, walk over to her, and extend my hand. "You're what matters," I tell her again.

Jessica places her hand in mine. "I know."

As though I've shed my cloak, I feel lighter. I look at my parents without hatred, more pitying because they are the ones who are without. Even if they cut me off, I'll still have more than I ever could've had with my job and money. I have an amazing woman and a beautiful little girl.

"Mom, Dad, I'd like to say it's been a pleasure, but that would be a lie. I don't know why you can't get over this idea that you have a say in who I love, but I choose Jessica. You can both have each other."

My mother gets to her feet, her eyes shrewd and calculating. "I didn't want to do this," she says as she makes her way over to a side table, grabbing an envelope. "I wanted us to talk and discuss things that had nothing to do with Jessica, but you saw this dinner as something else."

I saw it for what it was, an ambush against Jessica and I. Still, I find myself asking. "Then what was it about?"

She looks to my father and back to me. "I asked you here tonight, Jessica, because regardless of your background and financial situation, I believe that you truly love my son. God knows he's going to need to feel that."

"What do you mean?" I ask.

"I wanted just you here for dinner before I talk to the rest of your siblings. In fact, I haven't even said a word to your father about this. However, he's been having an affair."

I laugh once. "You might want to change your singular to plural. You can't seriously tell me that you weren't aware of *them*."

My mother swallows and then straightens. "Don't be ridiculous, I've known for years. I've accepted it, dealt with the embarrassment, and turned the other cheek because, what were my other options? Until now, it's never had need of my attention or brought embarrassment to this family in this way. That has changed, and after almost forty years of marriage, I'm leaving him."

"Why has that changed?"

"This. I will not allow this to go on." She hands me the envelope. "Open it. It's all there."

When I do, I see the photo of him, and . . . *her*.

Before I can even understand what's happening, I punch my father in the face and I see nothing but red.

Thirty

JESSICA

Grayson hasn't said a word in fifteen minutes. He keeps clenching and unclenching his bloody fists. I want to talk, to ask him who was in the photo, but I stay quiet. The scene was something out of a movie. There his father was on the floor with blood coming from his nose and Grayson screaming in his face.

He wasn't making much sense. It was a lot of yelling and threats before I was able to pull him off his father. Then he looked at me, grabbed my hand, and practically ran out of the house without a word.

The silence is eating me alive.

We pull into his driveway, he throws the shifter in park, and just sits. Each breath is labored—clearly, the drive did nothing to diminish the anger.

"Grayson?" I keep my voice even and calm.

290 | CORINNE MICHAELS

He shakes his head. "Don't, Jess. Please don't."

"Don't what?"

"Don't . . . fucking ask me what I saw."

In all the years I've known him, I have never seen him like this. He's always been the level-headed and collected guy. This version of Grayson, I don't know.

"Okay, I won't ask." However, I will make about a million assumptions and all of them don't end well.

He releases a very heavy breath and then slams his hand on the wheel. "He's fucking Yvonne."

Oh, okay, well. I don't know what to say. My jaw is hanging, and I blink a few times. "Your ex?"

"Amelia's mother."

And then a new sense of panic hits me. If he's sleeping with Grayson's ex, where the hell is she? "In France?"

He pinches the bridge of his nose. "It appears the property that he's been looking into buying is overseas."

His father has always been a pig, but this is a whole new level of wrong. To sleep with your granddaughter's mother. I mean, who does that? Seriously. I can't understand the rationale he had to use to justify something like that, even if just to himself.

"I don't know what to say, Grayson."

He laughs once without humor. "Yeah, me either."

All the plans I had for us tonight are shot. There's no way I can tell him any of my news now. Tonight, he's hurting, and . . . as much as it kills me to keep this from him, I know it's not the right time, but I wish it was.

I mapped it all out in my head with preparation that he may not be happy that I'm cleared, but at least he'd know how I feel about him and that I *want* to stay. I want him.

Almost unconsciously, he grabs my hand. "I need you, Jess. I . . . I know I'm a mess, but I just need you."

"You have me," I tell him. "You always have me."

We exit the car, walking up the stairs without speaking. I know he's in a dark place right now, and I just want to be here for him. I know how hard it is when your thoughts are jumbled and you can't make heads or tails of them.

Once inside, we remove our coats, tossing them over the back of the chair. He stands there, looking at me as his fingers slide against my cheek. I can feel the charge in the air, the mix of anger and need swirling between us. Before I can part my lips to speak, his mouth is on mine. The crashing feels like thunder, and his touch scorches like lightning. His hands in my hair as he backs me up against the wall. I let him kiss me, take my love, and feel that I'm here with him. My fingers are at the hem of his shirt, and I lift it up, throwing it across the room. The two of us move quickly, pulling at each other.

"Fuck, Jess." He moans against my mouth.

He tries to nudge my legs apart, but my skirt is tight at the knee. Grayson's hands slide down my body, pulling the skirt up to my hips. There's no sweetness, no finesse, as he moves my underwear to the side, sinking his fingers in roughly.

I groan in pleasure as his teeth nip at my neck. The pressure increasing as he fucks me with his hand.

"You're so wet."

"Only for you."

That response must be what he needed because he kisses me harder, moving his fingers in and out while his thumb circles my clit. "I can't wait," he says as his other hand fumbles with his belt. "I need to fuck you right here."

"Good. Hurry."

I don't want to wait.

I want him to take me, remember that I'm here with him and that I'm his.

My fingers go to his waist, pushing his pants along with his boxers down. We're barely undressed before he lifts me, and I sink down onto him. Grayson's breathing is hard against my neck.

"Wrap your legs around me."

I do, and he positions himself to go even deeper. I lift his face so that he's looking in my eyes. "I'm yours, Grayson. I'm yours."

I need him to know that, in this moment, no truer words can be spoken. I love him, and I will only ever be Grayson Parkerson's.

He jerks up, using all his strength to fuck me. This might be primal, but it's ours.

"Jessica. You. Are." He pants hard as he pushes into me again. "So. Perfect."

My head falls back as the picture falls from the wall. Neither of us care enough to look. If anything, the crash pushes him harder.

"I'm close," he warns.

I am too. His fingers are digging into my ass as he lifts me higher. I kiss him hard, wishing I could crawl inside him and protect his heart from any more hurt. He healed me, and I wish I could give him the same. A deep rush of emotion comes over me as I think about all that's happened between us. How lucky I am to have this once again. Grayson, my Grayson, has given me everything and more. He's loved me so much even when I wasn't at his side. I love this man so much it's too much for my body to contain.

Our lips move together, and then I scream, my orgasm hitting me so hard that tears run down my cheeks. "I love you," I say over and over as Grayson follows with his own release.

We sink to the floor, him still inside me as I cling to him.

I'm not sure how much time passes, but Grayson lifts his head first.

"Are you okay?"

My eyes lift to his. "I'm definitely okay."

"That was . . . not my plan."

"Are you okay?" I ask.

"No, well, I wasn't, but now, I feel . . ."

"You feel what?"

He gives me a crooked grin, the one I love because it makes his dimple deepen. "I feel much better."

I kiss his nose. "Good. Ironically, I do as well."

Grayson lifts me in his arms, carrying me like we're in a scene from a movie into the bedroom. He helps me remove the rest of my clothes, and then we climb into bed. Once settled, there's an awkward silence around us.

"I'm sorry . . . about before."

"You don't owe me an apology."

His arm is around me, fingers splayed against my back as we press closer. "I shouldn't have reacted that way."

"You were pissed. I would be pissed."

"I'm still not sure what the hell to think. I don't care about Yvonne," he says quickly. "I swear, it's not about her. I don't care what she does or with who."

"It's that your dad betrayed you."

He moves onto his back, staring up at the ceiling. "It's just not how I planned for tonight to go."

"Well, I don't think either of us did."

His head shifts, looking at me with a sad smile. "You said you had news? Something that you wanted to talk about?"

My throat goes dry and nerves take over. I don't know if I should say anything, but I'm not quite sure how to get out of it either. I feel like I've lied to Grayson enough and . . . maybe he will be happy? I mean, it's good news. I'm cleared to drive, and we can travel or ride bikes.

At least I'll start there.

"Are you sure you want to talk about this?" I ask. "You've had a crazy night."

He smiles, his hand cupping my face. "I could use some good news, don't you think?"

Right. Yes, we both could. I mean, I've only been spending the last few weeks dreading this and now I've sort of stepped into it. I have it all mapped out, how to make it clear to him that this changes nothing except that it's a choice for me. One that I'm making without any fear.

"It doesn't have to be today, the news, I mean, we can wait."

"Jessica, I want to know."

All right. Here it goes. "So, I went to the doctor, and they gave me the news that I'm cleared to drive again. It was really unexpected, but the headaches have really lessened, and I can't remember the last time I got dizzy. The doctor thinks that my brain has healed a lot. I'm not stuttering much . . ." I trail off, feeling the emotions getting strong.

"So you can drive?"

I nod. "I can."

"That's great." He leans in, kissing me. "That is good news. I'm glad that you got cleared."

Relief like I can't express fills me. He's taking it so well.

I smile, feeling like telling him the rest is the right thing. "He said I could fly too. That I'm free to go back to normal, and . . ."

Grayson shoves the covers off and gets to his feet. "You're allowed to fly? So, you can what . . . leave?"

I sit up, pulling the blanket around me. "Yes . . . but—I—"

"Great. You thought this was what I wanted to hear? That tonight you'd let me know you're leaving?" He pushes his legs through his pants with angry movements.

"I didn't say that. I just said I'm cleared to fly not that—"

"But that's what you've wanted from the day you got here. To leave. You've never hidden it. Now it's right there for you to go."

The shift in his mood is so abrupt I'm momentarily stunned. "Grayson, I didn't say I wanted to leave."

"You didn't say you wanted to stay."

"You didn't let me get there!" I get to my feet, moving toward him.

"When? When did you go to the doctor and get this clearance?"

I release a heavy breath. "A few weeks ago."

"So you've been lying to me."

"No, I just . . . I wasn't ready to tell you. I worried you'd react badly, which clearly I was right." I pull the blanket tighter around me, wishing it was a shield that could stop his words from piercing my heart.

"Because good news like this was better left unsaid? No, it's because you were planning your next move, trying to find the perfect time to let me know that you're leaving again."

I shake my head. "You're wrong. I was trying to decide how to. You. No. Leave." I let the tears fall. Hating that, for the first time in weeks, I'm stuttering. I wipe them away and try again, but he cuts me off.

"I'm glad we found out now." He runs his fingers through his hair, looking out at the vista.

"Found what out?"

"All of it. That my father has been fucking Amelia's mother, that you're cleared to go, it makes it all so much easier to end things now without any complications."

I take a step back, my chest aching as his words settle around us. "End things? You want to end things?"

He turns, his eyes filled with anger and disappointment. "It's not going to work. It's clear that things are too complicated for us. What a fucking joke this all was, right? Who finds love like this twice? You and I both knew this wasn't going to last, and now we can at least admit it."

"We did? When did we decide this because I wasn't there for it?" I ask, not really knowing what the hell is going on.

"Sorry, I guess I did. It's a good thing we didn't tell Amelia. She doesn't need another woman in her life who was going to just leave. I think she's had enough pain, and I've seen enough of the signs to know what this is."

Tears prick as the anger rises. "I never said I was leaving, Grayson. I was telling you that I'm cleared and I want to stay."

"I don't want you to stay! I'm telling you to fucking leave!"

"What are you talking about? I love you!"

He laughs. "Right. You love freedom. You love to travel. You are just like everyone else I've loved, you love to leave."

My lip trembles as I stare at him. He's angry—I get it. It's why I didn't want to say anything, but this is ridiculous. "You're hurting me because you're in pain."

"I'm waking up from the fog, that's what's happening. I

was so fucking desperate to love you that I convinced myself it was all real. You're cleared, Jess. Go. Just go."

I'm stunned. Absolutely fucking stunned. Who is this man? The one who needed me is now pushing me away. "This is what you want? To push me away when I'm clinging to you? How does this make sense? I'm telling you I want to stay, and you're not listening! I want you and us and Amelia and this . . ."

"I'm telling you to go. Go back to the life you left, and we'll go back to ours. Just as it should've been."

"So, because you're afraid, you're pushing me out?"

Grayson turns. "I'm not afraid. I'm realistic. I watched you walk away once. I watched Yvonne do the same. This clearance is the excuse we both needed and knew was coming. There's no reason for you to stay, and I'd rather you go now before we break my daughter's heart too. We're done, and I'll be just fine. It's not like we had plans."

My hands move to my stomach as the knot grows there. Only it's not a knot, it's a baby—our baby. I think about how tonight was supposed to go and how horribly wrong it went. The things he's saying, though, I can't stand here and listen to any more. He's ripping me apart, and I have to stop it.

Tears fall unabashed as the pain lances through my heart. "I was never leaving you. I was sharing with you."

He turns his back to me. "No one ever stays. Why would you be any different?" He laughs once. "I fucking knew it, I was just a fool."

"No, you're an asshole," I say as I gather my clothes, getting dressed because, no matter what, I don't deserve this.

I send an emergency text to Delia, asking her to come get me, which she replies almost instantly to, telling me that she'll be here in five.

Once I'm dressed, I walk toward the door, feeling so much pain it hurts to breathe. I stop, hoping he'll at least look at me. But Grayson doesn't turn, he just stands, looking out the windows, his back to me.

"So, this is it?" I ask.

"I'm doing what you did before. I'm walking away before you get the chance to do it to me."

"Right. Hurt me before I can hurt you?" He stays quiet. The text comes from Delia that she's here. "The sad part is that I was excited to be cleared, not because I was going to leave but because all I could think about was our life here. I saw our life together, not me getting on a plane to leave. What I didn't see was this reaction. I never thought you'd end things, but I'll give you what you want, Gray. I'll go. I'll do what you expect but not because it's what I want. I'm walking out of this house because I won't let you treat me this way. I won't let you villainize me when I've done nothing wrong. I'm sorry your father is an asshole. I'm sorry Yvonne is doing this to you and Amelia. And I'm even sorry that, when I was younger, I didn't see just how much I loved you and that we could've tried. This time, though, this is on you. I'm not leaving because I want to. I'm leaving because you pushed me out the door."

I wait. My heart pounding, praying that he'll turn around and . . . anything. Stop me, beg me, tell me that he's just scared, but he doesn't.

He just stands there, facing the outside world and closing me off.

So, I turn and do as he asks, leaving him with my heart shattered on the floor as he lets me go.

Thirty-One

JESSICA

I pull up to the house, needing some time to myself. I have cried more tears than any human should be able to shed.

I'm alone.

I feel bereft and hurt in a way I didn't expect. There's nothing to do but take some time and figure things out.

A part of me knows he was angry at the situation, but it doesn't negate the fact that he said what he did. It's been twelve hours since our fight, and I haven't heard a word from him.

There is nowhere else I could think to go where I could feel close to him while also being alone.

I look up at the yellow door, feeling the warm tears falling down my cheeks.

"Well, baby, it's just us," I whisper to my stomach as I carry my bag up the stairs.

It seems crazy that it was just a month ago that I was here.

How different the drive was that time with Amelia chattering away and Grayson holding my hand. Now, there are tears and heartache all around me.

I get inside and call Delia.

"I'm here," I say when she answers.

"Are you okay?"

"No," I answer honestly. "I'm not."

When she picked me up, she knew I couldn't talk. Tears were relentless, and I sobbed so hard my chest physically hurt. I just kept saying, "Please, beach house."

So, she drove to Stella's, tried to relay what little she knew, and Stella pulled me into her arms and gave me the key. I slept for maybe an hour and then got in the car to drive here. Funny how the first time I actually drove again was to come to this place.

"Can you tell me what happened?"

I sit on the couch, turning the light on and pulling the blanket around me. It's freezing in here, but I'm too exhausted to get up. "He ended things. It's complicated, and I'm . . . I don't know, but it's been hours and he hasn't called."

"Did you tell him about the baby?"

"No, I didn't get that far, and then . . . I couldn't. He was adamant about us being done and telling him felt like it would be a way to hold on to him."

Delia sighs deeply. "So, now what?"

"Now, I nurse my broken heart and figure it out, I guess. I'm pregnant, that's a fact. I'm cleared, and I need to come up with a plan."

"Are you going to leave?"

The question hangs out there, heavy and unsettling. "I don't know. A part of me kept waiting for him to call and beg

me to forgive him, but he hasn't. I thought that he was a ratio-
nal man who didn't act like this and that he would wake up and
see what a dick he was."

"It could still happen."

"Each hour that passes makes it harder to believe that."

"Well," Delia's voice is soft, "if it makes your decision any
easier, I want you to stay. I know that you're hurting, but the
truth is, once Grayson finds out about the baby, he's not going
to walk away. That's not who he is."

"I know that."

"He expects you to leave. I think that's why he was being
such an idiot. He's watched person after person he loves turn
away."

"He pushed me out, Deals."

"I know, and he deserves to deal with that, don't get me
wrong, but you both love each other."

She's right. Even now, when I feel like I could curl into a
ball and cry a river, I love him. He's angry, and that's fine, but
I am not going to be his proverbial punching bag.

"He has to realize that himself."

"Are you going to hide at the beach house until he does?"

That would be all too easy, but I came here because I hoped
he'd come for me. He'd know that I was here, waiting for him,
because it's our house. We might not own it, but it's ours.

I rest my head back on the pillow, wrapping the blanket
around me tighter. "I don't know."

"Okay."

"I just need a few days. Maybe then I can get my head
straight and form a plan that doesn't make me sob. I want to
tell him about the baby, but only after I know what I'm doing.
That way, the choice is what it is and not based on him and

what he wants."

"That makes sense."

"Does it?" I ask with a laugh. "I feel like it's all crap. The truth is that I want him to see that I'm not his ex or the same girl as I was before."

Delia covers the phone, speaking to someone and then comes back to me. "Sorry, I have to get back to work. I'm here if you need me."

"Thanks. Just . . . please don't tell him where I am."

"Your secret is safe with me."

We hang up, and the cold is too much. There's a blustering wind that is sending a draft through the house, so I get up and turn the heat on, hoping it kicks in quickly.

I refuse to sleep in that room. I can't . . . it's hard enough being here and not thinking of Grayson. This house holds memories that no one can take. It's where we made love the first time and where we conceived this child. It's where we laughed, smiled, and found hope. I need some damn hope right now.

I go into the pink room and grab the comforter off the bed and go back to the couch.

My eyelids are heavy because, between the tears and the pregnancy, I am always tired.

I look at my phone, the screen filled with a picture of Grayson, Amelia, and me smiling as we stand by the ocean. We were so happy and I truly believed we'd become a family.

"You stupid man," I say to him, feeling the sadness building again.

I close my eyes as a tear trickles down my face, hating that this hurt won't ebb.

My lungs hurt. Each breath feels labored.

Jesus. This dream. I can't handle it right now.

I open my eyes, but it's too dark for me to see anything. I cough, trying to get air.

This is a new dream, one where everything is too real. My heart races as I move from side to side, trying to wake. My body is hot, sweat all around me.

I try to see again, but there's . . . smoke.

Oh my God.

I'm not dreaming. I roll off the couch, hitting the floor hard and pulling my blanket over my head to try to protect my breathing. My phone. It was in my hand. I feel around for it and touch the screen. It lights up, but I can't see anything. I press where the phone is, hoping I get it right.

It rings and rings, at least I'll get a hold of someone.

"Jessica . . ."

Of course it's him. I called Grayson. As much as I want to cry, I know I'm in trouble. "Grayson, there's a fire."

"What?" His voice changes. "Where are you?"

"I'm . . . it's everywhere." I cough harder. "I can't breathe."

"Jessica!" he yells into the receiver. "Where are you?"

"Beach," I say before another coughing fit takes over. I need to get out of here. I pull the blanket off from over my head, staying low and covering my mouth. "I'm at the beach house."

His voice changes to being almost eerily calm. "Okay, where are you in the house?"

"The living room. Under a blanket."

"All right. I need you to try not to breathe too much. Just

take a deep breath now, and then I want you to orient yourself to find a door or a window."

I nod, even though he can't see me. As much as I wish I had called my sister or Delia, there's a strange relief that it's him. If something happens, his voice will be the last one I hear. Grayson is also a firefighter and can tell me what to do. He'll figure this out. I can't . . . I can't think about it.

"Lift the blanket and look where you are."

I do as he says, but the smoke is so thick that it's hard to see. I go back under. "Gray, I can't see."

"Okay. Stay low, and we're going to crawl to where the door is. I'm on the phone with 9-1-1 now, just stay on the phone. Help is coming. I'm coming."

"I'm scared."

"I know, love. God, I'm . . . listen, if you're on the couch, the door will be to the left. Can you feel along the side of the other couch?"

"Yes."

"Okay, keep under the blanket, but crawl and feel the way around. You know this house, Jess. Hold your breath. Try not to breathe unless you absolutely have to."

I do as he says, staying as low as I can, praying that I can get to the door. I feel my way across the living room, hugging the couch. I'm so dizzy. Everything around me is hazy, and my eyes just want to close.

I hear him talking, and my lungs are screaming for air. It's so hard to move, and I'm fighting for strength.

"Gray," I say his name, but it's quiet. "Hurts."

"Keep going, Jess, get to the door."

I want to cry, but I know if I let myself, I'll stop moving. I have to get air. I need to breathe, and then I think about the baby. God, the baby.

I need to save us both.

I push with my legs, going as far as I can while holding my breath. I can do this. I have to.

Something crashes to the ground to my right a second before glass shatters somewhere. "Jess!" He is yelling, but I can't breathe, the smoke is getting lower.

I swear, I can see the door, it's right there. I push again, but it feels as though someone is holding my feet, not allowing me any forward progress and pulling me backward.

"Jessica! Please, baby! Talk to me!"

I suck in a huge breath, but it doesn't relieve the ache. Using the last bit of energy I have, I claw my way closer, and then realize it's not the door, it's the hallway.

I was going the wrong way.

Thirty-Two

GRAYSON

I drive. I drive, and I don't know how many miles pass, but I drive.

My mind races, and my heart won't stop pounding.

I'm so far from her.

Too far.

I should've been there with her. No, fuck that, I should've had her in my arms at home.

I was so stupid. So selfish and—angry. When she walked out, my heart broke not because it was her who did it this time but because it was me. I stood there, wanting to run after her but not sure what to say.

All I kept thinking was: she will leave me.

Now, God, now, she really might, and it's all my fault.

My phone rings, Stella's name on the screen.

"Grayson? Grayson! I just got a call from Dad." I can hear

my sister crying. "Jessica. Please tell me you heard from her."

I clench my jaw as fear and anger rise again. "I'm on my way to her."

"She came here. She came here, and she was so upset. She said she needed the keys and what you . . . please tell me you heard from her!"

The sheer panic in Stella's voice makes the tears I've been holding back flood forward.

I relay the phone call, tears coming faster than I can wipe them away as I try to focus on the road. I failed her in every way.

"Oh," Stella pauses. "Oh, I don't even know what to say."

"Yeah, I don't either."

My sister goes quiet. "What about the fight?"

As much as I don't want to talk about it, I find myself pouring my heart out to Stella. She and I aren't the closest in age, but we're closest in heart. I tell her about Yvonne, Dad, Mom, and then the fight with Jessica.

It allows me a very, very brief break from worrying that I will never see Jessica again.

"My sweet brother, I am so sorry, but you'll fix this, and once you're home and you have Jessica in your arms, we'll figure out what to do about the rest of this mess."

I hope she's right, but the truth is, I have no idea what the hell I'm going to find once I get there. My stomach is in knots and my chest is tight as I race down the highway, praying she's all right.

"If . . . if . . . she . . . I can't talk."

"Okay." The defeat in her voice is almost too much to bear. "Please call me."

"I will. I can't . . ."

"I know. I love you, and I'll be here."

"Call Jack," I tell her. "Tell him. And Winnie and her family."

"I can do that," Stella says quickly. "I'll keep Amelia in the dark and just say you had to go see Alex or Josh."

I end the call, unable to think about this. If she's not okay . . .

If . . .

If I get there, and she's gone, I don't know how I'll go on. My life will simply cease to be the same.

It was one thing to lose her before. It was hard, but the obliviousness of youth worked for me. I didn't know any better. This, though, is different. Loving her the way I do now isn't young or naïve. It is the most beautiful thing I've ever felt, and the void will never be filled.

Pushing the accelerator down harder, I race to get to her. When I pull up to the scene, my heart drops.

I'm out of the car, running toward the house, but a police officer grabs me. "Son, you can't go in there."

"That's my house!"

"Okay, but you can't . . ."

"There was a girl inside. My girlfriend. Her name is Jessica Walker. Can you . . . is she—" I barely get the words out. I'm shaking because of the adrenaline flooding me. "I'm a fireman. Here." I give him my fire badge, and he looks over at the fire chief before waving him over.

He heads toward us, soot all over his face. "This is the owner and also a fellow fireman. I thought you could talk to him."

I shake my head. "The girl. Did you find a girl? She . . . she called me and . . . the phone. Please, just tell me."

"We found her, and she was transported to the hospital."

"Was she alive?" I ask, my hands shaking.

"Yes, she was alive," he says. "She was pulled out before we got on scene, but . . . I don't know her prognosis."

"Where is the hospital? How . . . I need to . . ."

The police officer places his hand on my arm. "I'll take you there."

I release a heavy breath as I stare at where the house we loved once stood. The place that held so many memories for us is now ash. I drop to my knees, feeling so much loss I can't stand under its weight. Jessica was in there, and I couldn't do anything. I have no idea if she's still alive and I can't take it.

There's a hand on my shoulder, gripping. "Come on, let's go," the police officer says. He helps me to the car, and we ride the ten minutes without talking. I'm glad he doesn't try because I have no words.

If I try to speak, I will fall apart. The only thing keeping me together is that they found her and she might be okay.

I send a text to Stella, letting her know the name of the hospital, and she lets me know Jessica's family is on their way.

When we get inside, the police officer informs the staff of who I am and asks about Jessica's status. She explains that right now they have no information other than she's in ICU and that I will have to wait until they talk to her next of kin.

I'm not family, and they can't release anything to me.

I have no idea if she's awake or unconscious. Is she hanging on or letting go? Is she asking for me or hopes I don't come?

If you're listening, God, just don't take her. Let her live and let me spend the rest of my life making it up to her.

My head rests in my hands, and I cry. I just fucking cry

because I did this to her. I pushed her away, made her run because I was so sure she'd go because that's what happens. She is everything to me, and I gave her away.

Now, she might really be gone.

How can I live with myself? How do I ever look at the skyline again and not die a little inside?

Hours pass. Hours and no matter how much I beg, no information will be released to me.

My phone rings, and it's Delia.

"Gray, we're at the hospital. Where do we go?"

She must've gotten in the car right after I did. "I'm on the fourth floor."

"Okay," she says panting.

A few minutes pass before the door opens, and Delia, Winnie, and her mother enter the room. Her sister rushes toward me. Her arms wrap around me, and we both start to cry.

"I'm a fucking asshole," I say. "I did this to her."

"Stop it. She'll be okay. She has to be. Who the hell survives a plane crash to die in a house fire?" she says as though that makes anything easier.

Then her mother is next to me, looking at me with red-rimmed eyes, and I pull her close. "I'm sorry. I'm so sorry."

Mrs. Walker brushes my cheek. "My daughter is a fighter. She won't give up."

"They won't give me any info."

She nods. "I'll go see what I can find out."

Delia rocks back and forth, chewing on her lip, and while her eyes are on me, she speaks to Jess's mother. "Be sure to ask about the baby."

And then I sink to the ground, no longer able to hold myself up for the second time in as many hours.

Thirty-Three

GRAYSON

I walk to her room and stand at the doorway, thankful that the curtain is drawn and I can't see her.

I'm not ready. I've seen burn victims. I've watched people struggle to breathe after smoke inhalation, and I curse the knowledge that comes with this. They are preparing another short session in the hyperbaric oxygenation chamber because, even with her being pregnant, it's the safest and fastest way to treat her lungs. They've already done several tests, and are finally allowing us to see her before they put her in this round.

The nurse stands behind me. "We gave her something for pain to help her rest easier, so she's sleeping."

I'm standing outside, terrified to see her in pain. I count to three and push the curtain over. The tears form instantly.

She's on the bed, looking so small and frail. There are some burns on her arms, but overall, it's not as bad as it could be.

The tests show she has moderate damage, and they are doing everything they can to help her, treating not only the smoke but also possible carbon monoxide poisoning. Because of the pregnancy, they are doing things meticulously and monitoring both of them.

I thank God for the fireman next door who smelled the smoke and was able to get her out quickly. That man . . . he saved her life.

I will never be able to thank him.

I get to the edge of her bed, taking her fingers that aren't wrapped in mine. She moves subtly, and as much as I want to see her eyes, I keep my voice just barely a whisper so I don't disturb her. "I'm so fucking sorry, Jessica. I love you so goddamn much, and I don't deserve you," I say, my head resting on the rail. "I messed up by pushing you away, and if you come back to me, I'll give you the world."

I move my other hand to her stomach, looking at the fetal monitor that silently blips along with the baby's heartbeat. "You, you fight. You stay there, and you—" I break off. Words becoming too much. My palm covers our child. A baby we made and I want more than anything.

Losing them. Losing either of them isn't an option. They need to fight. They have to be okay. If love is enough to save someone, then these two have more of it than they can ever need from me.

"You have a sister. Her name is Amelia, and she needs you." I look up to Jessica. "She needs you, and I need you. I need you more than I need air, Jessica. I was so wrong. Please," I beg, "please forgive me. Please let me make this right."

The sound of a throat clearing comes from the door. The

nurse gives me a sad smile, and I turn my head and breathe, trying to get a grip on my emotions.

"We need to take her to the chamber now."

"Yes. Of course."

Another person enters. "Hello, I'm Dr. Ryan, and I'm monitoring any changes with the baby."

"I'm the father. Can you tell me anything?"

She smiles. "The first round in the chamber helped, which is why we're doing it again. As of now, I feel hopeful."

The nurse finishes attaching things to the side of the bed before patting my shoulder. "We're ready."

"We'll be out to let you all know how it goes."

And now we wait—again, and I hope she fights and returns to me.

Winnie reaches over, taking my hand. "It'll be okay."

I close my eyes, resting my head back on the wall. "I heard her during the fire. I listened, and . . . I just kept thinking that I was going to hear her die. I'm hours away, and I can't get to her. She's going to die, and I can't save her, and the last thing I said to her was to leave."

"You guys fought?"

"I found out something that . . . well, it caused me to be a dick. I hurt her."

"Jessica has guilt too, Gray. She felt awful about being cleared and keeping it from you."

"She's also pregnant," I say, not wanting to remember the awful argument about her being cleared to fly again.

Winnie smiles softly. "I know. Does that change things?"

"Of course it does."

"I think she was worried about that too."

I look at her sister, a younger version of Jessica. "Why?"

Winnie sighs and shrugs, pulling her hand back. "You're both idiots. I want to go on the record here. Your last girlfriend got pregnant and left you. Here she was, pregnant and given the all clear to leave. She was terrified."

"And I did exactly what she feared."

She doesn't dispute it. "Delia filled me in on what Jess told her, which wasn't much. I'm sure your side is different."

I tell Winnie everything. It's like once the first word is out, they won't stop. I tell her about the dinner, the fight with my father, the argument I had with her, and then the call from Jessica. I'm not sure how long I speak, but my voice is raw and I feel broken by the end.

"That's . . . a lot to take in," Winnie says as she looks at the door. "I'm not sure what to say, but you and Jessica? You guys are what people write songs about. You're why love stories exist, and I have to believe *that* kind of love makes people stronger."

"Look what it did to her. If that baby doesn't survive, then what?"

"Then you guys pick up the pieces—together."

She makes it sound so damn easy. "I broke her."

"Maybe, but does it matter who broke who? Honestly, Grayson. Does it?"

I look at Winnie, pondering her question. "I don't know."

Her shoulder nudges mine. "I want to believe that when you love someone, it really doesn't. You don't keep score because it's not about that. Will she be devastated if she loses the baby? Of course. You both will. However, there will be enough blame to go around, and yet, what you'll both need is each other. Be there for her."

"I will never let her go."

"Good. When she's awake, tell her that. Tell her until she believes you. And then tell her again for good measure."

An hour passes, the treatment went well, but they aren't letting us back in because she's resting. As I was pacing the hallway, I got a call from the fire chief to come back to the house.

I take Delia's car, and when I pull up, my brain struggles to process the scene in front of me.

The entire left side of the house is gone, just a burned wall stands. There is water and burned furnishings everywhere. It's completely destroyed.

"Grayson Parkerson?" a man calls my name and I turn toward him.

"Chief."

He nods. "How is your wife?"

Wife. The word vibrates through me, settling in my chest. It's what she should be. "She's doing okay."

"Good." He clears his throat and points over to the house. "I thought you may want to see what we found as the cause of the fire."

We make our way over to the electric box. "It was the furnace that caused a flame rollout. It's location and age caused the perfect storm."

"She never should've been here," I say more to myself.

"We're going to seal it off, so if there's anything you need, go ahead and grab it now."

"The only things I need are in the hospital."

The house may have burned down. I may have lost the place where so many wonderful memories were made, but I won't lose her.

I won't let anything else go up in flames.

I look back at the structure one last time before leaving to save what really matters—us.

Thirty-Four

JESSICA

My hand rests on my stomach as tears fall. I'm so tired. I'm so . . . overwhelmed. Everything feels like it weighs a hundred pounds and I can't move any of it off my chest.

I think about how he begged for me to fight and what he said to the baby. He knows, and now I don't know what to do about it.

Nothing feels real, and my head is too jumbled to decide anything.

There's a knock at the door, and Delia enters.

"Jess." She rushes forward, tears in her eyes. "Oh, Jessica!"

"I'm okay."

"Are you sure?"

I nod. "I think so. They said if I had been inside a minute

longer, we'd be having a very different discussion."

She sniffs and wipes under her eyes. "I swear, you have the worst luck, so you can't leave the bubble we make for you."

"I think a bubble sounds good."

Her hand grabs mine. "We've been so worried. The doctor said you'll need to be on oxygen for a while."

"Yeah, they're still monitoring things, but the chamber helped a lot. Where is Grayson?"

She looks out toward the door and then back to me. "He's in the waiting room. He's been beside himself, Jess. I've never seen him so afraid before. And then, I'm so sorry, I told him about the baby."

I squeeze her hand. "It's all right."

"I just . . . I know you didn't tell anyone else, and I wanted the doctors to know."

My hand moves to my stomach as more tears fall. "You did the right thing."

"Did I?"

"Yes. You . . . you were . . ."

The emotions become too much, and I start to cry. Delia grabs some tissues and hands them to me. The two of us cry together as I struggle to deal with all that's happened. I almost died. I almost died in a fire in the house that has meant so much to me. It's all so damn much.

Delia moves to the side of the bed, wiping my face for me. "Jess . . . I have to ask . . ."

My eyes look up as someone comes to a stop just in front of the doorway. Grayson stands there, looking exhausted and yet so damn gorgeous at the same time. He watches us, and Delia stands.

"I'm going to go out there. You guys have a lot to talk

about." She leans over, kissing my cheek.

He steps aside so she can pass and then moves closer to me, looking a little nervous, and I can feel my pulse rising. "Please don't be nervous. I just . . . I'm so sorry, Jessica."

"I am too."

He moves to the side of my bed. "You have nothing to be sorry for. I was such an asshole. Everything I said to you, it wasn't true. I don't want you to leave. Ever. I want . . . well, I want it all with you, and I was angry and scared I'd lose you."

As much as I want to be angry, I'm not. I love him, and I may hate what happened, but I also know what it's like to live without him. I never want to do it again.

"I wasn't going to leave," I say the words that he wouldn't hear before. "I was happy because I knew that staying with you was all I wanted. Not because of the baby but because of us. Because of you and Amelia. I wanted the future before us, and . . ."

"I love you," he says matter-of-factly. "I love you, and I didn't want to watch you walk away again. I thought that pushing you out would give you the life you really wanted."

I shake my head. "You're the life I want."

"Then stay with me, Jess. Let me make it up to you."

If he were any other man, I might not give in so easily, but it's Grayson. The other half to my soul and the only man who has ever held my heart. We had a fight, and instead of giving up, I'm going to fight for him—for us.

"Grayson . . ." I say as tears fall. "The baby . . ."

He steps forward, his hands cupping my cheeks. "Did we lose her?"

My tears fall harder, and I wrap my fingers around his wrist. "No." I look over at the monitor. "He or she is still in there, but they've warned me. I'm very early in the pregnancy, and this has been . . . traumatic. We need to be prepared."

Listening to the doctor explain the risks and possibilities was incredibly hard. If we're lucky, we will have a healthy baby. But it'll be weeks of testing and monitoring to make sure that neither of us have residual issues.

Grayson's forehead drops to mine. We breathe each other in. "No matter what, I'm right here. I won't let you go." And then he climbs in the bed with me, his arms wrapped tightly around me, holding me to his chest. "You will never lose me again, love, because there's no one else in this world who ever had my heart. Rest, I'll hold you and keep the nightmares away."

I close my eyes, listening to the sound of his heartbeat, and sleep dreamlessly for the first time in months.

"It's great to meet you, Grayson," Dr. Warvel says. She asked if Grayson would come to this session with me to discuss all that went on.

"I've heard a lot about you."

She smiles. "I hope all good things."

"Of course."

I snort. "Don't lie to a therapist."

Dr. Warvel laughs. "I'm going to pretend he's telling the truth."

"It is the truth," I say with a grin. "We're both . . . coming to grips with all that happened."

"First," she says looking at me, "I want to say how happy I am that you're okay. I was worried and seeing you here right now is a miracle."

"I seem to be using the world's allotment up this year."

Her smile is warm. "I will say that I don't know anyone who has survived a plane crash and a house fire in a six-month period."

"Yes, I'm an anomaly."

"That much is true," Grayson agrees. I was released five days ago with very strict instructions to stay calm and relaxed.

Dr. Warvel nods in agreement. "Second, I want to say that I'm glad you're both here today. I'd like to get a feel for how you're both doing."

"I'm okay," I tell her. "I'm doing well, the doctors are very happy with my lung function, and I'm not having any issues with my TBI. I worried that would be triggered, but so far, I'm healing and I haven't lost the baby."

That is probably the only reason I am so okay. The OB-GYN explained what to watch for and said that all my tests, including the ultrasound, showed nothing abnormal. If I did lose the baby at this point, it may not have anything to do with the fire and just be a miscarriage. She said to take it easy, keep myself as calm as I can, and contact her if anything changes.

"That's great."

"I agree. I was told that I should take it easy and know my limits," I say, glaring at Grayson.

Grayson is taking the calm thing to an extreme. The first day, it was cute. He was so caring and waited on me hand and foot. The second day, it was . . . well, still a little cute. Amelia also took the role of being a nurse very serious. She stayed next to me, feeding me noodles, and making me drink my water each time the alarm went off.

By the third day, I was no longer so amused.

I wanted to get up, take a walk, but all I was "allowed" to do was sit on the deck while Amelia and Grayson hovered.

I informed him that I wanted to take a walk, which he was adamant about being too strenuous. Then he almost lost his shit when I was in the kitchen, preparing to do some baking, which calms me.

Yesterday, when he sat in the bathroom while I showered, asking if I needed help, I lost it. To avoid a fight, I went to bed at six o'clock, feigning exhaustion.

He raises both hands. "I'm just making sure you don't do too much."

"You're making sure I don't do anything." I turn to Dr. Warvel. "I love him. I love that he wants to take care of me, but I'm not an invalid."

She shifts, which means she's settling in to give it to one of us, and I'm hoping it's him. "Jessica," she starts, and I groan, "you know what it's like to suffer a trauma. You lived through the plane crash, dealt with crippling nightmares, stuttering, and a host of other physical issues. What you're living right now with Grayson is another version of it."

"I understand that."

"Do you?"

"You just said I should."

She smiles. "But that doesn't mean you understand it. I'm pointing out that being overprotective is a part of him dealing with his trauma." Her eyes move to Grayson. "Did you tell Jessica what you went through regarding the fire?"

He looks to me and then to her. "Not really."

"Why don't you try?"

"It was nothing compared to her being in the fire," he says.

Dr. Warvel nods slowly, I can see her brain working on

the best angle. "I'm sure that's true, but you lived it as well. Maybe not the same way as she did, but there is still your version of it, correct?"

"Yes. I wasn't in the fire, but I listened to it. I had to drive to her, not knowing anything. Then, when I got there, I had to wait until someone would tell me if she was even alive. I had to wait and worry, seeing the fucking house burn. Literally, the house was on fire. Not just the beach house, but us as well. Our relationship was going up in flames."

Man, she's good. Just a few questions, and he's letting it out.

I turn to him. "We weren't going up in flames."

"No? It sure felt like it. I lost you, Jessica. I thought you were dead. I listened . . ."

My fingertips move down his face. "I'm right here."

"I know that, and I am trying to tell myself to stop hovering, but I lost my fucking heart when you wouldn't answer the phone. I screamed for five minutes, racing for my keys, trying to find my shoes, and the whole time, I was calling out your name over and over, listening to the sounds of glass breaking and what sounded like bombs exploding in the house. And then the line went dead, and I had no idea . . ."

I didn't know that. During my stay at the hospital, it was a lot of focusing on my prognosis and monitoring the baby. We didn't talk about the fire other than when I relayed the events to the fire marshal. My mother and sister went back to Willow Creek two days after the fire, and Delia left the next day, leaving me with Grayson.

Stella came down with Jack and Amelia because she was struggling with him being gone so long and had overheard Jack and Stella discussing the fire.

Each day, I healed a bit more both mentally and physically. I had Grayson. I had my life. I was okay.

But he wasn't, and I didn't see that.

"Why didn't you tell me?" I ask him. "I knew something was wrong, but you didn't tell me any of that."

"You are supposed to stay calm and stress free."

I rub my thumb over his cheek, the scruff longer than usual. "We have a bad habit of trying to protect each other by keeping things from the other."

"I wasn't trying to keep it from you. Honestly, I didn't realize it until we started talking."

"Dr. Warvel does that. She makes you say things even when you don't know you need to."

She grins at us. "I try, but you two just did my job for me. Your relationship has a wonderful foundation. You know each other in a way that many couples only dream of. Your love hasn't faded through the years, almost as if you've been waiting to return to each other all along. Now, you're here and your house has the framing and the walls. Trust in that. It didn't burn down, it's not on fire, it just needs you to trust each other and keep building."

Thirty-Five

GRAYSON

"I'm selling my part of the company," I tell Stella.

"Umm, you're what?"

Jessica squeezes my hand in support. The last two weeks have been busy. Since the dinner with my parents, I haven't returned to the Park Inn. One reason is that I needed to take care of Jessica, but the other is that I'd like to set it on fire, and arson isn't really my thing.

Since the meeting with Dr. Warvel, Jess and I have focused on us. We talk about everything, and one thing we both agree on is that working for my father isn't possible for me anymore.

I'm going to give up my role as well as any holdings in the family company because it's time to start doing what I've dreamed of—fixing up Melia Lake.

"A few years ago, I purchased a plot of land. It has an old hotel—or, what might have been one, on it, and it sits on a lake. It's the perfect place to open my own inn."

Stella leans back in her chair, staring at me. "Years?"

"When Amelia was born."

"Wow. So, you mean to tell me that for almost the last five years we could've walked away from our shitbag parents and been making money for ourselves?"

"Stella, you're not leaving."

"The hell I'm not. If you're going, I am too."

"It's going to take me years to get it up and running, and I need to get investors. Jessica and I are already going to New York City next week to attend a premiere with Jacob Arrowood. While I'm there, I'm going to ask him if he'd be interested."

She gets up and grabs her phone. Before I know it, my phone is ringing with a video chat from her.

"What are you doing?" I ask.

"Answer the call, Gray." Then I see my brothers one by one get on the call. Stella looks over at Jess and adds her in. "You too, Jessica."

She swipes the call open, looking at me with confusion. I shrug because, with Stella, one never knows.

"Well, this is one hell of a good-looking crew," Oliver says with a grin.

Alex laughs. "Most of us, anyway. Grayson is a little dicey."

Josh chimes in. "At least he doesn't look prepubescent like you, Alex."

That earns him the middle finger.

"Hi, Jessica." Alex's voice is a little too sweet for my liking.

"Hello, Parkersons."

I move over closer to Jess, throwing my arm around her. "God, I forgot how possessive Grayson gets over her," Ollie notes.

"Right, as though she ever looked at us like we were datable." Alex shakes his head.

My brothers keep going, poking fun at us, and I really don't care. She's here, next to me, and we can have this conversation. I'll take all their bullshit and then some.

"All right, assholes." Stella clears her throat. "I'm calling because we need our own sibling meeting, and since Jessica and Grayson are a foregone conclusion, then she's family as well. We need to talk about something."

"Stella," I warn.

She continues. "We all know our father is the biggest piece of shit. We all hate him. We all want nothing to do with him, but we've all felt like we had no choice. Grayson is leaving. He's giving up his shares, and he already owns a piece of land."

Josh just looks into the camera, echoing the stunned silence coming from all my siblings.

Alex speaks up first. "You own land?"

"I own about two hundred acres with a lake on it."

"You own a fucking lake?" Josh asks.

"I do, I bought it when I had Amelia."

Oliver laughs once. "That's one hell of a birthday gift. How come I only get an empty card?"

"Because you're the spoiled brat," Stella says. "Focus. This is about Grayson opening his own inn—without us."

"Guys," I break in, "this isn't what I planned, but I can't be around him. I'm done, and I don't want his money or anything to do with him."

"Grayson, none of us want that," Josh speaks before any-

330 | CORINNE MICHAELS

one else.

"No, but if you're opening your own inn, why the fuck wouldn't you take us with you?" Alex asks. "Also, fuck not taking his money. He's got enough of it. We can all sell our shares."

Jessica looks to me, and I don't know what to think. They want to do this too. They want to leave my father's company and start over with me?

"Wait. You all want to leave your very comfortable lives and jobs making good money to come open an inn that we have no idea will do well?"

In unison they all speak. "Yup."

I turn back to Jess, who is smiling. "You could all be partners."

"And they'd all be here," I say.

"If we needed funding or another investor, I know Jacob would come on."

As great as it would be to get the money from outside, it would be awesome having my brothers all back here. We loved running the Park Inn before my father started branching off.

I turn back to the screen. "You know that this isn't going to be easy. We will be competing against a very well-known establishment."

Joshua's smile is wide, and he looks almost giddy. "Yeah, and how sweet will it be when it closes and his kids are who brought him down."

"Exactly," Alex says. "Plus, I've missed home."

Oliver nods. "I have money saved, this is a much better investment than a boat."

I laugh. "Stella?"

"I have been hoarding money since I was eighteen. There's nothing I'd love more than to own an inn with my brothers. Plus, our shares have value, Gray. A lot of value."

Well, it looks like I'm going into business with my siblings.

Jessica and I watch Amelia run along the lake. "Do you think I can have a house here?" she asks.

"No, Monkey, we're going to fix up that house and have our own inn."

"On Melia Lake?"

"Yup."

"Can we call it Amelia Inn?"

I laugh. "We'll put it on the list."

The last two weeks have been a whirlwind. We told Amelia that we were together, and she started crying because she was so happy and wanted Jessica to be her new mom. Since that went well and Jess was already there every night, I asked her to just stay with me.

"You okay?" Jess asks as we walk holding hands.

"Yeah, just . . . I don't know. If you had told me six months ago that this would be our life, I would've laughed."

"I know that feeling."

"It's just too good to be true."

Jess rests her head on my shoulder. "I don't know about that. Maybe it's just how it should've been and happiness is what we are meant to have."

"How very Dr. Warvel of you."

Jessica's musical laughter echoes in the trees. "I'll be sure to tell her you think she's rubbing off on me. Tell me, how was your talk with Jack?"

"I think it went well. We discussed your idea, and it seemed like he was intrigued."

She perks up at that. "You think he'll run his company from here?"

Jessica had a great suggestion that would help us to set ourselves apart from your typical inn surrounded by woods. She talked about how the pilots and flight attendants went on a company retreat every year and thought this would be a perfect location for them. Jack would be able to expand his business by offering a bonding experience to the groups who book with us and hopefully that would lead to them wanting to return.

"He didn't say no."

"I think what's going to set us apart is being able to offer many options here. If we aren't just one thing, it'll help us in the beginning."

I smile at the one word she used. "Us."

Her gaze meets mine. "What?"

"You said us."

"You've implied . . ."

We stop at the edge of the water, and I wrap my arms around her from behind, my hand resting on her stomach. "It's always us, love. It'll always be us."

In the last few months, my entire life has been upended. I found Jess again. I'm going to be a father again. I'm opening my own business and building on a piece of land I never thought I'd develop. All of it feels like it's because she came back to me.

One gift that has multiplied and become more than I could've hoped for.

I kiss the crook of her neck, and she sighs. "As much as I love the house, I love this place too."

"I do too. I feel like it needs a good name."

"Any ideas?"

She tilts her head back. "I don't know. I keep thinking about us and how to combine it all together. Plus, your family since you're all owners too."

"So, what are your words for us?"

Jessica laughs softly. "Fire. Plane. Fly. Crash. View. Mountain. Return."

"Well, I don't know that crash is a good word for a resort."

"Agree."

"But, what about Firefly?"

Her head rests on my shoulder. "Like what we used to catch as kids?"

"Well, and you were in a fire and you fly."

"This isn't my place. It's yours."

I want to argue with her, but it's much better to just let it drop for now. "Keep thinking, love. We have time, but we do need to think of another name."

Her hand moves to mine over where the baby is safely growing. "We have time for that too."

"We have months at least."

Amelia comes running over, and Jess steps forward to look at the small bunny she's carrying in her hand. "Do you think I can keep it?" Amelia asks.

I scoop her up in my arms. "We have a monkey already, we don't need anything else."

She pouts her lower lip. "I want a rabbit."

"I don't think so."

Jessica moves closer, her eyes dance with mischief. "I

thought you said something about a dog?"

I glare at her. "I love you, but don't encourage her."

Melia's eyes brighten. "I love dogs."

"I know, and I said when you turned five, we'd talk about it."

"I'm almost five."

"Yes, I know, but I was thinking we could talk about getting something else." I try to divert her attention to what I came out here for. "Do you remember what we talked about?" I ask Melia.

Her eyes widen, and she nods.

"What are you two up to?" Jess asks, looking at Melia since she's definitely the one likely to spill it.

"Nothing," she says with a coy smile.

"Hmm, I don't believe you."

Amelia covers her mouth and giggles. "I can't tell!"

Jess's eyes widen. "So, there *is* a secret?"

She nods.

Jessica creeps closer, keeping her voice low. "What if I promise not to tell your daddy?"

I give Amelia a grin and shake my head. "Don't do it."

"Daddy! You tell her."

"Fine. I'll tell her our big secret." I sigh dramatically, putting Amelia back down on the ground and dropping to my knee. Amelia kneels next to me.

I reach back, grabbing the ring from my jacket pocket.

"Oh my God." Jessica gasps as I lift it.

"I guess it's not a secret so much as a question. A long time ago, I met a girl, and she stole my heart. I thought I'd learned to live without it, but then she brought it back, and I realized how much I needed it—but mostly I needed her."

Amelia whispers, "He means you."

Jessica laughs and wipes her tears as she whispers back, "Thanks."

"When I thought I lost you, well, I didn't know that I could ever feel pain on that level. You are my heart and soul—our heart and soul. Amelia and I decided that we want to keep you, and we're hoping that you want to keep us too. I have loved you for over half my life, and I'd like to spend the rest of it loving you still. I will do anything to make you happy, Jessica. We just have one question for you."

I look at my daughter, who is smiling brightly. "Will you marry us?"

Jess drops to her knees, pulling Amelia and me into her arms. She's crying so hard she can only say one thing over and over. "Yes. Yes. Yes."

Thirty-Six

JESSICA

"**J**acob!" I yell and rush toward him. I can't believe it's been four months since the crash, and here we are, in New York City, for dinner before the big premiere tomorrow.

"You look beautiful," he says, pulling me in for a hug.

"Thank you. You look rather dashing yourself."

He laughs. "I'm nervous about this damn premiere, that's what I am."

"Well, you can't tell."

"This is Brenna," Jacob says as a gorgeous redhead steps forward.

"I feel like we're old friends," she says with a laugh as she pulls me in for a hug.

"Me too."

Grayson and Jacob shake hands, and then Brenna and

Grayson do as well. We came in a day early to spend some time with Jacob and Brenna and to talk to him about a business opportunity that he demanded we discuss.

"Your ring is beautiful," Brenna notes.

"Ring?" Jacob says, grabbing my hand. "You didn't say anything."

"He just asked two days ago."

"Congrats, you guys. This is great news." He raises his hand for the waiter. "Your best champagne."

We're in the back room of a restaurant that allows us privacy to talk and catch up. Jacob tells us about the kids and how it's been being back in his hometown. I laugh and explain my own experience.

"So, is this a thing?" Brenna asks. "People in small towns all leave and then come back to fix their lives?"

Jacob laughs. "I guess so."

"I've been telling patients the wrong therapy all this time."

Grayson drapes his arm around me, his fingers just grazing the skin on my shoulder. "I'm not sure that instructing patients to get in a plane crash is the best therapy either."

"No," Brenna agrees. "Definitely not. Although, it did seem to knock both of these two in the right direction."

Jacob leans toward her, his voice low. "I was always coming back to you."

There is so much love in this room it could choke someone. Jacob and I had a lot of regrets when the plane was going down. I remember him begging for me to tell Brenna how he felt if he didn't make it.

It was a terrifying time that really forced me to see my life through a different lens.

Now, I'm here with Grayson and can't help but be grateful

for it all. Had things gone differently, I wouldn't be engaged and pregnant.

Brenna smiles warmly at me. "How is the pregnancy going?"

"Okay. We have another ultrasound, and if that one goes well, we'll feel much better."

"Because of the fire?"

"Yeah," I say, feeling the nerves again. "The baby's growth rate is what we're watching now. So far, the tests they've been able to run have come back in our favor, but . . ." Grayson's eyes study me. The blue-green warmth infuses me with strength. "We'll know more next week, so we're just staying cautiously optimistic."

"No matter what, though, we'll be okay," Grayson reassures me.

"We will."

"You both are really handling this well," Brenna notes.

Jacob laughs. "Please don't do your shrink thing with them."

"I'm not. I'm just saying the truth. You've all been through a lot, and I'm just glad everyone is handling it well. That's just an observation, not therapy."

He takes her hand, kissing her palm. "Sure, dear."

"You're trouble."

"But I'm *your* trouble."

Her lips part, and she groans. "God help me."

The food and champagne, which is my favorite vintage, are brought out. Since I can't drink any, I sip my apple juice in a flute and pretend.

We eat and talk about the movie and Jacob's plans for living in California and Pennsylvania. Then the conversation circles to what we wanted to discuss with him.

Grayson does all the talking since it is business and not about the friendship I have with Jacob. "Basically, my siblings and I want to destroy my father."

"Well, now I'm interested."

Grayson launches into the story, leaving some information out but explaining enough on why this is important to him. I listen, seeing him in a way I haven't gotten to before.

This is a man who commands the room, and even though I know all the details, I'm hanging on every word.

This is freaking hot.

"So, are you asking for capital to buy out a company you want to basically fold?" Jacob asks.

"No, and yes. I want to force him out, not necessarily have the company collapse. He gifted us our shares, which we're going to make him buy back or we will sell them. We're proposing that you be the buyer. The shares have value, and we could sell them to anyone interested, but we'd like to control who the buyer is if we can. Either way, we have all decided to sell if he decides not to buy us out."

Jacob leans back in his chair. "Let me talk to my brothers. Oliver and Devney have some history, and I don't want to make things awkward."

Grayson accepts with a nod. "Oliver does know this is part of my plan. He wasn't happy, but he understands the need to have a backup."

"I get that, but my brother is who scares me a little." We all laugh. "Either way, I think there's potential. I owe Jessica a lot, and I think Sean feels the same toward your brother. While owning a chain of inns has never been a goal, I understand horrible fathers and the hell they cause in our lives. I'll let you know either way."

"No matter what we are getting out of the company, but if you buy it, my siblings and I will help make sure you don't lose your investment."

He nods. "I'll think about it."

And with that, we turn the conversation to family and friends.

"When do you want to get married?" I ask Grayson while we're lying in bed at the hotel in New York City.

"Tonight."

I roll my eyes. "You're insane."

"I am. But that's what I want."

His hand runs up and down my spine, and I melt into him. "I don't want to wait long."

"I think it's best for Amelia if we do it before we tell her about the baby."

"I worry we're changing so much in her world too fast."

Grayson gives a short grunt. "If she was showing any signs of being upset, I would say we should hold off, but she's not."

Amelia has been more excited than anything. She tells everyone that she asked me to marry them and I said yes. At school, she was the center of attention with that story. My heart didn't know it could love like this, but Amelia and Grayson have given me so much to care for.

"Still, I want to protect her."

Grayson kisses the top of my head. "And this is why I want to marry you now. Because you don't just love me, you love my daughter."

I lean up, looking in his eyes. "How could I not? She's a part of you."

"Seriously, Jess, I don't want to wait to have you as my wife. I want us to start our new life raising both kids as a married couple. Call me old fashioned, I don't care, but it's important to me."

"It is to me too. So, let's set a date."

"I want to do it before this crap with my father goes down."

Soon, the Parkerson siblings will walk away from everything they've ever known and band together. I know that Grayson is grappling with not only what he found out about his father but also that his siblings are giving up so much.

I don't think they feel that way, but he does.

They've lived a very privileged life and have done very well. That will change for them. There's going to be a period of time where finances could be difficult. Thankfully, they are talking and planning to make things as easy as possible.

Since the land that Grayson owns is huge, Alex and Joshua are going to stay on the property. Once construction starts, it will ensure that someone is always there, and they will also have privacy.

Oliver is going to stay with Stella, which should be hilarious.

I shift so I'm on my stomach, looking at him. "Okay, well, we don't have a lot of time then."

"Which is part of my plan."

"Oh? You have a plan?"

His grin deepens and that dimple I love becomes prominent. "I always have plans for you, love."

"Good to know, but what about the wedding?"

"I want to get married at the lake."

"Really?"

"Where did you think I'd want to marry you?"

I lift one shoulder. "No clue, but . . ." I sort of thought he'd pick the beach house. It's where we became Jessica and Grayson—or Gressica, as I like to joke to make his head explode. I wasn't actually excited by the idea, but this is, well . . . "I think that's perfect."

I love that lake. The lake is new. The lake is where our future is. It's where we'll build this new life.

"It's why we have to do it soon, before it's ruined by trucks and construction."

"You have very sound logic."

He laughs. "I will say just about anything to get you to agree."

I push myself closer to him, kissing him softly. "You don't have to say anything more."

Epilogue

GRAYSON

"Calm down," Jack says as he claps me on the back. "She'll be here. Chicks take a long time for these things."

"Is this coming from all your experience with women and weddings?"

He snorts. "No, but it was meant to be comforting since I'm your best man and everything."

"Well, it wasn't."

Choosing Jack to be my best man was a no brainer. I have three very competitive brothers, and having to decide between them felt like a minefield where I was surely going to get blown up, so I avoided it.

Plus, Jack is like a brother. There is no one who isn't blood who I trust as much as him.

"Well, have a shot then, that should calm you."

I'm not nervous. Not the way he thinks. Jessica will be here, I have no doubts about that. It's more of an anxious excitement. I'm ready for this. I love her, and I want to start our lives as husband and wife.

Jack hands me a shot of whiskey, and I take it before we raise our glass. "To brotherhood."

It's what we've said each time we toast. "To brotherhood."

The liquid burns its way down, warming me along the way.

"Did Amelia get ready with Jess?"

"Yeah, she said she's a girl and needs to be with them."

Jack laughs. "It's really funny that pretty much everyone attending your wedding is actually *in* the wedding."

He's not wrong. Our bridal party is four groomsmen and four bridesmaids, which is more than half of the invited guests.

"We wanted it intimate."

He nods. "Can I ask you something, Gray?"

I turn, finding the normally carefree air around him is different. "What's up?"

"How did you . . . well, how did you guys decide to move forward?"

Okay, now that's a surprise. "You mean try again?"

He nods.

"I don't know, I guess it was just always meant to be. It wasn't easy, but I don't think it's meant to be."

"Right."

"Is this about a few weeks ago?" I ask, remembering the night he showed up completely blitzed.

"No. That was just me being drunk," he says a little too quickly.

"Who was the girl?"

Jack shrugs, looking away. "No girl."

"Jack, you were going on and on about some girl."

"She's no one. I honestly don't remember half the night, and I . . . it's nothing."

"She doesn't sound like it."

Jack's entire demeanor shifts, and he smiles widely. "We're not talking about drunk hookups today, brother. It's your wedding, and it's about damn time we get out there. I see the Jeep coming down with your bride now."

I want to push him, but this is Jack, and I know him well enough to know that it's pointless to keep at it. Whoever this girl is, she clearly has him torn up, and until he's ready to deal with it, he'll just deny it.

Josh, Alex, and Oliver walk over in their sapphire-blue suits that match mine and Jack's. The only difference between our outfits is that they have gold ties and mine is white.

We didn't go all out with the wedding, but we wanted some of the traditional things to still happen.

I see Stella get out of the car, and she waves.

"It's amazing that none of the guys we've chased away from her have pressed charges," Josh notes.

Jack huffs. "Yeah, no guy wants to be in between you idiots."

Damn right. We know Stella is beautiful and too good for any man.

"Which is why we left Gray here to make sure the wolves didn't descend."

I roll my eyes. "Please, I think Stella is the wolf."

Oliver shakes his head. "He's not lying. She's scarier than the four of us."

"Well, five if you count Jack, he's like a brother."

Jack laughs and nods. "You could say that."

Next is Delia, and I look at Jack, who is staring at the girls. He hasn't taken his eyes off them. I'm starting to think Jess was right when she said that he has a thing for Delia.

Josh clears his throat. "Aren't you supposed to go help your bride?"

"I don't know, Jess said something about no aisle and that she was going to walk here?"

Oliver slaps me on the back. "Way to fuck up your wedding before it starts. Didn't you pay attention?"

"No," I groan. "I was too busy making sure you fuckers didn't get so drunk you couldn't get here."

Before I can argue or try to think about what the hell the directions were, Amelia hops out of the car, her hands going back and forth quickly as if she wants me to walk to her. When I move to take a step, I hear a chorus of, "No!"

"See, I am to stay here," I say as though it was my plan.

And then . . . then my heart stops. The world stops turning as she exits the car.

The sun is behind her, peeking through the trees and casting the most beautiful halo around her, making it seem as if she's glowing.

I know I'm supposed to stay here, but my legs want to go. It's not until I feel Jack's hand grab my forearm that I realize I was moving.

Jessica takes Amelia's hand.

My sister comes toward us first, and when she gets to me, she kisses my cheek. "I'm proud of you."

I laugh. "Thanks."

Then she smiles at the rest of the crew behind me.

Next is Delia, who gives me a playful wink as she passes.

Winnie, Jessica's maid of honor, waves her fingers as she

passes.

Her mother is last, and I pull her in for a hug when she gets to me. "You take care of my girl."

"Always."

"You know," she says softly, "I always hoped it would be you. You're a good man, Grayson Parkerson."

"I think it was always going to be us, no matter what."

Mrs. Walker smiles. "I think so too."

And then it's just her and Amelia. The two of them start to make their way to me, carefully avoiding rocks as Amelia waves randomly. They are both smiling, and I swear, my heart could fly out of my chest. I've never known a person could hold this much love.

"Hi," Jess says first.

"God, you're gorgeous."

She beams. "I'm glad you think so." Amelia looks up at me. "And you are so pretty."

"Thanks, Daddy. Are you ready to get married?" Melia asks.

I look to Jessica, our eyes locked and I nod. "Yeah, Monkey, I sure am."

"Never thought I'd see the day," Josh says as he hands me a beer.

"That I'd get married?"

"No, that you'd convince Jessica to marry you."

I laugh. "I did something right."

"I notice you invited Mom."

She's currently dancing with Oliver, and we've barely said

a handful of words to each other.

"I didn't want to regret it later."

"I get it. Does she know we're all about to wreck her life?"

It's doubtful that she does. When the five of us demand a buy-out or threaten to sell our shares, my mother is going to have a rude awakening. The lifestyle she's been afforded will be gone because my father will have to scramble to come up with the money, which means less alimony.

That house will probably be the first thing he tries to sell.

"Not really my concern today."

"I know, I just . . . I'm glad you invited her, that's all."

"It was the right thing to do."

"Yeah, the women in our lives are pains in our asses, but we love them," Josh says before taking a long pull of his drink. "Speaking of, where did Stella run off to?"

"I don't know, I wanted to dance with her."

"Me too."

I look around but don't see her. "I'll go find her," I tell him.

As I start to walk over to the tree line, Jessica comes rushing over from across the tented area. "Where are you going?"

"Nowhere. I'm just looking for Stella."

She peeks around. "Well, she's not here, we should dance."

"You said you wanted to sit."

"I did. I sat. I'm fine. Let's go. I like this song."

I look over to the floating dance floor in confusion. "There's no music playing."

"We make our own music," she says a bit too quickly.

"Jessica, what are you talking about?"

She laughs, and then I hear something in the woods. Her hand grabs mine, tugging me away. "Come on, babe. It's our wedding day."

"So you're going to pretend? Like . . . it's nothing?" Stella's voice is muffled, but I know it's her.

There's a low reply, but I can't make it out.

"We have to deal with this. We can't . . . we can't pretend anymore." There is a layer of hurt and desperation in Stella's voice.

I turn to my wife with a brow raised. "Is that why you want to dance?"

She releases a low breath, which is much more of a defeated sound. "Let your sister work this out."

"You know what's going on?"

Jess snorts. "I know everything."

"Then who the hell is at our wedding that she—"

I'll kill him.

I'll fucking kill him.

I turn, moving quickly in the direction of where the voices are.

"You still have feelings for me, I know you do!" Stella says, and I pick up the pace.

Still?

"I don't." I hear Jack, clear as fucking day. "I do . . . I *can't.*"

"You can't pretend with me, Jack."

"We can't," he says.

When I get to the clearing where they're standing, his hands are on her arms and she's clutching his shirt. My heart is pounding as I stare at my best friend, staring at my sister as though he's broken. "God, Stella, we can't." Then, before I can say anything, he crushes his lips to hers.

Jessica is trying to pull me back, but I see red. How the hell could he do this? He said it over and over again that he didn't like her. I never imagined the *her* would be Stella.

He doesn't like her? Then allow me to remind him.

"Get your fucking hands off my sister," I say, my voice sounding foreign to me.

They break apart, but Stella is the first to react and take a step toward me. "Grayson—"

"How could you?" I ask Jack.

"It's not what you think," Stella tries to step in.

I know if I open my mouth again, I'll lose it. Instead of making a scene on what is one of the best days of my life, I shake my head, glaring at Jack the whole time.

He steps forward. "I know you're pissed, and I get it, but you have to know—"

I raise my hand to silence him. Jessica gives me a sad smile and says, "Come on, love, let's dance and let them talk."

"Talk? Did you see that? It didn't look like talking when he was kissing her."

Jessica tilts her head to the side, staring at me. "Yes, and it's not our business. Your sister can handle it."

The anger I thought I felt before doubles. My best friend and my baby sister. It's an image I sure as hell won't get out of my head anytime soon. They've been fucking lying, and I can't even bring myself to think about all the shit he was drunk rambling about. Well, if he doesn't like her, then he better never touch her again.

Stella steps forward. "Go with your wife, Gray. We'll talk tomorrow."

I give one last hateful glance at my worst man and allow Jessica to pull me away. I can't believe this.

Jess doesn't say anything, she just walks carefully and I keep my arm around her so she doesn't stumble and hurt herself.

My wife, knowing me better than I know myself, leads me to the dance floor where she wraps her arms around me so I can't gather my other brothers to deal with Jack.

"Well, that was interesting," she says after a few seconds.

I raise one brow. "That isn't happening."

She laughs as though I said something comical. "Oh, Grayson, you silly, sweet man who thinks he can control any of this, haven't you learned anything? Life is unpredictable, but what's meant to be will be."

"Like us?"

She nods. "Exactly. Now kiss me and tell me I'm pretty."

I do as she asks and vow to spend the rest of tonight pondering the best place to bury Jack's body.

Thank you for reading Jessica and Grayson's story. I hope you enjoyed their second chance romance as much as I did writing it.

Next up is Stella and Jack.

There is nothing I can say to prepare you for their story. It took me by complete surprise. You have NO idea what's coming. That's all I'm going to say. Jack is freaking amazing. Stella is a spitfire and they have quite a bit of explaining to do . . .

Preorder Could Have Been Us and be ready for a story like I've never told before!

Acknowledgments

To my husband and children. You sacrifice so much for me to continue to live out my dream. Days and nights of me being absent even when I'm here. I'm working on it. I promise. I love you more than my own life.

My readers. There's no way I can thank you enough. It still blows me away that you read my words. You guys have become a part of my heart and soul.

Bloggers: I don't think you guys understand what you do for the book world. It's not a job you get paid for. It's something you love and you do because of that. Thank you from the bottom of my heart.

My beta reader Melissa Saneholtz: Dear God, I don't know how you still talk to me after all the hell I put you through. Your input and ability to understand my mind when even I don't blows me away. If it weren't for our phone calls, I can't imagine where this book would've been. Thank you for helping me untangle the web of my brain.

My assistant, Christy Peckham: How many times can one person be fired and keep coming back? I think we're running out of times. No, but for real, I couldn't imagine my life without you. You're a pain in my ass but it's because of you that I haven't fallen apart.

Sommer Stein for once again making these covers perfect and still loving me after we fight because I change my mind a bajillion times.

Michele Ficht and Julia Griffis for always finding all the typos and crazy mistakes.

Melanie Harlow, thank you for being the Glinda to my Elphaba or Ethel to my Lucy. Your friendship means the world to me and I love writing with you. I feel so blessed to have you in my life.

Bait, Crew, and Corinne Michaels Books—I love you more than you'll ever know.

My agent, Kimberly Brower, I am so happy to have you on my team. Thank you for your guidance and support.

Melissa Erickson, you're amazing. I love your face. Thank you for always talking me off the ledge that is mighty high.

To my narrators, Andi Arndt and Sebastian York, you are the best and I am so honored to work with you. You bring my story to life and always manage to make the most magical audiobooks. Your friendship over these last few years has only grown and I love your heart so much. Thank you for always having my back. To many more concerts and snowed in sleepovers.

Vi, Claire, Chelle, Mandi, Amy, Kristy, Penelope, Kyla, Rachel, Tijan, Alessandra, Laurelin, Devney, Jessica, Carrie Ann, Kennedy, Lauren, Susan, Sarina, Beth, Julia, and Natasha—Thank you for keeping me striving to be better and loving me unconditionally. There are no better sister authors than you all.

Books by Corinne Michaels

The Salvation Series

Beloved

Beholden

Consolation

Conviction

Defenseless

Evermore: A 1001 Dark Night Novella

Indefinite

Infinite

The Hennington Brothers

Say You'll Stay

Say You Want Me

Say I'm Yours

Say You Won't Let Go: A Return to Me/Masters and Mercenaries Novella

Second Time Around Series

We Own Tonight

One Last Time

Not Until You

If I Only Knew

The Arrowood Brothers

Come Back for Me

Fight for Me

The One for Me

Stay for Me

Willow Creek Valley Series (Coming 2021)

Return to Us
One Chance for Us
A Moment for Us
Could Have Been Us

Standalones
All I Ask
You Loved Me Once (Coming 2021)

Co-Written with Melanie Harlow
Hold You Close
Imperfect Match

About the Author

Corinne Michaels is a *New York Times*, *USA Today*, *and Wall Street Journal* bestselling author of romance novels. Her stories are chock full of emotion, humor, and unrelenting love, and she enjoys putting her characters through intense heartbreak before finding a way to heal them through their struggles.

Corinne is a former Navy wife and happily married to the man of her dreams. She began her writing career after spending months away from her husband while he was deployed—reading and writing were her escape from the loneliness. Corinne now lives in Virginia with her husband and is the emotional, witty, sarcastic, and fun-loving mom of two beautiful children.

CPSIA information can be obtained
at www.ICGtesting.com
Printed in the USA
BVHW042323190221
600699BV00005B/21